THE VOLUPTUARIES

THE
VOLUPTUARIES

Betty E. Ullman

G.P. Putnam's Sons • New York

SBN: 399-12084-X

Library of Congress Cataloging in Publication Data

Ullman, Betty E
  The Voluptuaries

    I. Title.
PZ4.U398Br [PS3571.L55]   813'.5'4   78–2187

Printed in the United States of America

There are several people I want to thank for giving me the encouragement I needed tc finish this book: Professor Astere Claeyssens, who also happens to be the most charming man I've ever met; Christopher Conkling, who edited my first draft; Patricia Bandak, my persevering typist; and Q.T., my Yorkie, who sat up with me as I worked late into the night.

CHAPTER 1

I stepped from the street, hot as a sauna, into the air-conditioned lobby of the famous Mayflower Hotel. I was in Washington at last, and it was home. After six terrible months, the days and nights on tranquilizers, mood elevators, sleeping pills, every medication they could find, they had finally brought me back. Six months locked in a sanitorium, and now I was whole again. God, it was wonderful to be able to laugh and enjoy the world again without counting the hours and the minutes to the next pill. It had taken months, and all my courage, but I had left California—and everyone in it—behind. Only James and his phony friends had mattered anyway, and now I knew I didn't need them. What would they think if they could see me now? Only five days in Washington and already I had made an elegant friend who promised to be my entrée to the circle of genuine Washington society. What was more, someone—someone very special—was also going to call me. Already.

Heading directly for the desk as I did every evening, I checked to see if I had any messages, any reward for another long day of job hunting. Each time the puffy man at the desk was all detachment, expression blank as he said, "Nothing yet, Mrs. Crane," shaking his jowls over his starched white collar. But today was different. He started smiling as he saw me crossing the lobby. As I reached the desk he bowed slightly and, with a mock flourish, handed me the note.

I tore it out of the envelope. There were only a few words on expensive engraved notepaper.

> Will you join us for dinner this Saturday. A car will call for you at seven. Please wear *no* scent. (No one wears scent at our dinner parties.)
>
> Cordially,
CORINTHA

There was no request for a response. No address or telephone number. Only the stark "Corintha Byrom" engraved at the top. It was a command performance, even to the odd, peremptory request about the perfume.

It didn't matter. Mrs. Byrom's party would be my debut in Washington. I'd have to buy a gown. It was the last thing I'd thought I would ever need when I left California. But Mrs. Byrom had been very explicit that all their affairs were formal.

Most of my clothes were still in Los Angeles, waiting to be shipped after I settled somewhere. The next morning at Garfinckel's I found just what I wanted—a simple yellow and white gown striped from shoulder to hem. The yellow was so pale it almost matched my hair. Though it was starched organza, it was perfectly cut to my figure, with a low, square neckline. Even at my slender five feet four, I felt regal and tall, ready to meet anyone Mrs. Byrom could present.

When Saturday finally came I was ready and waiting an hour ahead of time. Exactly at seven the call came from the lobby. I grabbed up my bag, swinging it in delight until I stepped into the crowded elevator.

The doors opened in the lobby and people crushed their way out. A huge man dressed in a black chauffeur's uniform came directly to me, as if he knew exactly who I was the instant I appeared. He didn't say a word, merely nodded his head, then gestured me toward the street. He followed closely at my heels until we reached the revolving doors; then he raced ahead to open the door of the long limousine at the curb. Still saying absolutely nothing, not even a hint of expression on his blank face, he tucked in the hem of my gown and closed the door, then hurried to the driver's seat. I was relieved that the glass partition between us was up. Perhaps Mrs. Byrom demanded this kind of silent deference but it wasn't the California style, and certainly not my own.

We seemed to be barely creeping along, though the traffic seemed light. But it was hard for me to judge our progress; the back of the car had swallowed me up. The seat was so deep that all I could see were the tops of office buildings, all the same height, all as unreal as a set of children's building blocks. I had nothing to do but think about the party, and as we drove I found my confidence giving way to jitters. To reassure myself, I thought about Mrs. Byrom. There was no reason to be nervous when Corintha so clearly wanted me to be there—had wanted to know me, in fact, from the first moments we'd met, on the plane from California.

Under normal circumstances we never *would* have met. But in my excitement at leaving the sanatorium and setting out for the new world that Washington would be, I'd splurged on a first-class ticket, and found Corintha sitting across the aisle.

She was probably in her early sixties and certainly not helpless, but the stewardess was treating her like a fragile flower. The woman was visibly annoyed as the attendant fussed with the arrangement of her coat and flight bag. Lips barely moving, she murmured across to me:

"These commercial lines are so boorish. They always make me uncomfortable."

I was enjoying the special treatment, but I smiled at her anyway, as if in agreement, and she immediately smiled back, as if we shared a confidence, a superiority over the peons around us.

A few minutes after takeoff the stewardess came down the aisle towards us, taking orders for drinks. She served me first, then turned to the woman across the aisle, hovering and fussing until Mrs. Byrom dismissed her with a freezing glance.

For the first time in months I found myself curious about somebody. There was something intriguing about this woman who had so confidently established her presence. Her face was fair, with a pinched, patrician nose and thin lips. Her hair was pure white, short, and set softly, expertly. She was wearing an immaculate light-blue linen suit, and her hat and gloves were probably the only ones on the plane. The dress emphasized the aquamarine in her eyes. It was obvious that nothing about her was inexpensive or accidentally suitable.

As I reached down for my bag to get another cigarette, my companion reached down simultaneously for her own. We both smiled, even more companionably than before. I reached for my lighter. She reached for hers. I lit my cigarette and noticed she was having trouble with hers.

"Use my lighter if you like," I said shyly. "I'll just leave it here on my tray."

The woman stiffened her neck and stared straight at me. "My child, you certainly don't look old enough to smoke, much less drink martinis. You can't be over seventeen."

"Oh, thank you, but I certainly am." For the moment I felt seventeen.

"Well, thank you, then," she said and leaned across for the lighter. The next moment she jostled my tray and the martini tipped over, splashing into my lap.

"My dear, I'm so sorry," she said, her lacy fluff of handkerchief ineffectually dusting at my soiled dress. "Go to the restroom instantly and put cold water on it. I insist. You can't spoil that lovely dress. Now go!" she exclaimed.

As I left my seat I could hear her calling a stewardess to re-place my drink. I washed the spots as best I could, and as I returned down the aisle I saw that my new drink had been placed on the woman's tray. My new seatmate had something in her hand which looked like a chased pill box encrusted with rubies. As I dropped into the seat beside her she slipped it back into her bag.

"How nice, my dear, our little accident hardly shows." She extended her hand. "By the way, I am Mrs. Corintha By-rom."

"I'm Sharon Crane," I answered.

"Will you be in Washington long?" It was a natural ques-tion, but somehow it seemed that she was encouraging me to talk.

"Permanently, I hope. I've just been divorced, you see, and I want to get as far from California as I can."

"You must have married very young," she said, sympathy suffusing her voice.

"Yes, I did. I was eighteen. Only five years, but it seems my whole life."

"You have friends in Washington?"

"No. I won't know a soul. I hope to get a job there right away, but I can manage for awhile till I find something."

"You're leaving all your friends behind you in California! Won't they worry about you, my dear, being so far away?"

"They're mostly James's friends, Mrs. Byrom, and they'll worry about me as much as a used paper cup. I gave up all my real friends when I left college to marry him. Since then, it has just been a merry-go-round going too fast, and I was finally pushed off."

"Your parents? Won't they worry?"

"They're both dead. . . . Is Washington your home?" I asked. Her interest flattered and relaxed me, but still I want-ed to turn the subject away from James and my parents.

"Well, I suppose it is," Mrs. Byrom answered, "but I travel frequently. Actually my circle of acquaintances is quite limit-ed in Washington, but I do prefer the time I spend with them to attractions elsewhere. You must like Washington very much, to make your new home there."

"I've never been there before," I admitted. "I wanted to, but my husband didn't like Washington. He thought it provincial."

Mrs. Byrom chuckled. "Provincialism follows the provincial. We create our surroundings wherever we are." She paused a moment. "Why did you divorce your husband? How did you meet him."

Flustered, I gained a moment by fumbling around my feet for my bag. "I must get another cigarette," I apologized. "I can't even talk about James without a cigarette in my hand."

"Here, have one of mine," she said soothingly. I straightened up in my seat, grateful for her concern.

"We have these made up for us," she went on, holding out an exquisite gold case. My hand hesitated in mid-air, as I noticed the oddness of her cigarettes. There were two kinds of blue-papered cigarettes, one gold-tipped, the other silver-tipped. Mrs. Byrom laughed softly.

"Don't worry, my dear, they're certainly not marijuana. Try the silver tip, it's milder. The gold ones are rather strong, but both kinds are quite pure, you'll not be hurt by them."

Relieved, I took a blue-and-silver one while Mrs. Byrom chose one with the golden tip. Lighting up, we sat back. "It's very unusual, isn't it?" I said. "It has the flavor of a cigarette, but somehow, it's more satisfying." I nodded in definite approval, drew in a long, deep breath, allowing the smoke to slowly escape from my lungs.

The drinks and the cigarette slowly were relaxing me. I was floating in a pleasant warmth, but my head was perfectly clear and I wanted very much to go on talking. Though she said little, Mrs. Byrom was affecting me like a combination of the Queen Mother and my own mother—despite the fact that she looked nothing like either one of them. I trusted her, and wanted her approval.

"I met James when I was a freshman in college," I began

breathlessly, "the first year I was ever on my own. He was a guest lecturer in my journalism class. He was a screenwriter who'd just been nominated for an Oscar, but as far as I was concerned it could have been the Nobel Prize. After the lecture, he waited for me outside the hall and asked me to dinner. I was just eighteen and you can imagine how thrilled I was when the celebrity singled *me* out. James was ten years older than I, but he wasn't any more mature. I didn't realize it at the time, but he wasn't used to being idolized. Later, when he invited me to Beverly Hills for a weekend, I was really dazzled by his sophisticated crowd. They hobnobbed with the stars, tossed first names around. James made a special point to speak to every big name he saw. They barely noticed him, but it didn't matter—I was enchanted beyond belief. For months I tried to balance my life between James's magic world and the tedium of my classes. Finally he asked me to quit school and marry him. Without a word to anyone else we were married that week. I thought my parents would understand, but they never forgave me."

Here I faltered. I could hardly speak the words, but they tumbled out. "They both died before I made the effort to see them again. I have no other close relatives, so James became everything to me. His unreal, glamorous world on the periphery of movie making."

"You must have had to settle your parents' estate." Mrs. Byrom's soft voice urged me to go on.

"James did it all through their lawyer. I couldn't face anything at the time. I felt much too guilty. They didn't have much, anyway—only a few things I wanted to keep. They were sent out to me. I kept very busy, though. I concentrated on living up to what I thought James expected of me. It was difficult but I had no one else to turn to. We socialized constantly, always making contacts for James. I studied everyone I met. We spent the little money my parents left in no time. But James was doing well, so I had no reason to worry, or complain.

"He didn't want children, though. He kept putting me off.

He never seemed to want to be tied down—at least not with me. We lived for the moment, but his success didn't continue. He was one of those people who get all their breaks early, then—nothing. His first script was the only one that succeeded. After that, he did the screenplays for two 'artistic' flops. And after *that*, there were no more offers."

"You left him because of that?"

"Oh, no! He left me. He found someone else." I gulped, trying to swallow the lump growing in my throat, trying to explain it all away as the psychiatrist had made me see it.

"As a screenwriter's wife, I traveled with people who were always climbing over each other to impress everyone else. I fell into their pattern, became more sophisticated, learned a lot about the business. Trying so desperately to be what I thought he wanted and needed, I lost the whole game. I tried to become a sophisticate, but what I completely forgot was that James had married me because I *wasn't* sophisticated."

I stopped, embarrassed. But Mrs. Byrom seemed engrossed by my every word. She certainly wasn't bored. The next part was hard to tell but the words were spilling out anyway.

"Then, one day, out of the blue, James informed me he no longer wanted the woman I had become. He was in love with someone else. She was older than me, quiet, almost mousy. She wasn't part of our crowd, so she didn't know what a joke James's career had become.

"The whole bottom dropped out of my life. The only friends I had were James's. I had to leave his world of writers, actors, publicity hounds, the whole bit. I fell apart. It took me months to recover." I stopped again, took a deep breath. "But today I feel so much better. You're the first person I've really wanted to talk to about myself. You're so kind to listen to all this."

"Oh, my child, I want you to tell me. I feel like your mother, listening to her child's hurts. Please, do go on."

I kept on and on, telling this woman every intimate detail

of my life with my parents, with James. The only secret I kept was my stay at the sanatorium. I wasn't ashamed, exactly, but I didn't want her to know how completely I had broken down.

Darkness closed in and dinner was served. I was still talking. Mrs. Byrom was an audience I was holding spellbound. Several times her hand brushed like a feather over my bare arm, touching my skin as though she found pleasure in the touch.

The food made me ravenous for the first time in months. I was about to dig into the filet mignon with relish when I noticed the hesitancy of my companion. She carefully arranged her napkin, scrutinized the dish before her, then daintily cut a small bite. I couldn't help looking at her quizzically.

"I'm afraid, my dear, I'm dreadfully fussy about my food. In fact, I'm quite particular about anything that touches my mouth. In a commercial plane, of course, one can't be overly demanding, but I would much prefer to have my own food prepared for me."

"Aren't you going to eat anything? This steak is really delicious."

"Oh, yes, of course it is, but I prefer waiting until I reach my home. This wouldn't actually hurt me. It's just that I simply won't eat anything I can't savor. I never consider food merely as sustenance."

Then the trays were taken away, and we both sat back, waiting for the long journey to end. The closer the plane came to the East Coast, the stronger my excitement grew. But I dreaded leaving my new friend. Mrs. Byrom once again sensed my need and started talking. It hadn't occurred to me that she already knew almost everything about me and I hadn't given her a chance to say a word about herself.

"You would enjoy our dinner parties," she said reflectively. "I'll invite you to one as soon as it is convenient for you. Our gatherings are always quite formal but I do believe you will find them pleasant."

"I'd love to come, at any time you'd like," I said happily. We were to be friends, then, not just traveling companions. "Does your husband share your interest in food?"

"I am a widow of many years. My friends, however, share my aesthetic interests. We are devoted to enjoying the ultimate sensations of our senses—taste, touch, smell."

She paused and smiled, then motioned toward the window. "Look, Sharon—there's your first sight of Washington."

I turned excitedly, but I had barely glimpsed the lights when I felt a sharp pain in my chest. Excruciating! I couldn't breathe. Involuntarily I clutched myself and bent double.

"What is it, my dear?" Mrs. Byrom leaned toward me.

I couldn't speak. Then, just as suddenly, the pain was gone. I let out a shallow tentative breath and the pain came back, but not so strong. "I'll be all right," I managed to answer. But I was terrified.

"I'll see if there's a doctor on the plane. You're absolutely white. You must have help. It could be serious."

"No, no, please. I'll be all right," I gasped. "It was just indigestion. It's gone already." I didn't dare let this new friend think of me as a burden she wouldn't want to assume.

"Where will you be staying in Washington? I don't think you should be alone."

"At the Mayflower. But I'm sure I'll be all right."

"Nevertheless, you must have a doctor check you. Those pains may return and you'll be in a strange hotel. One of my neighbors is an internist and he's near the Mayflower. I'm going to give you his name. You must promise to call him if you have even the slightest recurrence. He'll come to you immediately. Now I insist you be sensible about this. You must promise me you'll call him."

She wrote something on the back of a calling card and slipped it into my purse.

We were approaching the airport already. Mrs. Byrom had seemed to anticipate and fill my every need. And one day soon she was going to give me the chance to meet her friends. I sat back to relish the thought. The memory of the pain, the idea of seeing another doctor, were forgotten.

"My nephew is meeting me. We will drop you off at your hotel. It is not far from my home," Mrs. Byrom announced.

I weakly remonstrated, "I don't want to impose on you or your nephew. I'm perfectly all right now. I enjoyed the trip with you so much and I'm so looking forward to being with you again."

She seemed coolly affronted. "If it were an imposition, I shouldn't have mentioned it. Philip will have to get my luggage. Yours will be with it. I *said* we live quite near your hotel. We will drop you off." Her statement was a command and I sank back in relief at having all the difficulties of arrival assumed by my new friend.

CHAPTER 2

As soon as we entered the airport, a tall man separated himself from the mass of people milling around the waiting room. His grace and vitality overshadowed everyone around him. He glided up to Mrs. Byrom while I floundered in her wake. The aunt handed him both of our checks and he was off instantly. She hadn't introduced us, but she was probably just waiting until we emerged from the pushing crowd.

He reappeared quickly, a skyhop at his heels with the luggage, and we all rushed toward the entrance. As we walked, or sprinted, Mrs. Byrom quickly introduced us. "Sharon, my nephew, Philip Hawk. Philip, this is Sharon Crane. Mrs. Crane was unwell on the plane, and she'll be staying at the Mayflower. We'll drop her off. It was a most satisfying trip. I'll tell you about it later."

As I gave a hurried "How do you do," I got my first clear view of the man. The impression I'd had as he disappeared to the luggage area was of a large, muscular man dressed in a dark blazer. But Philip Hawk was much more than handsome—he was sensuously contrasting darks and lights,

18

strongly masculine, skin ruddily tanned, eyes light aquamarine, even lighter than his aunt's. Dark, thick lashes fringed his eyes and their heavy lids, making them seem half closed. His hair, the texture of an Indian's, was dark and thick, hanging low over his forehead and framing his face. Deep lines around his mouth saved him from an almost pretty symmetry of features. Assurance was in his every movement. He was the most dizzyingly attractive man I'd ever seen, and his eyes seemed to light up in appreciation as he quickly looked me over.

By now I was nearly running to keep up with Mrs. Byrom, but we didn't have far to go. A long Mercedes waited between two No Parking signs directly at the entrance. After helping his aunt into the front seat, and giving me another perusal, he firmly held my arm as I slid into the back. Philip Hawk started the car and was soon threading through the heavy airport traffic. Nephew and aunt started talking, not once attempting to include me, but I was too excited at the prospects opening before me to care about their rudeness.

"You found the Tokai Aszu?" I heard Mrs. Byrom ask. "How about the Chateau St. George?"

"Certainly. All we wanted. And the agent is returning to Tibet tomorrow for the other items."

Mrs. Byrom's voice expressed both satisfaction and discomfort. "Then your task is working out well this time?"

"Perfectly, Corintha." Philip had the kind of laugh I liked in a man: low, throaty, and free.

The Mercedes glided to the curb at the hotel before I was ready to arrive. I wanted to go on listening to Philip—and hated the thought of being alone again. Before the doorman could reach the car, Philip had jumped out and held the door for me.

"Well, here's home, little one. We'll get you registered and up to your room, but then I'm afraid my aunt and I must be off. Unfortunately, we both have busy schedules this week." He took my hand quickly in both of his and smiled, his teeth white in his dark face. "It's people like you who make me hate my commitments. I'd give a couple of bottles of Chateau-neuf du Pape to be able to buy you a drink. The bar off the lobby of the Mayflower is dark and cozy, I seem to recall, and they have an old-fashioned, four-piece band." His smile gleamed again. "Sometime soon I'm going to have you there all to myself. You may expect frequent calls. Don't be angry, though, if I wake you at three in the morning. I'm impulsive that way, so humor me."

"I'd be honored, your excellency," I answered. "Call day or night. But if I growl at you at three A.M., just be glad I can't bite over the telephone."

Philip chuckled, his hand touching my shoulder as if to acknowledge his bad manners. I instantly forgave him.

Then Mrs. Byrom was between us. "Dear Sharon, Philip and I must be off. I know we'd both like to stay and show you an exciting first night in the city but I'm a little tired, as I know you must be. Do you mind terribly?" She didn't expect an answer, or pause for one. "You get settled and comfortable and become acquainted with our lovely city. If you need anything—anything at all—you have my card. Come, Philip."

Philip blew me a kiss, and I knew I would sleep very well. I could still feel the warmth of his brief, affectionate touch on my shoulder.

CHAPTER 3

We were driving through a large business area, passing one boxy office building after another, with only minor variations and hundreds of dark windows. Mrs. Byrom had definitely said she lived near my hotel. Had the chauffeur been driving me around in circles all this time? Was he deliberately trying to confuse me? I grew more and more apprehensive with every passing minute.

At last, to my great relief, the car stopped. We were in front of a building that seemed like all the others. The block was completely deserted—well lit, but empty. On the street level of the building were a savings-and-loan company and a pharmacy, both closed and dark. The building occupied most of the block, but except for those two businesses, the rest of the street level was darkened glass storefronts with drapes drawn.

No sooner had the chauffeur opened the door to help me out than Philip came bounding from nowhere and grasped both my arms. He gave a long, low whistle. "How beautiful you are, Sharon. I didn't realize. To think, I've allowed almost a week to pass without seeing you."

21

Putting my arm through his, he led me across the wide empty pavement to a recessed doorway all but hidden on the right end of the building. The car and chauffeur had silently slipped away. I didn't see or even hear them leave.

Pulling a large ring of keys from his pocket, Philip unlocked the door. The key he used, and all the keys on the chain, seemed to be sterling silver. But I didn't have time to wonder about it; in a moment the door was open and we were inside.

Inside, to my right, was a bank of letter boxes, nothing else. Directly ahead was a set of double-doors. Philip led me to them and opened them with another silver key. Once inside the second doors I was astonished. The exterior of the apartment house looked like an office building, but this reception room was unlike the lobby of any office, hotel or apartment building that could be imagined. All the walls were dark mahogany, the panels carved and hung with majestic oil paintings. Dark, blood-red Oriental rugs covered the white marble floor, and interspersed along the entire length were pieces of heavy stuffed furniture, all upholstered in black cut velvet. There were ebony tables with huge Chinese Graviata porcelains and tall lamps of gold and black. And roses—huge, perfect roses in each of those vases. They were crimson, glorious against their stark background.

Philip led me to a bank of two elevators, their paneling matching that of the entry way. Once again he used a silver key. This time he inserted it in a nearly invisible slot next to the elevator button. He stood in the elevator quite at ease, obviously feeling no pressure to entertain me, make me feel welcome, or comment on the absolute grandeur. The elevator rose to the fourth floor.

"Sharon, you're going to enjoy the evening, I'm sure," he finally said. "Some of these people may seem a little unusual to you, but they're all interesting. Tops in every one of their fields. So have a good time. And please don't be angry if I have to leave you on your own. My mingling is for business purposes and you should circulate, too. You can make very good contacts here, maybe hear about a job. But whatever happens, don't think I won't find you again. There won't be so many people here that you can be lost easily. I'll find you."

Philip's hand was at my elbow as the doors slid open soundlessly. Here was another foyer, but entirely different. Another huge, empty area, but this one radiated warmth. A room at least thirty feet long stretched out ahead of us with ornate columned double doors at the other end. The whole room was carpeted in deep gold, the walls completely covered with golden brocaded drapes, and the Louis XIV furnishings were sparse. A strange kidney-shaped motif was everywhere—the chairs, the drapes, the rugs—but I couldn't quite make out its significance as Philip hurried me along.

It was oddly quiet and, for the moment, as Philip walked on without saying a word, I had the eerie sensation I was entering a dream. The absolute stillness, the absence of people, made the whole venture seem terribly unreal. Then, as we neared the end of the corridor, reality returned. The muffled sound of voices penetrated the doors.

Once again Philip reached ahead and used a key. The hushed hum of voices became more distinct, but still muffled, as if the room were a funeral parlor where everyone could speak only in hushed tones.

At least thirty people stood clustered in groups throughout a large windowless room that could have accommodated hundreds without crowding. They seemed almost lifeless, frozen in a tableau. Crystal prisms hanging from the ceiling and walls dotted the whole room with hundreds of golden flickering pinpoints of light. Not one of the assemblage turned to greet the new arrivals.

At last Mrs. Byrom emerged from somewhere, floating in blue chiffon, deep sapphires and diamonds sparkling from her fleshy arm.

"Sharon, my dear, sweet child. I'm so happy to see you. You are so lovely. I shall certainly enjoy presenting such a sweet thing to my friends."

She urged me forward and I had to go, noticing with

annoyance that Philip was already drifting away toward a glamorous foursome grouped by a fountain bubbling in the center of the room. The couple Mrs. Byrom was ushering me toward seemed much more solemn.

"Dr. and Mrs. Ahnesbach," she crooned, "this is Mrs. Crane, the young lady I found on the plane. I have been telling my friends about you, Sharon. Dr. Ahnesbach is our surgeon and Mrs. Ahnesbach assists him. Our second floor is their domain. You see, we all live in the building and the doctors have their offices on the second floor. We almost identify ourselves to others by our locations here. It has become our little idiosyncrasy."

Two tall persons in impeccable finery stood waiting to exchange pleasantries with me. They were both slim and probably past sixty. The man's hair—long, white, and swept back—was trimmed so the thinning edges weren't stringy. His face and neck were long and deeply creviced. Strong bones showed through the skin of his nose, cheeks, and chin. Even in the dim light, he had a distinct gray pallor, the look of a death's-head. Even so, he had the bearing of a patriarchal symphony conductor looking down upon the world.

"I approve your taste," he told Mrs. Byrom in a strong, resonant tone. "Mrs. Crane is a charming addition to our little party. I am sure you will appreciate our delicacies, my dear." He bowed to me and gravely kissed my hand. As I tried, startled, to pull away, he gripped my hand tighter and pressed his hard, thin lips down. Then he lifted his face slowly, baring his teeth in a winner's grimace.

Ahnesbach's wife was equally overwhelming. She was as gaunt as her husband, but where his appearance was enhanced by his thinness, she simply looked skeletal. The high-necked silver gown was the most flattering she could have chosen. Its severity transformed her ugliness into a ramrod of glitter. Her coiffure was unusual as well: silvery gray hair parted in the middle, drawn tightly down to plaits that were wound meticulously into knobs the size of apples over her ears.

To my relief, Mrs. Byrom saw someone else she wanted me to meet. But the man walking toward us did not wait for an introduction before thrusting a golden goblet into my hand.

"Here," he said, "you'd better allow our guest her cocktail before the new wisps begin." Mrs. Byrom approved.

"Sharon, our Dr. Pavel. He owns the pharmacy downstairs. The doctor is quite right. You must meet our friends, but first you must enjoy the smells in the air before they disappear. You must have noticed the aroma through the room. Soon there'll be even more provocative scents. One of our little fetishes, you understand. You'll learn to appreciate them."

"This is my small contribution," Dr. Pavel said smugly. "Drink of it and your taste buds will never be the same."

I slowly took a sip of the green liquid in the goblet. It wasn't crème de menthe, or wine, or any other liquor I knew, but it was so delicious I held it on my tongue a moment before letting it slip down my throat.

The pharmacist was watching me carefully. "We don't serve hors d'oeuvres before meals. We simply don't believe in distracting the sensations of our taste buds. The 'cocktail' tonight is my latest concoction. I do hope it pleases you." He nodded, without even letting me compliment him.

Dr. Pavel did not look like a pharmacist. He was slim, with delicate long hands that curled daintily around his own goblet, and a thin moustache curling down around his pink lips. His bright blue eyes were strangely penetrating. He reminded me of a temperamental artist. I couldn't imagine him behind a counter measuring out prescriptions, but guessed the pharmacy was his plaything, a toy laboratory where he could concoct any creation that titillated his imagination. He wasn't effeminate, but his appraisal of me seemed at the same time intense and strangely asexual. He was no older than Philip, but he examined me as if I were another species.

I didn't usually stare at people, but there was something special about this whole gathering. Each person was different, but their differences seemed to knot them into a very tight society. I couldn't quite understand why I was being so graciously accepted as a guest, but I wasn't going to question it.

Mrs. Byrom was quickly guiding me along to meet others, while I was intently looking for Phillip. He wasn't hard to find. He was with the only beautiful woman in the room. I almost tripped over my own feet, trying to keep up with my hostess and still get a better look at the girl claiming his attention.

She had almond-shaped eyes, porcelain skin, and black, shining hair pulled up from her face and wrapped into a high crown. She had to be Eurasian, but she was very tall—her eyes were almost level with Philip's—and her full breasts were barely enclosed in a low, white, clinging gown. She was sensuous, sophisticated, and certainly accepted by the group. As she and Philip laughed, I felt a real tinge of jealousy, jealousy of a man I barely knew, and then I caught the strange expression on Corintha Byrom's face. Mrs. Byrom was enchanted by my obvious attraction to Philip, and pleased by my jealousy as well.

We came to another group. I was introduced to Dr. Romano, an internist. He was an albino. Like Mrs. Ahnesbach, Romano's wife served as her husband's nurse, also, in an office on the second floor.

Then I met the retired General MacDonald, who imperiously called himself the Managing Director, with capital letters. He looked like a puffed-up bulldog, and he proudly recited for me his responsibilities in the building. He was in charge of the amenities, but his primary duty was to purchase all the tenants' staple supplies. He explained, head loftily high, that they each contributed a monthly sum to keep up his storeroom, which was on the fourth floor. He lived on the fifth.

Mrs. Byrom was right. Each had his domain. And to each, it was a kingdom.

We finally reached Philip and the group around him. The

beauty I so envied was Cheena Wescott, a ceramicist, whose kiln was in the basement. She lived here, too. Her voice was soft and pleasant, a touch of Vassar in it, which did nothing to please me. And I was so intent on her that I was barely aware of being introduced to the others standing with her and Philip.

Mrs. Byrom kept ushering me from group to group. The handshakes began to puzzle and irritate me. Each person slid a hand over mine as if to prolong the feel of my skin. I was the only outsider and knew I was being given special attention, but it was beginning to get on my nerves. They spoke little of themselves, but turned all the questions on me, drawing me into their conversations as though my opinions and my interests were as important as their own.

I was desperate for a cigarette, but embarrassed to bring out my Kents. Everyone was smoking those strange gold-tipped cigarettes I'd seen on the airplane, and I didn't dare offend this critical assemblage with my ordinary brand. Mrs. Byrom read my mind.

"Here, have one of mine, my dear." She held out her silver case.

Gratefully I lighted a silver one. One drag and there was the tantalizing taste I remembered. The smoke filled my lungs and gave me a sweet, heady feeling, yet it didn't detract from the smell and taste of my drink. I began wondering if I'd be offered another glass of the green liquid. But my goblet had not been refilled and no one was offering to freshen it.

Then a soft whishing sound distracted me. The air throughout the room seemed to be rushing up toward the ceiling, and fresh air was blowing in from somewhere. As I looked around, I saw everyone standing motionless, enthralled. For moments there was no smell of any kind. Then, in subtle wisps, a new essence seeped throughout the room. No one said a word. All savored the moment. I tried to emulate and appreciate their custom.

The new essence wafted about the room, blending, separating. The people kept shifting from one spot to another.
Gradually they began talking softly again. But not for a moment did they allow me to be left out of one or another of
their animated discussions. Each group treated me as one of
their own, questioning me, listening intently to the little I
had to offer. My nervousness began to dissipate as I suddenly
realized they approved of me. They smiled and nodded, at
me and at each other, and slowly I forgot the awe, the solemnity, even the strangeness of my first impression. I had made
a place for myself in James's tinsel world, but these people
were in another realm, and I wanted more than anything to
be accepted by them. I turned to put down my goblet when I
was startled by Philip taking my arm.

"I'm taking you in to dinner, little one," he said. I was both
pleased and annoyed—pleased he would be my partner, annoyed that his charming smile was gone now that he had left
Cheena's side.

A gong sounded. It was struck a second time, louder, then
stopped abruptly. Everyone turned in place to face the north
wall where the two high doors started sliding apart.

CHAPTER 4

The silent fraternity glided through the doors. Philip held me back, waiting for the others to file in before us. At last he moved me along to a landing which separated into two spiral staircases. He deliberately paused a few minutes before descending so I could do justice to my first view of the dining chamber.

Spread before us was a room at least three stories high, lit only by hundreds of flickering electric candles. It was at once magnificent and awesome. The walls seemed to reach forever upward, covered with diamond-shaped smoked-glass mirrors, beveled to reflect the dim lights. The ceiling, too, must have been mirrored and a deep purple carpet covered the floor.

One long, narrow table shaped like a C encircled the whole room. Majestic high-backed chairs, black and ornately carved, were set far apart around the table, all facing the center of the room. The only spots of lights were the white plates, the silver and crystal set on the dark-purple cloth.

Small, formal place cards marked each place. There were no decorations anywhere in the room.

The center of the room, faced by all those chairs, was a disappointment. There was only a huge, black velour dais, three levels high, with an outer rim at least twelve feet across. Not a thing was on it. It stood about fifteen feet from the table, and all the surrounding area was bare.

I jumped as Philip touched my arm again to indicate that I was to proceed down the stairway. He escorted me to a chair near the open end of the table. The first familiar face I saw was Dr. Ahnesbach presiding at the center of the tremendous table. I found his wife at the other end, almost opposite me. Philip sat on my left. On my right a large, dark-bearded man was already seated. I remembered him too. He was a pathologist whose laboratories were also in the building. But somehow I couldn't remember his name.

Philip leaned closer and whispered, "The essences haven't been brought in yet, but they will."

"Is that what we're waiting for?"

"Yes. You'll appreciate it. They enhance the intoxication of each course as it is served."

"I must say this is unusual."

"It's far more than that, Sharon. Everything we do builds to unbelievable satisfaction. The only sin is to fail in meeting our standard of perfection. Tonight's culmination will be the dessert course."

"You mean only one course has to be perfect?"

"Yes, but the other courses were passed upon at former occasions. We each have our turn in planning the menu. We each create one new masterpiece. That course must be perfect. It would be too taxing to develop several new courses for every dinner. The rest of the meal consists of formerly approved creations."

"Who does all this?"

"We each have a turn as host."

"Well, does the host have to do all this cooking?"

"Oh, no. Of course not. He just supervises the other courses, but he would never trust anyone else with the responsibility of preparing his new creation."

Again I wondered why I had been invited—certainly not for my cooking ability.

"Whose turn is it tonight?" I asked.

"Dr. Ahnesbach."

"He seems terribly on edge. Is it because of all this?"

Instead of answering, Philip put his finger to his lips. Something was about to happen. The whispers died down, and the room became deadly silent. A thin beam of light suddenly shone down from the ceiling onto the dais, which was slowly sinking into the floor. Then, as the spotlight grew, the outer circle of the dais soundlessly rose from the floor. Silver plates bearing small bowls came steaming into the light. I became aware of a luscious aroma. Waiters filed into the room. In seconds everyone at the table had his soup.

"Our version of Potage à la Windsor," Philip informed me.

The portion was small, but so delicious I already experienced the excitement of anticipating what was yet to come.

The soup was removed; the center spotlight went black. The light changed and the dais rose again, offering a fish dish. On the third rise of the dais, all three circles rose. The outer ring bore vegetables, each on its own small plate. The second circle held empty plates that were presumably to be filled with whatever treasure was yet to come into view. The anticipatory heavy breathing I heard confirmed my guess.

Finally the center section slowly rose. It carried a tremendous platter of what Philip said was suckling boar, shining and steaming, with the traditional apple in its mouth, bedded on a thick layer of yellow, orange, and green grass-like slivers that glinted in the light.

The waiters served small portions of the boar onto hot

plates wheeled in on a golden cart and then placed them on the plates from the center ring. A voice broke into my concentration.

"Mrs. Crane . . . "

The bearded man on my right was leaning toward me and whispering.

"I'm sorry to startle you, but I felt I should warn you. Be careful not to touch the table where the plates will be placed. They are heated so the food will continue to be warm. We are so attuned to our little amenities we sometimes forget a guest isn't aware of these things. . . . By the way, my dear, I'm Doctor Forrest Schine. We met hurriedly, but I am sure you will have no trouble remembering our names when you know us better."

Dr. Schine was enormous and solid. His head, shining bald, contrasted with a black beard trimmed meticulously down to two sharp points at his chin. His brows were heavy and black, his deep, inscrutable eyes almost hidden under dark red lids. His thick lips glistened wetly through his beard. I certainly hadn't forgotten him. Now I knew I'd never again forget the name.

Finally, his heavy lids lowered and he turned back toward the dais. As he did, his thick, hairy hand daintily patted his wet lips. He was wearing a large ring, intricately carved with the kidney design I'd seen in the outer hall.

At the far end of the table, Dr. Pavel, his small mustache twitching, his eyebrows lifting, acted as both sommelier and guest, examining each bottle of wine, checking labels, pinching and smelling corks. After sniffing each bottle, he allowed small portions to be served for each guest. No second portions were offered or requested.

Some of the vegetables were familiar, but their flavorings were foreign to me. Philip volunteered that the spinach had been cooked in coconut milk and herbs I'd never heard of. Even the grassy cushion under the boar was served, and it seemed to be needle-thin slices of fruits I couldn't recognize.

I ate slowly, but my companions were even slower, delicately savoring every mouthful before allowing anything to slip down their throats.

Only once during the main course did I happen to glance at Dr. Schine. He was so engrossed in his meal that he was not aware of anything else around him. His wet lips were busy, the thick muscles of his jaws working in circles. His tongue, darting in and out like a cobra's, was as red as fresh blood.

As the feast progressed, I forgot Dr. Schine and even forgot Philip as I became more and more absorbed in the taste, smell, touch, and sight of the food. I almost understood the fanaticism of these people. It was catching. By the time the plates were finally clean, my hosts sat back in their chairs, still without any conversation. The table was cleared. The accepted courses were over. They were waiting for the finale. I was as anxious, impressed, as I could ever remember being.

The room grew dimmer. The aromas of the previous courses were gone. Suddenly I became vividly aware of a savory, lotus-like fragrance teasing the air. A thin beam of light started to expand again from the ceiling as the dais rose. The beam grew stronger, and for the first time I could hear a soft trilling, a non-melodic sort of music—solemn, hypnotic. The volume of the trilling grew as the dais rose. At first the two outer rims appeared, laden with sparkling crystal dishes, each on its own small gold plate. And on each dish was what appeared to be a root, some fernery, and a single orchid. The central portion of the dais rose gloriously, holding a large glass bowl that glowed with a purple, bubbling liquid. The room stayed perfectly quiet as the waiters spooned the purple liquid around each orchid, dramatically bringing each serving to the table. Almost as one, every right hand reached for a spoon to bring up the first tiny bite. What looked like the orchid's base was a paper-thin almondy shell filled with a creamy substance. The stems were edible slivers of crust; the leaf was another creamy medley of flavors. The orchid itself tasted as luscious and distinctive as it looked. The purple liquid was evidently to be dipped into. It was thick and clear, with a distinct violet flavor.

When I had finished my portion, I saw everyone was facing Dr. Ahnesbach. He sat like a stone, waiting. Perspiration shone on his forehead; his hands trembled. Suddenly the entire gathering broke into enthusiastic applause. A smile spread across his face. He nodded to each side of the room. The other guests surrounded him, each one shaking his hand and then proceeding directly out of the room. The ceremony was over.

Soon I was alone in the room with Mrs. Byrom. She started to walk toward me. Philip had congratulated Ahnesbach and then left for the anteroom with the others without a word. Mrs. Byrom flashed her toothy smile.

"I was proud of you, my dear. Our little rituals are so important to us that we rarely introduce outsiders at these times. You passed our scrutiny admirably. We'll have luncheon sometime soon. Philip will be seeing you home, but he must leave for the Far East in a few hours, so I'm afraid he won't be able to dally. I shall contact you again shortly. It was gratifying having you here."

As she spoke, she was guiding me quickly into the outer room, and the moment she stopped speaking she walked off toward the elevator, leaving me standing nearly alone in the large gold anteroom with only a few people still chatting as they waited for the elevator. No one talked to me. A hand touched my shoulder. It was Philip.

"Let's go, little one. You withstood the formalities very well, but you can relax now. So can I. Come on, I haven't much time, but at least we can get to know one another a bit better on the way home."

CHAPTER 5

"Would you care to see a little more of Washington before I take you to the hotel? You haven't seen the city at night yet, have you?"

Before I could answer, Philip drove into the deserted street. I was surprised at the offer, but my spirits soared at the prospect.

"I'd love to. But I thought you were in a hurry. Your aunt said you're leaving for the Far East in a few hours."

"Yes, I am, but that's no problem. I commute. All over the world. . . . Anyway, Corintha's just being possessive. You're *her* new friend and she doesn't want me seducing you away from her."

I was flattered, but competition between Corintha Byrom and Philip for my friendship seemed incongruous, just a little too soon and too overdone, considering the company they already kept. Philip was just being gallant, but his kindness gave me the courage to satisfy my curiosity about that curious dinner party.

"Philip, would you please tell me something?"

"Certainly, Sharon dear, anything at all."

"I was wondering—why was the dinner so solemn, especially at dessert?"

"It's just that we like perfection at our dinners. Conversation interferes with the sensation of taste."

"But there seemed to be so much tension about the dessert. Dr. Ahnesbach looked as if he was scared stiff until they started applauding him."

"Oh, Sharon, you shouldn't exaggerate things. Oliver Ahnesbach is like that—a worrier. But it was important to all of us. We were trying a new dish which will be served at one of our international dinners. With our competition, we feel a great compulsion to measure up to the standards of our friends. It's quite important to us, but that's all."

There was still something nagging. "There's another thing, Philip. I felt all evening as though your friends were sizing me up. They were all very hospitable, but I felt on display and they couldn't have been all that interested in my mind. I'm certainly not in the same league with any of them."

He only laughed, loud and long. Then, still smiling, he answered me.

"You're imagining things, Sharon. You're a beautiful woman. Why shouldn't you interest them? Even women admire you. How can they help it? You were especially lovely tonight. I had to remind myself that you were really Corintha's guest, and she had to be allowed the pleasure of showing you off. But I can tell you, I resented every minute I wasn't able to monopolize you."

Philip's flattery didn't satisfy me. I knew I'd looked my best, but these people weren't taken in by a simple pretty girl. Philip reached over and took my hand, reminding me that this wasn't really the time or place to push the subject further. I tried to content myself with the moment and absorb the pleasure of being with Philip while I could.

We drove along the waterfront, then back to the Jefferson Memorial and finally to the Lincoln Memorial. He looked down at me and smiled. I was spellbound. He stopped before the Reflecting Pool.

"This is one time I'm not going to enjoy leaving so soon. You are doing something to me, Sharon. I'm enjoying everything about you. I thought you were a little sophisticate, but you're more like a novice from a convent. You are lovely, so refreshing."

He hugged me close to him. I shuddered, thinking suddenly of James. I couldn't face another man who could hurt me so terribly. I wanted Philip desperately, but froze at his gentle touch. He withdrew his hands abruptly.

"Anything else you'd like to see?"

I wanted to cry. "You'd better take me home. I can't help it. I wish I could tell you."

"Some other time."

"You've been so wonderful."

"It was my pleasure."

He drove in silence to the hotel. Walking me into the lobby, he briefly nodded, murmured, "Au revoir, ma chère enfant gatée," and was gone.

CHAPTER 6

I woke with a start. My chest was on fire. The pain, a thousand times worse than on the plane, bent me over double. Choking back a scream, I clutched at my chest. The room was still dark. I couldn't catch my breath. Bolting upright, freezing with cold sweat, I cried aloud: "God in Heaven help me!" The pain subsided. Without waiting to relax, I slid my feet from under the covers and, holding onto the bed, then the chair, made my way to the bathroom and leaned over the sink. I wasn't nauseated. Now hot sweat was bathing me and next everything was freezing again. I dragged myself back to the chair, found my bag, and had barely the strength to get it open. That doctor's number had to be somewhere. Would he come? Corintha had insisted that if I called him he would come at any time. How long had I been asleep? It seemed only minutes since I'd finally succumbed after hours of wakeful tossing, berating myself for Philip's cold departure. Was it only last night? Only a few hours ago? Calmer now, I looked at the clock. Only six-thirty—much too early to call that doctor.

I remembered. There had to be a hotel doctor. Dragging the telephone to me, I furiously jabbed at it.

Somebody came on the line.

"I need a doctor, I'm very ill."

"Just a moment, I'll connect you with the medical bureau."

"Hello, hello!!" I sobbed into the dead receiver, waited an eternity, and then, finally, another phone was picked up.

"Medical Bureau; may I help you?"

"I'm very ill. I need a doctor right away." The pains were returning. I could hardly speak between my clenched teeth.

"What is your name, and where are you?"

"I'm Sharon Crane and I'm at the Mayflower Hotel."

"I can get a doctor to you in about an hour, or you can go to the hospital emergency room. Can you take a taxi? Go to the George Washington Hospital."

"I can't. I just can't!"

"I'd better send an ambulance for you, then. Give me your room number."

"I don't want any ambulance!" I cried, and hung up.

I searched frantically through my bag. Maybe I'd lost that card. But I hadn't; there it was, big bold writing on its back. "Dr. Phineas Romano—KL5–4851." He was one of the doctors I'd met at Mrs. Byrom's. I'd have to call him, but I'd try to wait as long as I could. Maybe he would get up by seven.

My head began to pound, but as the time passed, the pain in my chest became at least bearable. Slowly, precisely, I dialed, fingers weak, damp and trembling.

A cool, precise voice answered almost immediately. "Mrs. Romano speaking. May I help you?"

"Is the doctor there? This is Sharon Crane. I was a guest at the dinner last night. Mrs. Byrom . . . I feel awful, and . . ."

"Yes, of course." Her voice softened, almost as if she had been expecting the call. "The doctor will see you. Can you make it to the office or shall he come to you now?"

"I don't think I can make it there. I'm in such pain."

"Where are you staying? I remember Corintha mentioning a hotel. Which one are you in?"

I told her and, without even hesitating, she said: "The doctor will be there shortly. Stay in bed and don't exert yourself. Don't even use the phone. The doctor will be shown to your room."

I thanked her as though she were saving my life, crawled back into bed and lay there shivering but bathed in sweat.

The bedside phone rang at last.

"Dr. Romano is here," announced the deskman.

In a few minutes, a hotel employee turned the latch and the doctor edged into the room. The light was on beside the bed, but he turned on all the other lamps as he made his way across the room. I remembered him from the party—the albino, so light of skin, with cotton hair and pink eyes, even his suit a colorless cream.

Methodically he checked my heart, blood pressure and stomach. His pink eyes looked deeply into mine. Sitting back, he shook his head as though perplexed.

"It is nothing as far as I can tell," he said with a curious expression. "It's not angina. You may have eaten something earlier yesterday. I'm certain it couldn't have been caused by our dinner."

Warning me to eat nothing before he saw me again, he practically ordered me to come to his office at nine precisely. He squinted down at his watch. "That is less than two hours from now. I want you to rest until then."

He gave me a shot in the arm, saying, "This will relax you. I'll leave the address here on my card. It's on the second floor of the building where you dined last night. Use the elevator at the center entrance between the pharmacy and the bank."

I quickly drifted into a deep euphoric sleep, but I kept seeing his white skin and lashless eyes hovering above me, like a transparent angel sent down from Heaven.

A few minutes later, or so it seemed, the telephone rang and I bolted out of a leaden sleep. Dr. Romano had alerted the desk to call me in time for my appointment. But all the pains were gone, as mysteriously and quickly as they had appeared.

"I've got to get dressed and get over there," was the first thought in my mind. "But I should be out job-hunting. I can't afford to stay here much longer. But what is wrong with me? I couldn't have imagined such pain. Suppose it happens again! I could die. And I am all alone except for Mrs. Byrom and her friends. I have to find out. I wonder what he'll charge me?" Still, I hurried to dress for the appointment. The doctor had been insistent, but I feared even more that Corintha Byrom would cut me off completely if I didn't appreciate her friend's concern. If I ever wanted to see Philip Hawk again, I had to keep that appointment.

CHAPTER 7

White-faced and rubber-kneed, I went down for a cab. The office was only a few blocks away. The center entry, the one Dr. Romano had told me to use, was easy to find. It had a small, businesslike marble lobby, cold and unornamented. The elevator took me to the second floor. Only four doors were marked: they were the offices of the doctors I had met the evening before. Other than these inconspicuous lettered doors, nothing broke the simplicity of the long hall. I wondered how Dr. Romano had managed to schedule me so quickly, then realized that he probably considered my condition to be very serious. Trembling with apprehension, I stopped hesitating and walked into his office.

Once inside I was certainly not reassured. The reception room was as stark as the hall, empty except for a few simple green leather chairs, a magazine rack with nothing in it, and a small, completely bare desk. Everything was spotlessly clean, not even a speck of dust. I sat down to wait, still trembling, and clutching both arms of the chair. What in the world was the matter with me? And how could I ever pay for my own care, without a job and so far away from anybody I really knew? If my illness was serious, I certainly couldn't impose on the charity of Corintha Byrom and her friends.

After a few moments the white door at the other end of the room opened and I recognized Mrs. Romano. She came toward me, hand extended, but there was no warmth in her movement or expression. The woman exuded breeding without charm. Even in her nurse's uniform she seemed to dominate the room. Her hair was a deep red, severely pulled back from her face and wrapped in a tight knot at the back of her head. She said good morning, nothing more—poised, abrupt, and efficient.

As I watched Mrs. Romano's approach, my heart started pounding again. It was exactly nine o'clock. The woman stood tall above me before she spoke.

"The doctor will be with you immediately, Mrs. Crane. Go into the first examining room and disrobe completely. A gown is on the door."

No sooner had I donned the gown than the doctor walked through the door. He said nothing, not even "good morning." He started the examination with such seriousness that all of my fears multiplied, flooding over me. Never had I been examined so completely, inside and out. My skin was scrutinized through a magnifying glass from head to toe. Dr. Romano's pink eyes, magnified by the glass, seemed like red torches. He scratched various parts of my body, for allergies I supposed. My blood was taken. Several times. I was attached to a dozen or more strange machines. Finally the doctor nodded, told me to dress and come into his office.

I didn't even notice my surroundings as I hurried into the adjoining office. I was only aware it seemed unprofessionally decorated, but that wasn't on my mind. I dropped into the chair beside the doctor's ornate desk.

"How long were you married?" he began without preamble. "You had no children? May I ask why not?"

"I used a diaphram, and then the pill," I half whispered.

"Was your husband impotent?"

"No."

"Sterile?"

"I never had a chance to find out. When he'd been drinking he wouldn't come near me. When he was sober, he made certain I was prepared. After a time I merely did it automatically. Mrs. Byrom probably told you we're divorced."

"Were there any other men? I don't mean to be personal, but I need to know whether you can conceive, if that is your problem."

"No! Of course not." I wanted to spit at him.

He rested back in his chair, and I thought I was through at last, but he went on. "Dr. Schine is just across the hall. I want you to take a few more tests with him."

"How much do you think all this will cost, Doctor? I have to start budgeting myself and I didn't anticipate this sort of expense."

He barked at me, "Young lady, do not worry about our charges. Why are you living at an expensive hotel if you can't afford to take care of your health?" Then he laid his white hand lightly on mine and leaned toward me confidentially. His voice was low and soft.

"I believe Mrs. Byrom mentioned you were looking for a job. Have you found anything yet?"

I relaxed a little. "No, I haven't had time. That's why I've been staying on at the hotel. It's convenient to the employment agencies and they all have that number now. I've never had to look for a job before."

"Well, after you've had Dr. Schine's tests, and if all is well, I think I may be able to offer you something to hold you over. We need a receptionist. I'll tell you more about it after the examination. Be in my office by nine sharp in the morning. I'll see you then."

He called the pathologist and told him to expect me across the hall. Then he curtly ordered me again to report back promptly at nine in the morning.

The huge Dr. Schine, dressed in spotless white, was waiting. He greeted me warmly, his pointed beard bobbing grotesquely against his white coat. The thought of being
touched by those fleshy, hairy hands that had fascinated me
at dinner was unnerving. But despite his size he moved
quickly and gently. In less than an hour, he was finished. He
looked me over carefully and then told me I could leave, but
again I was reminded to return to Dr. Romano's office early
in the morning. He assured me I needn't worry, then turned
his back in dismissal. He was now no less curt than Romano.
And after all that, neither of them had given me even a hint
of what was wrong with me.

No breakfast, no lunch. I was famished. It was three
o'clock when I finally reached the street again. The building's pharmacy had no lunch counter. Headachey, afraid
and near exhaustion, all I wanted now was the nearest coffee
shop, a cup of hot tea, and some food. I found one at the corner and slipped onto a stool at the nearly empty counter.

There were several girls behind the counter, all busily
scrubbing, moving things, or talking to each other, doing everything but noticing the few customers who wanted service.
I tried to attract their attention and became angrier when it
did no good at all. Tapping my fingers on the counter, I waited. My head was aching with hunger. I pulled out a cigarette
and lighted it. Drawing in the first puff was Heaven. A voice
distracted me.

"Excuse me, could I have the salt?"

Automatically, I handed the shaker to a man two seats
away.

"You're new around here, aren't you?"

Turning to the man, glaring at him as I had at the waitress,
I spoke sharply: "Yes, I am. Are they always this slow? How
can I get one of these women to take my order?"

"Marge," he called out, "this lady's starving. Come on, get
her order before she faints."

The lean, dancey black girl turned and beamed. "Sure Mr.

Dell. Right on. Been rushin' to get ready for the coffee stampede. They'll be bargin' in here like a rock concert any minute." Miraculously transformed into a pleasant obliging waitress, she came over immediately and took my order.

"Thank you so much," I murmured to the man, embarrassed at my overreaction. "What is this power you seem to have over women?"

"I'm a regular." He put down the book he was holding open in one hand and picked up his change with the other. "We regulars patronize this posh place every day at off hours. If you try lunchtime or coffee breaks you won't get near the counter."

"You always come in late, then?"

"Generally about two it's relatively peaceful. And when I work late, which is practically every night, their daily special holds me until I get home."

He was tall and lean and trying to balance himself on the flimsy stool. He was also well dressed in an expensive-looking buff suit. But his lemon-colored tie was askew, and an unruly lock of light sandy hair flopped across his forehead. When he caught my look, his brown eyes gleamed with amusement. With a laugh he said, "All right. I'm a lawyer. My office is across the street in that building in the middle of the block. I spend my life there. And I get awfully sick of this counter, but it's the closest I come to home cooking."

"You don't really eat your dinners here, too?"

"Yeah, sure. This is the only place open till seven. I grab something and take it back. There are plenty of restaurants, but it takes too long to get a decent meal."

I took the first bite of my sandwich and made a face. He laughed again.

"You're cute when you frown."

"Thank you, sir, and if you don't mind my saying so, I don't see how you stand it."

He looked at me blankly, then laughed.

"Oh, you mean the food."

"Yes, of course. For a starving woman like myself it's great, but a steady diet of it . . . Ugh!" I scrunched up my nose.

"It's better than nothing. I've got to eat. What about you? Do you work near here?"

"No, I've been to the doctor. As a matter of fact, I've been looking for a job and my doctor told me he might have a receptionist's position open soon. I just pray it works out."

"Which doctor is that?"

"Dr. Romano. He's in the building on this side in the middle of the block, the one above the pharmacy."

"I didn't know there were any doctors in that building. Nobody ever goes in or comes out of it. Several of us have noticed it. I don't understand how that pharmacy stays in business. It hardly ever has any customers that I can see. How'd you happen to go to that doctor?"

"A friend recommended him."

"Well, I guess it's none of my business, but my office faces that building. If anybody ever goes in or out, they certainly don't use the center entrance. The only signs of life I see there are at night, when I'm working late—it's the only building around here that's lit up every evening, even though I can't see anything through their smoked windows."

"People live there. Those are apartments on the upper floors. It's a cooperative."

"Weird place for an apartment house. Why in hell would anybody want to live in the midst of all these office buildings anyway?" He changed the subject. "You think you'll take the job?"

"If he offers it to me. I should know tomorrow."

"Well, I hope you get it if you want it. I shouldn't really make remarks about that building. I've never paid close enough attention to know, honestly, whether people go in there or not. It's just that people in the neighborhood get to know each other, coming and going as we do, and several of us play a sort of guessing game about what goes on behind those mysterious walls—you know, whether it's a bordello, or a front for the C.I.A. By the way, my name's Singleton, Wendell Singleton. Most people call me Dell." We shook hands and he held mine for a moment. "Well, hope to see you here again soon."

I turned and watched him scrambling toward the door.

Nice man, I thought. Somehow I felt better about the prospects for my new job, my health, my new life.

CHAPTER 8

The next morning I went directly to Dr. Romano's office. I woke early and timed my arrival perfectly, but when I walked into the doctor's office at the stroke of nine, there was no one there. I waited. Finally, after I'd squirmed for an hour, the doctor himself opened the inner door and summoned me without a word of explanation for his delay. He led me through a hallway of closed doors and motioned me to the deep leather chair beside his desk. I had barely noticed the office before. Now I was vaguely aware of the walls, two draped in brown velvet, the others filled with row upon row of books with antique bindings, beautifully scrolled and bound.

Dr. Romano's chin sank down to his puffed-out chest, his voice dolefully solemn: "Mrs. Crane, you have been neglecting yourself. You must have sinned against your body for some time. Have you been under any great stress?"

"Well, yes, for a few months, but that's all past now. All I need is a job and a more permanent place to live. But am I physically all right? What were those pains?"

"Organically I find nothing wrong with you, except possibly your susceptibility because of the run-down condition. I'll prescribe something that will help, but it must be taken religiously and you must regulate your habits as soon as possible."

"But the pains? What if they return? I can't call you out again in the middle of the night."

"The pains won't recur once your system is stabilized and your worries overcome."

I thanked him and started to get up to leave when he grasped my arm to restrain me.

"I think I may be able to help you," he said, "at least long enough for you to regain your health."

I felt tears coming to my eyes. I held my breath. This was going on like a drawn-out melodrama.

"I believe I mentioned the receptionist position you might fill," he went on. "Actually, Doctors Schine, Ahnesbach, Press and I all use the same receptionist. The position is simple, mostly answering the telephone and taking messages. We're all semi-retired, so we spend very little time in our offices. The salary is nominal, but I am sure it would be adequate if you find more suitable living accommodations."

He named a figure. It was a surprise, more than I'd expected—not much, but more than I felt I deserved for the inexperience I had to offer.

My answer was immediate. The weight of anxiety lifted while my heart raced. "When would you want me to start? I can start any time and I'm sure I can do it. I promise I'll try my best."

He smiled to put me at ease. "How about Monday morning, say about ten? Today is Friday, so that won't rush you."

"I'll look for an apartment during the weekend."

Another slow, tantalizing grin crossed his face. "I may be able to help you there, too, if your work proves satisfactory. We have several small apartments on the top floor and I think one of them might be vacated shortly. If you find a room, make temporary arrangements in case our apartment becomes available. I am sure the others can be persuaded to give you first preference, as we do keep those smaller places for the convenience of our employees. We'll see how the job works out."

He handed me a slip of paper. "I want you to take this prescription downstairs to Dr. Pavel the moment you leave this office. Have him fill it for you. It's a new drug and I doubt if most other pharmacies have it yet. Take it three times daily until I tell you to stop. You will notice an improvement almost immediately, but there can be a bad reaction if you aren't absolutely conscientious about the regimen until your system has recovered completely. See that you eat wholesome food, preferably home cooking, broiled, without seasoning. I'll see you here Monday morning."

I practically danced downstairs to the pharmacy. In one morning all my problems had been solved. Dr. Pavel came out of a back room immediately. Grinning at me, he took the prescription and, without looking at it, sauntered out of sight. He was back almost immediately with a large bottle of pills, my name already typed on the label.

"How much, doctor?" I had my wallet open.

"Oh, two dollars, please." His grin annoyed me. I threw down the money. He didn't ring up the sale, but stuffed the bills in his pocket and smirked his way back out of sight into the workroom.

How could he have anticipated that I'd be in? There hadn't been time for Dr. Romano to call. Why had that prescription been ready and waiting for me? I became more and more uncomfortable as I walked very slowly, deep in thought, back to the hotel.

CHAPTER 9

Saturday I found a room. It was in Maryland, quite a long bus ride from where I'd be working, and it was dingy compared to anything I'd known before; but I could afford it with my monthly checks from James and as soon as my job started I could begin to save for an apartment.

I walked into Dr. Romano's office Monday morning as if I owned the world. The pills he'd prescribed were already affecting me. It must have been the pills. The move and the prospective job couldn't have invigorated me and raised my spirits so much. I felt better than I had in years. Marvelous! As I bathed, my skin glowed and felt silky. I was confident now that I could make it on my own.

Mrs. Romano greeted me at the door. "Well, Mrs. Crane, you do look much better." The doctor's wife was again immaculate in her perfectly tailored uniform, but I realized for the first time that she was nearly nondescript. Your eyes caught her hair but missed the rest of her. Her skin, too, glistened with health.

"Here's your desk," she said matter-of-factly. "I'll show you how to use the telephones. Message pads and supplies are in the drawer. The closet and bathroom are for your use. All the doors have time locks so you needn't bother with closing up at the end of the day."

She swept me through the suite of rooms, explaining as we walked. "You'll limit your attention to the outer office. I take care of the rest of the suite." She spoke softly but firmly, with almost no inflection.

"You'll answer the telephones and record the messages. The doctors will call you for them."

"What about making appointments?"

"You won't make them. Just take the messages. I schedule the appointments. The other doctors do their own."

"What if an emergency comes in?"

"We rarely handle emergencies. I believe the doctor told you he is almost entirely retired from active practice. He sees only certain special patients."

I wondered to myself why he'd been so quick to come to me when I'd called. Aloud I asked only: "Do you want me to do some filing or handle the mail?"

"I handle all the files and mail. You come in at ten, leave at five. And the doctors prefer that you take your luncheon later in the afternoon, say about two. We have a buffet on the fourth floor. Use it any time. You may also bring whatever you wish back down here if you prefer. The buffet is restricted to occupants of the building. I'll show you where it is. Please do not wander about the building. It is a private residence, you know. Actually, we prefer that you use the buffet. You will not be charged for your meals, and it is open all day as a convenience to our residents. The food is excellent and it will take far less time than if you use the neighborhood restaurants."

We were back in the outer office. Satisfied that everything was in order, she abruptly departed, leaving me alone to face the empty office and my first day at work.

I sat for hours doing nothing. The door never opened. The only calls that came in seemed to be social; no one asked for an appointment. No one left his name. In my boredom I began looking through my desk. In the first drawer I found only telephone pads, some pencils, a few paper clips, and the first sign of dust. I tried another. Empty. I was feeling disgusted when I remembered I hadn't taken my pill. I had to swallow it without water, because I didn't know of a fountain and there were no cups in the bathroom. The pills were innocuous-looking, small and white, but they had a distinct, peculiar aftertaste of almonds.

I was famished. I slammed the desk drawers. The frustration of doing nothing was getting to me. The last drawer, the deep one, closed with a thud, but it wouldn't shut tight. Something was caught behind it. I pulled out the drawer above it and laid it on the floor. Getting onto my knees and stretching to reach the back of the desk, I maneuvered my hand until it reached the bottom. I felt paper, twisted and tugged, and finally got it out. It was only a paperback book—a gothic romance. The previous receptionist must have been just as bored as I was. It was better than nothing. As I flipped the pages, I discovered a tightly folded letter with no envelope. As I unfolded it, a photograph fell out. It was a picture of a young woman, blond and pretty, and she glowed like a girl deeply in love. The back of the photograph was blank.

Then I froze. I thought I heard footsteps in the hall. Squatting in my awkward position on the floor, I was afraid to move a muscle. Minutes went by, and my foot fell asleep under me, but whatever I'd heard didn't recur. "I must be imagining things," I thought as the muscles of my body relaxed.

I slid the picture and the book into my purse. The letter was in badly scrawled handwriting on cheap, thin paper, worn from refolding and handling. There was no address:

Dear Mary Etta,
    I am writing to you this one more time. I got your last letter almost 3 months past. You sounded like everything was going

so great I couldnt hardly believe it. I wrote you too times since then. At least I thought we was allways good enough freinds that you would anser me right back when I told you my own good news. I wrote you both times about me and Ben getting engaged so you must of at least got one of my letters by now. It dont seem like you to be cutting me dead.

It was the best thing ever happened when you took off. You was able to get yourself a good job and a apartment and everything right off. The best thing of all was you got that terrific boyfreind right away too. I allways knew you had it. You was allways the prettyest girl around and it was no wonder you hit it big soon as you got out of that rotten town.

This is why Im writing you this one more time. I thought you would want to know that Ben and me has got married and he got himself a good job in Arkansas where we are living now. It sure does feel great to have a real home as you found out and now I did too.

Well I wont bother you no more after this because I know you are really living it up but I wanted you to know about us getting married and I am sending you my address where you can write to me just in case you get the chance.

I know that boyfreind (or husband) of yours is keeping you so busy you must of changed a lot because the last letter you did write hardly even sounded like you. I honestly couldnt make out all the things you was saying.

No matter what reason you got for not writing, we both got ourselves out of that lousy foster house, and out of that one horse town and I know you are doing real good and so am I and I just wish you keep on with your good luck like it has been.

Your freind,
Elloise

The letter, the picture, and the paperback told me a great deal about the girl who had occupied the desk before me. Her life almost came alive to me, and I wondered where she could be now.

CHAPTER 10

It was already after two. Mrs. Romano hadn't come back and I couldn't wait any longer. I was starving. I decided to get lunch at the coffee shop. The mysterious free buffet would have to wait until I had some directions on how to get there.

The waitress knew me this time and brought my order in minutes. Mr. Singleton was evidently a favorite and any friend of his was accorded favored treatment as well. The food didn't improve, though, and a rubbery, over-seasoned hamburger was all I felt like eating. But I downed three cups of hot coffee trying to wake up. The almond pills seemed to have a tranquillizer in them, and I dreaded having to exist on drugs again. I lingered over the coffee, hoping to see Dell, but he didn't come. The coffee-break stampede was also beginning and I felt guilty about holding the seat, so I started back to the office with the frustrated feeling I was heading for more solitary confinement.

I was alone again the whole afternoon, feeling even more cut off than I had in the morning. At least then the phones had rung. The doctor strutted through the door exactly at five, self-satisfied and much too cheerful.

"How did your day go, Mrs. Crane? No problems, I hope."

"Very well, thank you, Doctor. There were a number of calls this morning but no one would leave a name."

He smiled. "That's perfectly all right. Perfectly all right." He seemed far away, as though he hadn't heard me.

While I had the chance I went on: "Doctor, there is one thing. I feel so useless. I know in time I'll be more helpful, but the patients—I can't even tell who they are. If I could get to know them, at least by name, I could . . ."

He cut me off. "Mrs. Crane, we've explained your duties fully. It is quite sufficient that you do as you are doing. I only see a few very special patients and most of them are housed right in this building. Of course, they are completely segregated from our living quarters, but the other doctors and I can see them quite readily."

"But doctor, couldn't I . . . ?" I just wanted a little more responsibility—anything to make the job less boring—but obviously the doctor thought I was overstepping myself.

"Our patients, my dear, are special research cases. All of them are deeply emotionally disturbed. You would never be qualified to deal with them, so you will only cause difficulty if you try to exceed the duties you have already been assigned."

"Well, thank you, Doctor," I squeaked. "I promise I won't bother you again. If you want anything, I know you'll tell me."

He flashed his broad, gummy smile, as mechanical as his words. "That's exactly right. I must be leaving now. Just came by for my mail. There's nothing more before I go? I am pressed for time, you know."

I hated to ask, but he'd given me an opening. "There is one thing, Doctor. Mrs. Romano told me she'd show me the way to the buffet. I guess she forgot."

For a moment it seemed as if he would lose his temper again. I felt like crying; I was certain I'd lose my job after only one day. But as he went on, I almost sighed aloud with relief. It wasn't I he was angry with; Mrs. Romano would be the one to hear about this.

As though speaking to a child, he gave the directions. Like a chastised and obedient schoolgirl, I listened.

"Just take the elevator at the end of the center corridor to the fourth floor. You can't miss it. It's clearly marked. But don't wander anywhere else on that floor. There are several private suites and you might disturb someone. And there are a number of private storage rooms on that floor. You could easily lock yourself into one of them. Our security measures are very rigid and many doors won't open from either side without the proper key." Without another word, he hurried out the door.

It was time for me to leave too. I'd been told the office doors had time locks, but surely I wasn't simply to walk out leaving the office open. I stood by the door for a few moments, but there seemed no way to lock it, so I stepped into the hall and pulled it closed. Testing it, I found it was locked. A few more seconds' delay and I would have been locked in. And I knew no one at all I could have called to get me out.

All the days were the same. Nothing but invisible patients and nameless phone callers. But still the calls came. Not once did I see anyone entering or leaving the building. If the doctors had patients, I never saw them. Only occasionally did Dr. Romano visit his office, and when he did it was only for a few minutes. The mail piled high, but for the most part he even ignored that. He rarely talked to me. Despite my instructions I couldn't bring myself to go to the buffet. At least not yet. I had to get outside the building and walk around for a few minutes to break the monotony of the long days. At first I was careful to take a short lunch period, rushing down to the coffee shop, and back, always hoping to see Wendell Singleton.

Dr. Romano didn't mention the buffet again and he was never around to know where I ate or how long I took for

THE VOLUPTUARIES

59

lunch. Soon I was spending more and more time at the counter. Finally Dell came in, saw me, and sat down beside me. During the next two weeks I made certain to go out when I thought he would be there. He always was. We lingered over lunch as long as possible, getting acquainted. I told him everything I had told Mrs. Byrom, but with Dell I didn't have to keep anything back. I found it easy to tell him all about the sanitorium. I brought him up to date, especially about the luxury with which I was now surrounded. The only things I couldn't bring myself to tell were my strong feelings for Philip, and the ride we had taken after the dinner party.

Dell's main topic was his work, but he loved to listen to me talk. The only time he seemed strained was when I told him about the possibility of getting an apartment right in the luxury building where I worked. He looked down and said nothing. That wasn't the reaction I'd expected, but I decided that he thought I was being unrealistic, and preferred to say nothing rather than ruin my hopes.

Most days we spent the time laughing a lot and talking. The lunch hours grew longer each day but none of the doctors seemed to care. He had a slightly crooked smile, and a funny way of twitching his nose when he laughed. He frowned quickly, laughed easily, his face full of animation. But I found as I studied his face that, no matter how pleasant he was to be with, my mind always wandered back to Philip Hawk. I couldn't help making comparisons and Dell just reminded me of how intensely I wanted just one more chance to make amends to Philip. I was glad for knowing Dell—he broke the monotony—but Philip was all that really mattered to me.

One day Dell was restless throughout most of the lunch. Just before we reached for our checks, he touched my hand to delay me.

"Sharon, how about dinner and a movie tonight?"

"Tonight?"

"I suppose you're busy."

"No, I'd love it, Dell. But I'd like to go home first and change."

"Okay, I'll pick you up at seven. If I can find my way to Maryland."

Dell picked me up on time. "You don't mind riding in a four-year-old Mustang, I hope, after those fancy foreign jobs you've become accustomed to? How 'bout a pizza?"

"I'd love it, but the doctor told me to be careful of what I eat since I had that upset."

"Is that why you're always taking those pills you tell me are making a new woman out of you?"

"Yes, and they have. I've been feeling absolutely terrific ever since I started taking them. It must be the pills. I never felt this well in all my life."

"Well, they must have *some* kind of magic. You've been looking better every time I've seen you."

I changed the subject. I didn't want to believe that my health was so dependent on the pills.

We drove back from the suburbs to an Italian restaurant on Wisconsin Avenue and Dell ordered a full dinner. I didn't give a thought to my diet. It all sounded so good: antipasto, minestrone, spiedini alla griglia, Italian rum cake and coffee. It was delicious, especially after Dell reminded me of the drugstore specials I'd been eating.

We were sitting over coffee and cigarettes when Dell put both elbows on the table and rested his head on his hands. He was staring at me. His animated face went solemn and his voice dropped. I could almost tell what was about to come and I didn't want to hear it. With all the talking we'd done, neither of us had talked about our feelings for the other. Dell was a cheerful note in the tedium of my working days, and that was all I wanted from him. But I couldn't stop him from speaking.

"Sharon, I lost my wife two years ago."

I hadn't even thought to ask him whether he'd ever been married.

"When it happened, I went right back to the office and practically lost myself in my work. It was an anesthetic and it helped, but it got to be too much of a habit. I cut myself off from all of my friends. But about six months ago I stopped and took a good look at myself. I was nothing more than a machine. So I moved into a new apartment and I made the effort to meet people who had nothing to do with my work. I even visited some of my old friends. It wasn't easy, but until then I had been letting myself drown. . . . A whole year and a half out of my life, burying myself in that office. . . . I still work long hours, but I make time for other things, too. I had to make an effort to be interested. There is a world full of exciting people wherever you are, but you won't find them hidden away in that building where you work. You'll be locking yourself into a situation where you will have to depend entirely on the few people who live there. And you're not in their league, whether you'll admit it to yourself or not. You're liable to wind up watching them the way you'd watch a television screen. They won't take you into their circle, and even if they do, you'd go crazy trying to be one of them."

"Oh, for heaven's sake, it's not as bad as all that." I had to defend myself. "Think of all the advantages I would have. No commuting at all. And I'd be right across the street from you. And besides, you've practically got me locked in a cell, and they may never even let me have the place."

He smiled, but continued thoughtful. "I'd worry about it less if it weren't for all those pills you have to take. You know, it was pills that killed my wife. She took birth-control pills that her doctor thought were safe and died of a stroke at twenty-nine."

"But these aren't that kind of pill at all!" I spluttered. This was getting ridiculous.

"I don't know what they are," Dell pressed on, "and neither do you. But I don't like the looks of that pharmacy or the whole set-up. Okay, forget it, but about the apartment, just promise me you'll think about it very seriously before you do anything. Look around a little. At least see what's available."

"All right. All right, I will." It was a half promise I knew I probably wouldn't keep. I was thinking only of Philip and having an apartment near his. But before we said goodnight I finally agreed to see Dell again on Friday night. It was to be a special occasion for him and I hadn't the heart to turn him down.

CHAPTER 11

Mrs. Romano was waiting when I walked into the office the next morning. She was standing stiff, fuming, indignant, beside my desk. She came directly to the point.

"Mrs. Crane, I'm afraid I didn't make it perfectly clear, or you didn't take my suggestion seriously when I told you to use the buffet for your lunch. I've been away or I would have known it sooner. Well, I've learned that you still have not been there. And I know the doctor told you how to get there. It is for your own good as well as for the convenience of the people you are working for. We ask very little, but we do expect our employees to maintain their health. It is important to us that you follow the doctor's regime with absolutely no deviations."

With that said, she stalked out. I had been thoroughly reprimanded. How could she have known whether I'd been to the buffet, with so many other people using it? I didn't see why she or Dr. Romano should care, in any case. I was just the receptionist, as easily replaceable as Mary Etta. The suggestion was now an order. I dreaded staying inside the building all day, missing the lunches with Dell, but it had to

be done. Then it occurred to me that I might hear news
about Philip at the buffet. He might even eat there himself. I
hadn't heard from him or Mrs. Byrom since I had come to
work in their building.

By two o'clock, as usual, I was hungry. I wasn't looking forward to going to the buffet alone, but Mrs. Romano's order
certainly was not to be taken lightly this time. So I followed
the empty corridor that crossed the building and turned into
the hall leading to the back. I found the elevator and took it.
It was like following a maze in an empty hospital.

When I reached the fourth floor another lushly furnished
corridor appeared. The carpet muffled every sound. Each
heavy-looking door was inconspicuously marked in the lower
panel. It was simple to find the buffet door. I took a deep
breath, and opened it.

The room was warm and inviting, luxurious but informal
despite its great size. One wall was brick and had a fireplace.
Three walls were painted a sunny lemon yellow, broken only
by ceiling-high windows at one end. Tables and chairs were
grouped for sociable conversation. Copper and ceramic pots
brimming with freshly cut flowers hung everywhere. In every appropriate spot were Chelsea porcelain figures, African
carvings, Oriental tapestries and gold-framed Braques, Cha-
galls and Matisses. Near the back wall was a long table, obviously for the buffet, but now the cloth was bare. Not a soul
was in sight.

I thought Mrs. Romano had said the buffet was open
twenty-four hours a day, but obviously she'd been mistaken.
Then, as I turned to leave, a door behind the table opened
and a young black girl bustled through wearing a blank
smile.

"I'm so happy to see you," she said, without any inflection.
"Please sit down. I'll bring out the dishes immediately. This is
your first time here, isn't it." Her words rolled out as if they
had been recorded.

I really wanted to leave now. "Don't go to any trouble. It's
late. I'll come back another day."

The attendant stepped into my path, almost as though she would stop me by force if I made a move to leave. "It is no trouble. The food is kept in the kitchen until the guests come in. We have been waiting for you, Mrs. Crane."

Before I could say anything more the girl was gone. She had called me by name. Why should this waitress have known about me? I was beginning to think that the buffet was just a charade, played for my benefit alone.

In minutes the girl was back, loading the buffet table with appetizers, cold plates, hot dishes, salads, enough food for twenty people. I forced myself to take some lobster salad, muffins, and spiced ham, then sat down in a corner of the room in royal solitude, feeling terribly uncomfortable, as though something lay in wait for me here. At least my back was protected.

As soon as I was seated, the waitress removed the other dishes and left. Evidently nobody else was expected. The food was ambrosial but I rushed through it as though it were nasty medicine. If I hurried I'd have time to stroll around outside at least for a few minutes. But I was thwarted again. As I crammed the last bite into my mouth the waitress returned with a tray of pastries and a large pot of steaming coffee. My intuition told me I was expected to eat anything presented, and the food itself was tempting. But the situation was so unreal—like a dream that you wake from soaked in hot sweat.

By the time I started on my coffee, I had begun to enjoy the strangeness of the situation. With each sip the craving to go out for a walk was vanishing. I thought suddenly of my almond pills. Was it possible that even here the food was doctored with a mood elevator? It was a ridiculous idea, and the more surfeited I became, the faster my qualms slipped away. Then I remembered I hadn't taken my morning pill and quickly remedied the oversight. When I left the room the waitress was nowhere in sight.

Jabbing at the elevator button, I again felt the overwhelming urge to get out of the building. I had to see people. Five minutes passed and still the elevator hadn't come. I looked for a stairway. There were no exit signs, only those heavy closed doors with their quiet lettering. The only way out was a door, but I had no keys. Everything in the whole damned building was locked. There was nothing to do but find that waitress. When I turned around, the girl was coming toward me. Exasperated, I cried out furiously: "Don't you have a key for this elevator? I can't get back down."

She was annoyingly sympathetic. "I'm sorry, Mrs. Crane, I don't have one, but I'm to call the General. He'll come right after you."

"Isn't there any other way down? Must we bother the General just for me to get downstairs?"

Again she recited, "It is perfectly all right. He will be happy to do it."

She was gone and didn't come back, but in no time General MacDonald came marching down the hall.

"Hell-l-l-o, Mrs. Crane, I'm delighted to be of service to you. I'm so glad you finally gave our little dining room a try. Didn't you enjoy your meal?"

I controlled myself. "Yes, I certainly did. Everything was delicious, but I don't enjoy having to bother you just to get out of here."

"No bother at all. We want you to come here. The food is the best in every way, tasty, nutritional, balanced. We do insist our girls stay healthy. Any time you are ready to leave, just have the waitress call me and I'll open the elevator for you. I assure you it is no trouble."

"Couldn't I have a key so I wouldn't have to bother you?"

His smile hardened. "Afraid not. Security, you know. Only residents have keys. But I assure you this is one of my most pleasant duties. You must not deprive me of my pleasure." He was beaming like a Cheshire cat. It was out of character. The smile on his lips was not in his eyes. They were burning like dry ice.

He inserted a key and the elevator responded at once. I

thought he would accompany me down but he just stood there watching until the doors closed him out.

Something was wrong with what he'd said. The thought struck me as I watched his beaming, silly face disappear behind the closing doors. If the elevator was locked for security reasons, then why was it so easy to get upstairs and not down? Anybody who wanted to get into the building could come in at any time through the center entrance. There was no obstacle to coming in, only to getting out.

CHAPTER 12

By Thursday, frustration had me frantic. I couldn't wait another day for human contact. I had forced myself to eat every day in the buffet, and while it was fabulous and free, I would have preferred to eat off greasy spoons with Dell. That night I called his office and asked him if he'd please go to a movie with me. He had to work late, but he reassured me we still had a date the following night. I trudged wearily back from the hall phone to my room. I was lying across the bed, staring up at the ceiling, wanting to cry, when someone knocked. It was the landlady, and in her high-pitched, breathless voice, she called through the door to say a man who had called many times before was on the phone again.

She was still babbling when I managed to get past her and bound down the stairs.

It was Philip!

"I've tried to reach you several times, Sharon," he said, "but I was always between flights and I couldn't wait for your landlady to get you to the phone."

I was breathless. "Oh, Philip, I'm so glad you called. I wanted to . . . " He cut me off.

"How about tomorrow night? I'll be home for a few weeks, but they are booked solid. I want to see you while I have the chance. Is it a date?"

I remembered the date with Dell. "Oh, I'm sorry, but I have a date. I can change it if it's the only night you have free."

There was a long silence, and then I barely heard him. He spoke as though he were accusing me again. "No, don't do that. I'll call you the first chance I get. Try to make those dates a bit tentative for awhile, though, won't you please? We'll get together. Take care, and don't let that other fellow put his arm around you." He hung up.

The weekend was ruined. Friday's evening with Dell was flat and dull despite his efforts to bring me out of my mood. I tried but it was no use. All of Saturday and Sunday I stayed in my dreary room waiting for Philip to call. He didn't. The brass ring was still dangling just out of my reach. Why was he teasing me this way? Maybe this was just the jet-set's indifference to anyone who didn't belong.

CHAPTER 13

On Monday at eleven o'clock I closed the office door and started for a prearranged lunch with Dell. To hell with the buffet! Let them fire me. I couldn't take another day of it.

Then I saw the patient. The first one I'd yet seen. The girl was coming toward me down the corridor. Strangely, I knew her immediately to be a patient. It was a relief to see her. Until now the few people who came to the office were obviously only making social calls. They'd saunter through the office without a word to me and knock on the doctor's door. Dr. Romano would always throw it open with a wide, gummy smile on his face and usher his guest in.

This girl was not like them. Everything about her was all wrong. Heavy with pregnancy, not even aware of me, she waddled along slowly, her eyes cast down to the marble floor. Her concentration seemed entirely focused on reaching the proper door without mishap. She stopped short before Dr. Press's office. Even if she hadn't had such a big belly, nobody could have missed her in the tent dress she wore—a bright red with large white polka dots. Just before she turned away,

I caught a look at her face. It was the same girl whose photograph I'd found behind the desk drawer. The long blond
hair was now caught back from her face, pinned tight to control the curls, but her face was the same. Even without that
glowing smile, she was still lovely. As she reached for the obstetrician's doorknob, she glanced around. When she caught
me staring, she hesitated. Her face clouded. Her lips hung
open, her body seemed to move on its own. She opened the
door and disappeared.

I felt as if those puffy, dark-circled eyes were still staring at
me. For that one moment they had registered something,
and then they had gone totally blank again.

I couldn't bring myself to tell Dell about the girl. He would
have laughed at my curiosity, or worse, it would have further
convinced him I shouldn't even think of living in that building.

After lunch I was dreading the long afternoon ahead, or
the reprimand I'd get if they found I'd not used the buffet
again, but when I walked into the office, to my amazement
Mrs. Byrom was sitting in the chair beside the desk. She was
clearly provoked. Her face was redder than I could have
imagined. I tried to cover my surprise with a broad smile, but
I was annoyed with myself for not being at my desk on the
one day Mrs. Byrom chose to call.

"Why, Mrs. Byrom, I didn't expect you. What a pleasant
surprise. Have you been waiting long?"

Her frown was gone now, but her voice was still icy.

"Yes, Sharon, you are forgiven. I'm sure you don't do this
often or the doctors would call it to your attention."

She smiled in that artful, open way she had. "Please, my
dear, it's to be Corintha. I was most anxious to see you. I've
wonderful news and I wanted to catch you before it was too
late. The apartment has become available, just today."

"The apartment?"

She ignored my blank look. "It has finally been vacated. I
was so anxious that you have the first chance at it before it is

promised to anyone else. It's a large efficiency, furnished. We reserve it for our receptionist. Just perfect for you. Come, we can see it right now."

"But I'd never be able to afford a place in this building."

She was annoyed again. "I told you, you mustn't allow the rent to bother you. Our efficiencies are not expensive; they are for the convenience of our employees. The doctors prefer it this way."

Her timing was so unexpected that I wasn't prepared. She sensed my hesitation. Her face went tight. She was hiding her anger at my lack of appreciation.

"Philip's apartment is the only other one on the same hall as yours. The other efficiencies use another entrance. It maintains privacy even in the smaller apartments. The one next to Philip's is the choice one. It uses the main lobby. Come on, Sharon. I don't have much time." She knew the bait for me. Was I all that obvious?

"I'm so sorry, Mrs. By—, Corintha, I didn't mean to sound so ungrateful. You just took me by surprise. Of course I want to see it, but should I leave the office empty again? I took so long for lunch."

She waved the doubts away with her hand. "I'm certain the doctor won't miss too many calls. We won't be gone that long. Besides, this would please us as we are most uncomfortable having you live so far away. Our friends and patients know our customs; they'll call back as usual."

She bustled me out before I could even go near my desk. We went to the main elevators, where Mrs. Byrom used her key. The elevators opened at the eleventh floor onto a long hallway, thickly carpeted, papered in heavily flocked Wedgwood blue and hung with more original paintings. Another luxurious area of the building! A handsome chair and a console table with fresh flowers and mirror were set in a small alcove beside the elevator. Only two doors broke the long hall ahead of us, and they were both flanked with marble pillars. I already knew I had to have this apartment. Just getting to it was the essence of grandeur.

When we came to the first door, Mrs. Byrom fingered through a number of keys before she selected one, inserted it, and ushered me in.

It was a large, impersonal room, furnished almost too simply for the rest of the building, but it fit my style better than I'd thought possible. The small sofa, lounge chair, dinette set, desk, and chest of drawers seemed lost in the room. The bed and its small table with a lamp were set in the other branch of the L, separating them from the main part of the living room. Everything was a shade of brown or beige, making the room seem drab. It certainly wasn't lavish, but suitable for a mere receptionist. A small kitchen, large dressing room and bath completed the apartment. Four sliding glass doors opened onto a balcony.

We walked out onto a private portion of the roof, the full width of the apartment, at least ten feet across and completely walled in. All trace of the surounding office buildings was cut off. All you could see was the sky.

"You can sunbathe out here any time you like," Mrs. Byrom suggested. "The balustrade is high enough so you can't be seen from across the street."

The wall was of dark-red brick at least five feet high—I couldn't see over it. On the left was the windowless wall of the next building and on the right was another brick wall reaching to the overhanging roof. The roof came out over only a part of the balcony on which we stood, allowing the sun to come far into the room. It was almost like a private penthouse. It just needed some furniture—a few aluminum lounge chairs, a small metal table with yellow chairs, and the balcony would be a wonderful place for entertaining. It was just waiting for the right touches to make it charming. It was perfect for a person like me.

If only James could see me now. I had a job, an apartment, and I was going to live alone on the floor with the most fascinating man in the world.

There was only one question left. "How much is it?"

Mrs. Byrom lifted her finger to her lips. She didn't seem to want to discuss money, but then she brightened and replied: "One hundred and fifty a month. I'm not one for figures, I'm afraid, but I'm certain that's what the General told me. He usually takes care of these things, but I was so anxious for you to have your chance."

"When can I move in?" I found myself saying before I dared think.

"As soon as you wish. After all, it is vacant."

"My room is paid through this week."

"You needn't worry about that, dear child. You won't be charged here until the first of the month, naturally, and you might as well get yourself settled. I see no reason to wait. You haven't anything but the clothes you brought with you, have you?"

"No. Most of my things are still in storage in California."

"Well, simply pack tonight and move in tomorrow. I'll tell the Romanos and you can report to your office as soon as you get yourself settled. Now I'll take you back downstairs and lend you these special keys until the General issues you your own. You must return these to the General when you get yours. Be very careful with them. A lost or stolen key could cause us tremendous problems. All our locks are specially designed, and if any key is lost, all locks are changed immediately."

She dropped the keys into my hand. In my excitement I didn't notice until later that they were both engraved: "On loan—for use of apartment No. 1."

CHAPTER 14

On Tuesday I moved into my first apartment with mixed emotions. I didn't want to spend all my time with the residents of this building, but I was elated to be living in such style, and so close to Philip. I just had to run into him sometime in the hallway—no one else would come to this part of the building. I swung my arms around, hugging myself at the thought. I saw our floor as an island—a perfect situation to be in.

With my few belongings hung in the closets, the room still felt and looked like a hotel. I began moving the furniture around. A little better, I thought as I surveyed it, legs apart, hands on my hips. As soon as I sent for my things in California I could make it seem more like home. I hadn't taken much when I left James, but there was enough, and I'd be needing my fall clothes soon. I sat down immediately and wrote the storage company asking them to rush shipment, and as I was writing my new address, I realized I didn't even know the name of the building. Nobody had mentioned it and I hadn't seen it anywhere. It seemed curious, considering the building itself was such an object of pride to all the residents. In a flash of insight the import hit me. I was actually living here now, but I was still not accepted in their clique. Perhaps I never would be. I was an employee despite Mrs. Byrom, despite Philip, despite the enthusiasm with which they had all seemed to accept me at their dinner party. It now seemed so long ago. So I decided to slip down to the street, mail the letter, and at least satisfy my curiosity about the building's name.

I was still in jeans, a soiled shirt, and bedroom slippers. No makeup. Even though I'd transported so little, I was tired and sweaty from lugging clothes and shifting the furniture. It was nearly midnight. I was tired, but also anxious to get the letter in the mail. I could bathe and fall into bed as soon as I got back.

I made it to the lobby without interruption. No people, not a sound. Closing the front doors, I stepped across the sidewalk for a look. Unobtrusively set above the doorway was the address number, but nothing else. I put the letter in the mailbox at the curb, then hurried toward the center entry recessed between the bank and the pharmacy. There was nothing there either except another number. Standing protected by the windows of the bank and pharmacy, I felt foolish. I wondered if I should try the entrance at the other end of the building, but somehow I knew it would be useless. The street was deserted. Only a few speeding cars broke the silence. I ran down to the end of the building. It ended with a short alley that led to the third entry. I couldn't even see it from the street. It was pitch dark. But over the door was a third inconspicuous, dimly lighted number. This must be the address used by others who worked in the building and lived in the efficiencies at the other end of my floor.

As long as I had come this far, I decided to try to find out what this entry was like. But my key wouldn't unlock the door. I wasn't surprised. Leaning over, I peered through a nonexistent crack in the door and couldn't see a thing.

I trudged back toward my own entrance, not caring now if anyone saw me. Halfway to the door I heard voices coming from inside. One was Philip's; who was with him? I couldn't let him see me like this. I raced back to the entry between the pharmacy and the bank and backed into a dark corner where I could watch through the pharmacy window, straining to see who was with him. I could hear Philip's voice, low-pitched and compelling, but whoever was with him seemed to be mute. They were going to pass right by my hiding place. I didn't dare move now. I could only stay as quiet as possible and pray they'd be too involved with each other to look into the doorway.

The street lights shone down on them and I recognized her. It was the pregnant girl I'd seen in the doctors' hall. She was still wearing that awful dress, but a man's jacket had been thrown around her shoulders. Philip was leading her, nearly carrying her along. The girl staggered as if she were drunk or doped. She stumbled and fell. When Philip pulled her up, I saw his face, livid with rage. He yanked her to her feet and I finally saw her face—lovely, young, artless, but completely drained of all expression. Her mouth slack, eyes fixed on nothing, she was like the walking dead. Philip managed to get her to her feet again and she allowed him to handle her as if she were completely without volition. The spark of expression I had seen less than a week ago was gone. It was as though her will had shattered and she had given up. No, it was more than that. It was as though she functioned only on command. Maybe she was an alcoholic or on drugs. Was Philip trying to reassure her? He could have picked her up and carried her, but he didn't. He had some purpose in whatever he was doing.

Through the windows I could see them going toward the other end of the building, Philip guiding the girl's mechanical steps. I still dared not move. Philip might return at any minute. I couldn't see, but was almost certain they'd been heading for the other entrance. I waited, crouching back in the darkest corner for what seemed hours. He didn't return. He was probably staying with the girl until she revived from whatever had made her so ill.

I had seen a new and terrible side to Philip. God help me if he ever showed that side to me. And that pitiful girl—what could have been the matter with her? Philip treated her like an animal, and she behaved like one, sidling along beside him after her fall. I recalled the letter I'd found in my desk. She had certainly not been in this condition while she held my job. Perhaps it was her pregnancy that had changed her. And who had made her pregnant? Please, God, not Philip! I shuddered. Carefully, quietly, I returned to my apartment.

As I closed my own door behind me, I was shaking, terrified by the incident. I rushed into the bathroom and gulped down two of my pills, admitting for the first time that they contained tranquillizers. I distrusted drugs, but after the shock of seeing Philip and that girl, I needed something to calm me down.

Stumbling, I made it back to the bed and fell asleep the moment I crawled into it, almost as though I, too, had lost control over myself.

CHAPTER 15

I bounced out of bed the next day, laughing aloud with the pleasure of spending the new day in my new home, forgetting my fears of the night before.

I dressed quickly, looking forward to doing the chores that would make the apartment more livable. The bright sun gave it such promise that I could hardly wait to transform the whole place. No more luncheons with Dell until I had all my shopping done, but the sacrifice would be worth it.

Suddenly the morning glow was gone and I wanted to cry. I was out of coffee. It was a small thing, but it symbolized the fact that my apartment was still no more than a hotel room. I'd have to dress and go down to that teeming drugstore just to get a cup of coffee before going to work. What was happening to me? From heights to depths ever since I'd moved in. Then I remembered the buffet and my spirits soared again. I chose my simplest, most becoming dress, one I'd never worn to the empty office or even to meet Dell. One never knew who might be in the buffet that morning. I put on makeup, not much but enough. I wanted so much to look as lovely as the girl in the picture I'd found in my desk drawer.

I knew I'd have to take the back elevator to reach the buffet. Using the elevator nearest my door would necessitate my walking through the unknown, probably verboten, corridors of the fourth floor. Passing Philip's door I slowed and listened, but heard nothing. Going on down the hallway I turned toward the back of the building. Near the end were several doors. They were probably locked, but I instinctively knew they couldn't be apartment entries. I wondered where they led. I finally reached the elevator and pushed the button, but the car didn't come. The lighted numbers above the door showed that it was not moving from the fourth floor. In disgust I started to return to the front elevator, but I couldn't force myself to take that chance. What made me so timid about these new neighbors, or about what the Romanos would say? It was so unlike me. I stood there chiding myself for such nonsense. I was about to turn back to the apartment when my eye caught the panel above the button. There was another, almost invisible keyhole. There had to be one, then, for every entrance and exit. I tried the building key and the elevator responded instantly. Obviously, without the proper key one could not get around the building at all.

The elevator opened onto the familiar end of the fourth-floor hallway. As I neared the buffet, voices became louder. On opening the door I was taken aback. The room was completely filled with vivacious people, dressed elegantly, laughing and chatting across the tables. A carnival atmosphere pervaded the place. I knew most of the people by name now, but some were strangers. My eyes searched around. Neither Philip nor Cheena nor Mrs. Byrom was among them. Then I caught sight of a woman waving furiously for my attention. I acknowledged her with a smile and a nod and went on to the buffet table.

The buffet was as heavily laden as ever—trout, sautéed chicken livers, steaks, and at least a dozen other delicacies I couldn't name. A chef in white stood waiting to cook omelets to order with a choice of fillings. I wanted an omelet and a pastry. The chef waited patiently while I debated which of the luscious fillings I wanted most. But I couldn't decide, so I just waved my hand for him to do the choosing. He spooned up a lobster sauce and dripped it over the golden eggs.

When I turned to look for a table, the same woman waved at me again. By now she was sitting with the General and a red-haired man I didn't recognize.

"I'm Grace St. John," the bubbly woman announced with a broad British accent before I could get into my seat. "We met, but we hardly had a chance to become acquainted. At our dinner affairs we concentrate our whole attention on the wonders of the evening. I'm so happy you have joined us. I approved of you as soon as I saw you. You remember the General?"

He gave a quick, self-satisfied bob of his head and continued his meal.

Grace should have been breathless, she talked so fast, but she pointed to the red-haired man at the table. "And I don't believe you've met our Mr. Smith. Mr. Warden Smith. Warden was one of the founders of our organization. He designed all the marvelous innovations for our comfort."

The gentleman was still standing, waiting for Grace to finish her monologue, but he didn't seem bored. He was openly studying me. The expression on his face hadn't changed one whit; he looked deliberately blank as he turned his head and clipped out a "How do you do." Then, as he sat down, I noticed that he, like Dr. Romano, had trouble seating himself. Both men were slightly lame.

Grace was in her mid-thirties, with the complexion of a baby. Her haircut was mannish, but becoming to her long, thin face, and the sheen on her tawny blond hair added to her style. Her simple shirt and skirt had the same expensive tailored look I saw on all the other people there. I wondered what her talent was, besides talking.

Smith was a bit older than Grace, his complexion ruddy
and nearly as red as his crew-cut, rusty hair. He was a handsome man, tall and lean, and by all appearances my idea of a
tycoon. I imagined him spending his days settling global
problems which no one but he could resolve. After his first
scrutiny of me he didn't even look up from his meal. As soon
as he could, he excused himself and left. Even so, I had the
feeling Mr. Warden Smith came to quick decisions and had
made one about me.

Others came and left, but still Philip did not make an appearance. Maybe he never used the buffet. Several people
stopped by and welcomed me, but I couldn't place all of
them. Mrs. Byrom came in late, sat with another group, and
smiled brightly across the room, as though she approved of
my decision to join her breakfasting neighbors.

There was a subdued but real excitement in all these people. Quick giggles, deep-throated laughter, rose and fell,
breaking off suddenly. They were like new arrivals at a festi-
val, all trying to merge with the stream and get into the spirit
of the adventure.

Suddenly I heard the General's voice and realized he was
addressing me.

"I'll drop by your office very shortly to answer any questions you may have and to give you the house rules. Now if
you will excuse me."

Grace interrupted him almost before he finished speaking:
"Yes, indeed, the General handles so many of our special
conveniences, you'll appreciate him as we all do." The General simpered paternally at her, wiped his lips and his metic-
ulous mustache, and rushed through the blur of bodies.

Only Grace and I were left at the table. She suggested
another smoke and more coffee. I thought Philip might still
appear for a late breakfast, so I took the silver-tipped cigarette Grace pushed at me.

"I notice you didn't take your pill," Grace pointed out quietly.

"Oh, yes, thank you, I did forget."

"Perhaps it would be good to remember to take it before your meal. The men always take theirs before."

"Do all of you take the same pills?" I had never known such regimentation outside the mental hospital.

"No, of course not," she laughed." But whatever the doctors prescribe for each of us does marvels for the body and mind. Without their care, we could never keep up our pace. We're traveling all the time. Dr. Pavel is the real genius. You'd never believe what his prescriptions have done for me. Why, my youth has been completely restored. I can do anything—anything I want. I'd give up everything I own before I'd forego those little pills. Haven't you noticed the improvement in yourself since you've taken them?"

"Yes, I have," I had to admit. "But I didn't realize the pills had that much to do with it."

"Oh, my goodness, yes," she said. "Don't you ever forget to take them or you'll regret it."

"Are they some kind of vitamin?"

"In a way, I suppose they are." She changed the subject as she watched me swallow my pill. "Have you heard about my gardens? I'm quite a horticulturist, you know."

No one had mentioned it. "I'm afraid, with all the talents I've heard about already, I missed hearing about yours. Where can you garden here in the middle of the city?"

"On the roof behind your apartments. I take care of Philip's garden, too. The gardens are simply magnificent. You must see them. So lovely. Such exotic plants. Our friends have brought them to us from just about everywhere. They are such a challenge to me and I do marvels with them." She was getting carried away, as usual, by her own words. "But my real joy is my herb and vegetable gardens. You must see them. I'll show you this afternoon."

"I'm afraid I have to work this afternoon."

"This evening, then?" she insisted. "You can see them before it gets too dark. Artificial light doesn't do them full justice."

"I must do some shopping, Grace. I have so much to do to

get settled. Couldn't we make it the first chance we have later in the week?"

"You won't have to worry about shopping once you've had your interview with the General. But I'll wait and call you. It gives me such pleasure to show off a little. I don't suppose you realize that we all eat the vegetables and herbs I grow in my garden."

"You grow vegetables for the whole building on the roof?"

"Certainly. I suppose you wouldn't realize what my contribution means to me unless you were one of us."

She was upset and started sulking. But her mood changed when I got up to leave. She touched my arm as she smiled and said good-by, and I winced. Her possessive, slimy touch went too far for our brief relationship. Grace was one person I instinctively disliked.

"Now don't you forget, Sharon. I'll be calling you." Grace's piping voice trailed me out of the room.

CHAPTER 16

The back elevator was busy for the first time since I'd been in the building. I rode down to the second floor with several people I didn't know. They hurried off into the doctors' offices and there seemed to be more energy in the building than I had ever felt before. The sensation heightened as I entered my own office. The room was still empty, but the telephones were ringing madly. I began trying to take messages with both hands. Romano and his wife came in, followed by two people, and quickly disappeared into the inner office. The traffic and the telephones kept up throughout the day. Every time the door opened I could hear excitement in the corridor as I never had before—subdued, but electric with expectancy. In the midst of all this, the door opened and the General marched in and sat beside the desk to wait until the phones stopped ringing. The moment there was a break in the calls he began talking.

"Mrs. Crane, I'm here to fill you in on our conveniences and regulations and answer any questions you may have."

I was so relieved; I had a thousand questions.

"Well, first of all, I'd like to know how I pay my rent."

"I'll come to the office each month and collect it. You make out the check to G.U.C. Incorporated."

He stopped me before I could take out my checkbook.

"Wait until I tell you about our supply room. Supply room charges are included with your rent. You'll find yours at the rear of the fourth floor, across from the buffet. A sign marks the door. You'll find grocery carts in the storeroom. Take one and keep it in your apartment if you wish. We stock household items and you should take all you need. There are paper and cleaning products, dry food items, personal hygiene and other merchandise you will normally use, including our own prescribed soap. Since there are few supermarkets in this vicinity, the storerooms save our residents from traveling all over for staples. When you select items, check off on the forms you will find there whatever you have taken. Leave the slip in the box you'll also find there."

I asked about dairy products, meats, fruits, vegetables. His answer should have been anticipated.

"There are a freezer and a refrigerator there as well. Miss St. John supplies us with a variety of the best produce. I think you will find whatever we provide is far superior to anything you could locate elsewhere, and the prices are lower as well.

"We discourage outside deliverymen from entering the building, so you would have to carry in anything you purchase outside. Of course, we accept large deliveries, such as the one you will receive from California. Oh yes, there's one minor imposition we must make. None of the efficiency occupants may engage outside help. The apartments require little upkeep, and I'm certain that young people as competent as yourself can manage to do their own cleaning."

"But—" I began, when he went on as though reading my mind.

"The larger apartments and, of course, dinner parties, the buffet, and so forth, do require outside help. Those people are thoroughly screened before we employ them. I meet them at the entrance and escort them to their individual locations within the building. None of them have any of our keys. They remain in their locations until I escort them out when their duties are over. Absolutely none are allowed to stay overnight, and they are not allowed to roam from their places of duty until I relieve them. In your situation, please, under no circumstances should you have social conversations with the working help. They are well aware of this and will avoid answering if you press them."

"How do you keep them with such rigid rules?" I asked in mock admiration.

"They are selected carefully, as I told you, and they are well recompensed for their compliance. They also know full well the repercussions of disobedience, even minor infractions. Now, shall we go on?"

"It sounds like you people have thought of everything. Anything I'll ever need seems to be provided. I certainly don't need a maid, so that's no problem. I have never heard of anything like your setup—it's almost too perfect."

"We do try to please. We have planned quite carefully for minimal intrusion on our way of living." He was officious and slightly patronizing, but I supposed he was right. They certainly had worked out every detail and I had to fit into their regime.

He coughed to draw my full attention.

"By the way, here are your permanent keys. I would like the ones you have been using, if you please."

Scrambling through my purse I found them, handed them over. He examined them carefully before relinquishing the new set. Satisfied I'd given him the right ones, he handed me a ring with a white and a blue key on it.

"One more thing," he said emphatically, his hand on the doorknob. "Your telephone number is unlisted. Just a precaution, but it's for your protection as well as ours, so I am sure you will not give the number out to people indiscriminately." I thought of asking whether he would like to interview potential friends of mine before I gave them my number, but decided he wouldn't appreciate the sarcasm.

"The rules of the building are in this small booklet I will leave with you," he went on. "Most are similar to those of other cooperatives, but we strictly enforce our rules for the protection of our residents, and of the very valuable art objects we display here. I urge you to read over the booklet as soon as you can. What may seem unimportant to you may be essential to the security of the building."

He dropped a small, leather-bound booklet on my desk and was gone. The doctors had been covering their own phones all the time the General was there, and they went on doing so, apparently unaware that he had left. So I concentrated on the book. My name and apartment number and the serial numbers of my keys were printed on the cover. It read like an ordinary set of landlord's rules, until I came to the section about privacy and safety. There was a great deal of space given to the keys, how the white one opened the supply room, most of the elevators, and the buffet, and the blue one opened my apartment. And then there was an underlined warning:

> To use the white key for any locks not specifically mentioned is forbidden. Other keys fit those areas where residents require access for private purposes. Each key is serially numbered and registered and is to be returned to the General if you move.
>
> The keys are never to be loaned to anybody for any reason. If you plan to be away for even one night you are to leave your keys with the General.

I was sure that the pompous, bossy old General had had a wonderful time composing the booklet. A lot of the precautions and regulations seemed unnecessary, and even slightly paranoid, but I had to admit one thing: I would certainly be safe living here. Any second thoughts I'd had about moving to a city with a crime rate as high as Washington's were now alleviated. I did wonder how guests would enter the building. I certainly didn't want to go through some complex procedure dreamed up by the General every time someone wanted to drop by. The only outside person I knew so far was Dell, but there would be others.

I would have an extra set of keys made. I could use the new ones and keep the ones he'd issued me in a safe place right in the apartment, lending them to friends when that seemed convenient. What the General didn't know wouldn't hurt him.

CHAPTER 17

As soon as the clock tolled five o'clock, I searched out the supply room. I needed everything. As directed, I went to the fourth floor and spotted the discreet marker on the door opposite the buffet. The white key opened the lock and as the door opened, lights flooded the room.

Spotless white shelves were all around me, except at the back of the room, where refrigerators stood to the ceiling. There were limited supplies of every household item I needed. Each brand was quality. It was like shopping in a free supermarket.

On the forms provided, I checked my selections and dropped the sheets into a small box beside the door. My cart was crammed full. I wouldn't have to bother with the grocery store after all. Anything I might need would be just floors below me. This place was beginning to feel more like Utopia. My home on a luxury island. . . .

When I finished stocking the groceries in my apartment I went to the window to watch night fall. A few lights were on in Dell's building. Which ones were his, I wondered. Maybe he was in. I reached for the phone.

Dell answered. I hadn't expected that and giggled when I heard his voice.

"Dell, guess where I am."

"Sharon! Where the hell are you? And stop that silly giggling. Are you drunk? You had me worried as hell. I called the house and the woman told me you'd moved and hadn't even left a forwarding address."

"I'm right across the street from you. I can even see your windows from right where I'm standing. You'd better close your blinds at night."

I laughed; he didn't.

"You went ahead and moved into that building! You told me you'd at least look around before rushing into it. But you just couldn't wait, could you!"

His reaction surprised me. I was having so much fun being thrilled; why was he determined to deflate me? He knew nothing about this place; he didn't even know the people.

"Oh, Dell, it's perfect. Stop acting like an ass. Wait until you see it. Why don't you come on over right now and see for yourself?" His hesitation made me angry, suspecting the worst when there was nothing to suspect. I had to reassure him. "Look, I'll flick my lights off and on. You can see exactly where I am."

"That's silly. I know where you are."

"You don't know. Look out your window."

He grunted and I flicked the lights off and on a half dozen times. When he came back to the phone he sounded even more disgruntled.

"All I can see is the top of your windows. Nothing else. I don't like it."

"Why should you say that? I'm a lot safer here than I was traveling to that boardinghouse every night. Won't you please come on over? I'll fix supper for you. You probably haven't eaten, and I have food in already—everything I could possibly need. I'll come down and let you in."

As I hung up, I was torn between the thrill of having a guest for the first time and an uneasy feeling. He had agreed to come, but what would he think of all the barriers to getting in and out of the building? The time seemed endless while I waited, even as I busied myself tidying the few things in the chaste apartment, then hurried to the lobby to let him in.

Dell was fascinated, missing nothing as I led him to my own domain. But his lower lip still jutted out and he glared at everything he saw. He seemed relieved when we were inside the apartment, but having seen the rest of the building he was puzzled by its simplicity and drabness.

He pushed a paper bag at me.

"Here's something to toast your new home. Sorry it isn't full, but I couldn't get to the liquor store. I had this Scotch in the office."

His gesture touched me because I knew he was angry and ready for the least excuse to criticize me more.

"Thank you, Dell. This is probably the only staple the building doesn't supply. Wait till I tell you. You won't believe it. I won't even have to go to the grocery store. They have a place right here in the building and it carries practically everything, and the best, too; and what's more, it's not expensive!"

Dell was still sour. "Oh, come on, Sharon, don't tell me they also keep your pantry filled for you. That's too much. You're a stranger and they're handing you everything on a silver platter. You've got to admit it sounds funny. There must be a purpose. You're a pretty girl, but there are all kinds of women they could have showered with this 'luck.'"

Now I was angry again. "Dell, you don't understand. I pay for everything. Nothing is gratis. Look at this apartment. You can't say it isn't suitable for a poor working girl like me. It just happened—I was there when they needed somebody, that's all."

He didn't answer. He took the bottle and went to the kitch-
en, bringing back two half-filled water glasses with very little
ice. Here he was, my best friend, someone I could talk to as
though I'd known him forever. I had to make him approve.
He tried to be enthusiastic but I knew he still didn't feel it.

When he left for refills I tried to think of something to
bring back our old harmony.

"Dell, would you do something for me?" I called. "I want
to retain you as my attorney. James sends me an alimony
check every month and I want to let him know where to send
it next month. I just can't write to him myself. Would you do
it for me?"

Dell's sour mood cracked a little. "I'll be glad to, Sharon.
No trouble. Is there anything else you want me to tell him?"

"No, just the change of address."

After the steaks and a second cup of coffee, Dell was beginning to act his normal self. Now he sprawled out on the sofa
as if it were his own, his eyes intently probing the room from
end to end.

"You know, Sharon, you need something to perk this place
up. It's like a morgue. Why don't you get some plants?
They'd help. I'll take you to a place Sunday where you can
get all you want. You'll probably need Saturday to get mops
and brooms and stuff—unless they furnish all that, too. Besides, I've got to work Saturday."

"No, they don't supply mops, and yes, I would love to go
with you Sunday. I appreciate it. It's a wonderful idea. Just
call me when you're ready to come so I can let you in."

I gave him my phone number. "It's not listed. They don't
list numbers here."

"Naturally," he said. I had to laugh. "Look," he went on,
"you're probably tired. I'll call you Sunday and I'll get that
letter off this week. I'm very busy on a new case, but call me if
you want anything. And you can always flick your lights." We
laughed together, friends again.

Just as my door opened, so did Philip's. I hadn't seen him

in weeks. He hesitated, then stopped short. He seemed surprised.

"Why, Sharon, you're actually here. How wonderful." He saluted, grinned broadly, and hurried on. While Philip waited for the elevator, Dell suddenly leaned down, grabbed me to him tightly, and kissed me hard on my lips. Whether he did it simply to show off, for spite, or to embarrass me, I didn't care. Philip couldn't have helped knowing I was being kissed. Maybe knowing another man was interested in me would bring him around.

CHAPTER 18

On my way out in the morning I saw the note. It had been slipped under my door, and it had to be from Philip. I reached for it gingerly, my fingers shaking as I unfolded it.

Dear Neighbor— Please reserve this evening for a fresh start at seven, to plot strategy for sharing our floor.

P.H.

How infuriating he was. I read all kinds of meanings into his message, but it actually told me nothing. It could be an invitation or it could be just what he said—a conference to settle how we could share our close quarters without embarrassing each other. I was tense and excited, and more than that—the few vague words set off a round of daydreaming, followed by exuberance, followed by hopelessness. And then another round of daydreaming.

I decided to lunch at the buffet to avoid Dell. Somehow I couldn't face him today. When I opened the door, once again the room was humming and a place was noticeably vacant for me between Grace and Warden, the architect. Then, as I slipped into the seat, the last person I expected to join this group, Dr. Pavel, slid another chair next to mine and immediately started making cute remarks to everyone within his hearing. The aura of expectancy around the room was, if possible, more intense than it had been the day before. I was dying to ask Grace if something was in the offing, but she was giggling at something Pavel had said, so instead I just joined in their laughter, neither knowing nor caring what it was all about. At last I was able to get away to return to my office and my glorious daydreams of the evening with Philip.

Somehow the day passed, and when I finally reached my apartment there was another note under the door.

Don't eat. Dress for comfort. Wear rubber-soled shoes. See you at seven.

P.H.

Brief, but more informative; I smiled over the humorous peremptoriness of the note, then realized I didn't have much time. One minute I was rushing about trying to find something to wear, the next flopping into the chair in frustration, certain that what little clothing I had would be all wrong. In desperation I put on tight jeans and a loose pink cotton shirt, but became almost frantic because I had no rubber-soled shoes, only high heels and the scruffy bedroom slippers. I'd have to wear them. Trying not to pace the floor, I grew more nervous every minute. Exactly on the dot of seven, there was his knock at the door. Perfection in everything. Even punctuality.

"All ready? Let's go."

"Am I all right?"

His eyes examined me from head to foot.

"You are perfect, pink lady. Those shoes don't look too sturdy, but they'll do. We won't be walking much and they won't hurt the boat."

This time he had another car, a Porsche, and within minutes we were at the waterfront. He parked and led me through the maze of piers to one of the smaller boats. I helped throw off the lines, then Philip handed me the large picnic basket he had been carrying, ordering me to go down to the cabin and transfer everything from the plastic carton to the refrigerator. I had it done in minutes, and started back up to the deck. Philip was trying to start the motor, but each time it gave a feeble chug and then, pfflut, it died. He tried several times more. Standing at the top step of the ladder, I could see only his profile, but it was enough. Philip was rigid, biting his lips white. He didn't say a word. His hands shook. I was shocked at the violence of his reaction to such a minor inconvenience. At last the motor caught, and he went to the wheel and soon was steering expertly out into the channel. My shock was slow to dissipate, and I stayed below until I felt I could smile.

The boat was a little jewel, and it seemed to have been used very little. It was factory bright, scrubbed to a glowing shine, except that down beside the refrigerator I'd noticed a rusted old piece of junk jewelry, part of an earring, that somebody had missed in the last cleanup. I was surprised that Philip kept such a small boat. He seemed more the sailboat type. If he or any other members of the cooperative went yachting, it would only be with the various foreigners who were always calling, and I was certain their entertainment would have to be far more lavish than this little boat could provide.

Philip was now in command and his face was again composed. He turned to me only occasionally to point out a few sights along the waterfront as we cruised down the channel to the river.

The evening was sweltering, the sun blazing red and nearly at the horizon, but the breeze helped, and the small cabin was throwing out cooler blasts of air from an air conditioner inside which hummed along with the motor.

It was soon dark, and Philip steered down the river an

hour longer while I sprawled comfortably on the pad across the back. For a long time neither of us said anything, but then he called to me to come sit near him, and he began to talk. It was as if we'd picked up in the midst of things we'd been saying to each other all our lives. We talked mostly of ourselves, the things we liked, personal and private things, funny and sad memories. We even agreed on mutual pet peeves—like people who didn't say "thank you." In the wash of a few waves, Philip managed to transform us from strangers to confidants. He was a master at manipulating a woman, and though I was aware of being charmed, I soaked it in as though starved for the attention.

Eventually he turned into a narrow cove and we dropped anchor. I could see nothing but the black shadows of trees along the shore and pinpoints of light. We could hear the soft lapping of waves, the hum of crickets, melodies carried out from the shore.

"I don't like music at times like this," Philip whispered into the night. "The other sounds are so much more beautiful."

He came back to sit beside me on the long cushion at the back of the boat and as he slid down he slipped his arm around me. This time there was no memory of my past. I leaned back, eagerly waiting for his kiss. He didn't kiss me. Instead he leaned back with me in his arms and watched the sky, his thoughts completely his own as he smoked one of his gold cigarettes. Without a word he handed me a silver one. Neither of us wanted to break the enchantment of the moment. When we finally crushed out the butts, Philip got up, unfolded a table from a compartment at the side of the deck, and went down into the cabin. He had decided it was time to eat. As hungry as I was, I was surprised and a little disappointed at his timing. Philip was a genius at flirtation. Every move he made was tantalizing. Every word he spoke left me guessing what it really meant. Emerging from the galley, he opened the picnic basket. It held plates, utensils, every amenity, but nothing like any picnic settings I'd ever seen before.

The food was stored in separate compartments on the tray. A medley of aromas spread across the boat. Philip raced back and brought up iced beers and soon we were eating chunks of cold white crabmeat, spiced shrimp, caviar, and several other seafood dishes I never tasted before. There were bowls of special sauces for each dish. At least the beer was picnic fare, I thought as I watched him pouring it into the frosted glasses. At last he did something human, too. He picked up a shrimp with his fingers. He looked at me and we both burst out laughing. He knew exactly what I'd been thinking.

"We'll save dessert for later," Philip announced, reaching under the table and producing two finger bowls with pieces of lemon floating in them.

"That does it," I howled. "I thought I'd seen everything. But fingerbowls! Now I suppose you'll bring out the gold engraved toothpicks."

He played along.

"And why not? We have one for each tooth, engraved with your name. What do you think we are? Peasants?"

Again we laughed, and when I was completely spent and taken unaware, he suddenly pulled me back against the cushions and looked down into my eyes. He held me in a firm but gentle grip. Slowly he moved his face down. His lips brushed softly over mine, his tongue rubbing them to open. Then gradually his lips became more passionate and hard. I returned the kisses until at last I felt something cutting into my inner lip. Whether it was his teeth or my own I couldn't tell, but it hurt, and I couldn't help but flinch when he kissed me again. He recoiled, and a look of irritation instantly replaced his tenderness. Then, as he saw the trickle of blood on my mouth, he became all contrition.

"Why, my darling, I am a dog." He smoothed back my hair, whispering, "Please let me kiss it away."

His eyes swallowed me. Before I could answer, his mouth was completely over mine. His tongue went into my mouth and sucked away at the small cut. As he drew away he gave me a far-away look, then stood up, leaving me perplexed, but wanting more.

"We'd better be getting back." He was calm now, and distant.

We came home slowly. I stood beside my captor, his arm around my shoulder while he steered. Every so often he leaned over and kissed me lightly before turning back to watch for debris in the water. We'd forgotten about the dessert. His passion was gone and we talked desultorily and inconsequentially all the way home. Foremost in my mind was the question of whether we would see each other again. With someone else I would have recognized the signs, but I couldn't interpret anything Philip said or did. We docked, and he handed me the box containing the dessert.

"You might want this later, little piggy. By the way, tomorrow night is formal, so wear that lovely yellow dress. Be ready by six."

Tomorrow night!

"I have to wear the yellow dress if it's formal. None of my things have arrived from storage yet. I haven't much choice until then."

"They haven't arrived yet!" Suddenly Philip was angry. "Where are they? For God's sake, Sharon, why have you put up with such treatment?" He was furious, and again I was shaken to see him expend such rage on such a small matter.

I tried to calm him down. "It's only been two days since I wrote, Philip. It takes at least a couple of weeks for any storage company to send things across country. They wait for a full van. They wouldn't just send my things even if I asked for special service."

My excuse didn't impress him. Such petty annoyances were an insult in his world. His attitude upset me. I wondered if I could ever bridge that gap, not knowing how little this problem really mattered to Philip or his friends.

"You just give me the name of that company. It's absolutely ridiculous! I can do something about it. No wonder you had to wear bedroom slippers! Why didn't you say something about it?"

His attitude was becoming insufferable. I spoke sharply. "Why should I? These things are routine. I've written them. Why should I have bothered you?"

"Routine? You are living here now. We don't put up with inconveniences. Just remember, in the future, I won't have you expecting anything to be routine."

He followed at my heels into the apartment; he eyed it with distaste.

"This is not you, Sharon. Even for a day it doesn't become you. It is cold and inhospitable. It is demeaning."

"I told you my things will be here shortly. They'll make a big difference."

"You also need plants."

I started to tell him that I would be buying some on Sunday, but Philip cut me off.

"All the plants you need are right on the other side of your balcony wall. I have an immense garden. Grace takes care of it. I'm sure she's told you about that. She has enough growing out there to furnish ten apartments. You choose whatever you want and we'll bring them over tonight if you like."

"Not tonight. I'm a working girl, remember. We can get them whenever you're free. Whenever you want, but not tonight. I'm bushed."

"All right. I'll help you select them. There are many exotics given us by our associates around the world. Grace could tell you how to take care of them. She'll even do it for you if you prefer. We'll get them Saturday."

He wouldn't leave without the storage company's name and address, but he still had the scowl on his face. If I wanted to continue with Philip, I could see I would have to acquiesce in his plans entirely.

CHAPTER 19

Early Friday morning I called Dell's office. I wanted to tell him about the landlord supplying the plants I needed, but he wasn't there. I said I'd call back. I certainly couldn't leave a message breaking a date. At exactly five I rushed from the office up to the apartment. Showering quickly, I pulled my hair up into a French knot with the bangs still covering my forehead, the most flattering style I knew of. Dressing was an ordeal. I knew that this night I'd be on display before Philip's contemporaries, those he socialized with, his real friends, and he would expect perfection. I had to meet those expectations, or it would be the end. And without Philip, this fortress I'd gotten myself into would be hell itself.

I couldn't find my cigarettes. I was getting nervous. Then I remembered my "almond" pill, rushed into the bathroom and swallowed one down quickly. I waited for it to calm me down, not even last night had I been this jittery. I was ready and waiting long before six. The pill was working.

At last I heard Philip's knock, dashed to open the door, and stood with arms flung wide to welcome him. He gathered me close, held me to his chest. Then, thrusting me back, he inspected me, the turquoise eyes intense between the black lashes. At first he was solemn, noncommittal, then gradually a smile crept over his face.

"All ready and so lovely, just for me," he said, his eyes gleaming.

"Philip, have you any cigarettes? I'm afraid I'm out and I know I'll need some later."

He chuckled. "By pure coincidence I knew you'd say that. Here's something I thought you'd like and you have the audacity to ask for it before I even have a chance to surprise you."

He held out a small package beautifully wrapped in silver and yellow paper. I tore away the wrappings to find a slim, silver case, an unusually shaped rectangle with intricately designed corners. They were curious, indecipherable designs. Opening it, I found it full of the silver-tipped cigarettes. Philip picked one out and lit it for me.

"Sharon, if you must smoke, I insist you smoke nothing but these. Promise to do that much for me. They won't harm you as regular brands do, and you can get all you want from the supply room. It's for your own good or I wouldn't ask."

His concern touched and reassured me.

"Of course I will, Philip," I answered without hesitation.

We headed for the garage. I was giddy with anticipation. Philip couldn't have known how badly I wanted to get out of the building and be with other people. And even more, I wanted to know that Philip did have friends other than the peculiar assortment gathered in our building. Driving through heavy traffic into Georgetown, we finally reached a block that had a high stone fence built around it. Philip pulled through brick-pillared gates and squeezed into a crowded parking area near a large, dark red brick house. Behind the house was another wall, the same brick as the house. From the other side of this wall came the welcome noise of music and many voices.

A smartly dressed young woman stood at the front door greeting guests. Her face was familiar, but I didn't remember her until Philip mentioned her name. She was probably the best-known hostess in Washington. She welcomed Philip with a kiss and a warmth reserved for special friends.

"Anita, this is my girl—Sharon Crane," Philip said as the beautiful blonde held both hands out to me. I glowed at Philip's introduction and happily followed Anita through the charming old house to the garden. Among the crowd outside I recognized women I'd seen or read about in society columns even on the West Coast; rival politicians drinking and joking together like bosom buddies; and prominent journalists out in force. Every one of them knew Philip. I sensed they even courted his attention. But he held me close to him and I was ecstatic. He was real. All this was real. There was nothing ever again to keep me in a constant state of nerve-wracking suspicion.

A bar was set up at the edge of the garden serving Scotch, bourbon, and other pleasantly ordinary drinks. Philip brought me a double Scotch and water and didn't frown when I drank it with relish. Some of the guests had obviously already had more than a few and, in these surroundings, I felt comfortable and normal. This party was just like what I'd always known as entertaining, and it was such a contrast to dinners at the cooperative that I had to laugh out loud.

Later we went inside to a buffet in the huge dining room. A string quartet played romantic themes and old favorites. Philip and I filled our plates with party food, and then he maneuvered me into a corner where we ate, chatted, and laughed as though we were the only two people in the room. Being with someone whose electricity ran through me so intensely made this party different from any I'd ever attended before. Even with James. The evening was over long before I wanted it to be, yet I was becoming more and more eager to be alone with Philip. He had said nothing when I'd taken the third Scotch and began to act lightheaded and careless, partly from the excitement, partly because I hadn't had Scotch for some time, and largely from this newly awakened sensuous intoxication with Philip.

As we rode the back elevator to our floor, I could hardly believe how perfect everything was. We went to my door. I was searching through my bag for my keys, both of us laughing for no reason at all, when Philip said, "Why don't we go over to my place for a nightcap? It's still early. And you don't have to work tomorrow. I want you to see my sanctum sanctorum under the best circumstances, and what could be better than tonight?"

He didn't have to persuade me. I trotted behind him as he strode down the hall. He hadn't waited for an answer.

Philip's door opened on to a large, rounded entry, panelled with dark, mottled brown leather, unadorned except for dim, antique lanterns. He led me through this striking foyer to the living room. Three steps down was a room at least sixty feet long and nearly as wide. He stood aside like a sentry, allowing me time to appreciate my first impression.

Straight ahead, across the room, was a huge granite fireplace, so artfully designed that the stone appeared to be in its natural state. Before it were three deep oversized leather sofas embossed with geometric designs. The room was dimly lit by carefully placed old brass, pewter, and copper lanterns. Tables were scattered everywhere, all displaying a variety of strange, ancient-looking figures. There were several grouped seating arrangements, but the central point was the fireplace and sofas. The room was littered with priceless artifacts and artworks with no consistency in period or place of origin. Bookcases covered two walls, crammed with books of old tooled leather and more recent ones with their jackets still on. Objects of art were squeezed between books whenever possible. Off to the right, steps led up to a balcony with heavy, dark railings around its edge. There his dining furniture seemed stark and formal in contrast to the clutter below.

High glass doors flanked the fireplace. Through a loosely woven dark net, hundreds of tiny lights flickered.

Philip took my hand and led me to one of the sofas, and I

saw the table for the first time. Beneath it was a hand-made rug, woven to resemble a primitive version of the zodiac. The table was octagonal and at least six feet across. It was beautiful and hideous.

Philip spoke for the first time since we'd entered the apartment. "That rug was used in rituals in Yorubaland in ancient times. It was presented to me the first time I was there." His eyes were glowing with recollection. But, as he had expected, I was spellbound by the table. As I stared at it my lids dropped and I found that my eyes were barely able to focus.

"You are astute, my love. That table is the receptacle of my hardest-won rewards."

"You display them here where you can sit and recall what they meant to you, don't you?"

"I certainly do. I made the table myself and filled it with the gifts I most treasure. The legs, as you can see, are carvings depicting the tortures of life, made by Dyaks, natives of Borneo. The glass top protects the other pieces. It will take hours to tell you about all these ancient fetishes. I want you to appreciate them as I do. You are one of the few women who could understand their profanity as man's true nature. This table stands as evidence that man was thus from the beginning of time and still is the world over."

On a black velour shelf under the immense glass top were dozens of hideous reproductions of living creatures, some intricate, others crude, but all of them depicting torture—people and animals devouring, killing, fornicating, grotesquely gratifying themselves in every manner possible. Philip stared down at the shallow glass case, supported by its seven carved legs. His passion was almost frightening. He was so engrossed he gripped my hand, and walked me around the table so I wouldn't miss a gruesome detail. I was repulsed, but I had to follow. Each leg was different, but they all were hand-carved ebony figures of women in various contorted positions. Each had a huge belly and breasts, as in the last stages of pregnancy. Small figures crouched at their feet, with arms upstretched to take the babies. The faces were out of proportion to the figures. All were distorted, in ecstasy or pain. I gagged at the pornographic depiction of childbirth.

Philip could see that I had had enough. "Come, little one," he said, drawing me away. "Let's have a drink." But the table held me hypnotized. Groggy from the Scotch my dizziness was heightened by the horror I still felt.

"Sharon, *come*." Philip stood before me, offering me a glass. He held a glass of his own, and a ruby-colored decanter. The glasses were simply deep-cut garnet, glistening like jewels. I sniffed my drink and found it unfamiliar. Carrying his own glass and the decanter with him, Philip led me back to the three sofas. I was floating, happy, but all my senses seemed numbed. Philip pulled me down onto the center sofa facing the fireplace, which now was only a black cavern. He laughed as he crossed to a cabinet and turned on soft music. It spilled from all sides of the room. The music began to climb as he returned to my side. He draped his arm loosely over my shoulder and leaned back, giving himself up to the fantasia. It was so very strange—drums, trills, and shrill notes, no melody. The drums beat faster and faster until they seemed to race the beat of blood in my veins. Each time I swallowed deeply from the cool drink, Philip refilled my glass. The fever pitch continued, then suddenly dropped away into a throbbing rhythm.

"You may not like this at first, but it gets to you. It's something I recorded at secret rites in one of the remotest areas I ever entered."

His thoughts were a million miles away and he was talking in a hushed voice, as though he were reliving the excitement it had aroused in him. He spoke under his breath with such fanaticism he seemed alone, arousing himself through his recollection.

"They crowded around me like lions about to pounce when I brought out the recorder, but they tolerated it because they were fascinated by the spinning of the reel. It was a curiosity for them, but the naked, magnificent bodies stood with knives and spears ready to cut me into pieces if I made the wrong move. It was so challenging, trying to convey to them that I wanted to take part in their rituals, that I wasn't ridiculing them. I had to prove I was serious. I had to gain their acceptance; I wasn't afraid to take part in their rituals no matter how vile they were or how far they went."

I wondered how he had managed to prove himself, but he didn't explain.

"I had to, but I kept the recorder going and they ignored it once they began testing me. I stayed with them for weeks, and it was . . . " His voice drifted off and I never heard the effect it had on him. But one thing was clear: Philip had been fascinated by the atrocities he must have seen and participated in. But he didn't seem to care what I thought of his revelation. Maybe it wasn't as bad as I imagined. . . .

"I'll tell you all about it—but some other time, Sharon. Now let's just be with each other. Just let the music carry you with it. I'm the only thing I want you to think about. Only me. Sharon, I've fallen in love with you. All I can think about is you. You must feel the same."

My whole being was pounding, throbbing. If there was euphoria, this was it. Philip spoke little, only to mouth words I could barely hear. His hands were all over my skin, caressing, rubbing me with his tongue, even softly nipping me with his teeth. The tips of his fingers lightly traced the flesh of my face, my throat, went down carefully under my arms. He held up my fingers to the dim light of the table lamp, as if his eyes could penetrate my skin to the blood, bone, sinews beneath.

Philip pulled back and sat erect on the edge of the couch, staring down at me where I lay among the dark leather cushions. His pupils seemed to grow until I could see nothing but the blackness of his riveted stare. I unbuttoned my already half-open dress and let it slip to the floor. He made no move to help me undress. He merely waited, standing over the sofa now, watching my every movement. Those eyes never left me, but his hands stayed at his sides.

At last all my clothes were strewn around the couch, on the floor. Only then did he kneel beside me, his hands surveying and probing my entire body, as if he were a blind man, probing all the soft and firm places. I was at once freezing, then feverishly on fire, trembling in ecstatic pain, yet thrilled to the point of trembling from head to foot.

Philip didn't pick me up and carry me to the bedroom. Instead he simply rose and turned in that direction. I arose and followed him, in rhythm with the beating tom-toms, on into the bedroom. As we moved, as if in procession, the cadence became more fevered and frenzied along with my pounding blood.

I lay on the bed writhing; Philip pulled my arms harshly out toward the sides of the bed. He was still only kneeling on its edge. He was nude now. The muscles of his beautiful brown, satin skin were glowing in the dim amber light that flowed down from the ceiling. My fingers clasped the bed cover in an agony of desire. Philip let go of my arms to pull my legs apart. He held them in that position with iron strength. He made no further move except to mouth silent laments between his teeth. I lay waiting. At last, as I began to feel I was going mad, Philip's hands began moving. They came up from my legs and rested above my belly. Then they began a strange tracing of patterns over me. He seemed to be exploring my pelvic region, tracing on it the outline of something I couldn't understand. Then he reared back and slowly opened the big ring he still wore on his finger. He dipped his fingers into it and then I could feel a hot liquid he was pressing deep into my navel, down through the pubic hair between my legs, and thoroughly inside me as far as his fingers would reach. The tension was now unbearable. Everything but Philip was hazy. He loomed like a giant above me in full erection. At last he came closer, and down, until the glorious surge of relief drove everything from my mind.

Hours later I clung to him, thrusting my body against his to keep touching every part of him while I drifted off into a half-sleep, whispering: "Philip, do you know this was the first time I've forgotten about using my diaphram? It's such glory to make love without it."

He was smoking a cigarette. "My sweet Sharon. You've made me so happy. You'll never use that stupid device again."

"But what if I get pregnant?"

"Some things happen for the best. It could be marvelous. Imagine the perfection of a little Sharon or a little Philip."

Dawn arrived much too quickly. It was time for me to get back to my own apartment. Philip slipped out of the bed and handed me a long black robe. He donned another robe that clung softly around him, making him seem more naked than before. He walked me down the hall. When we reached my door he stopped me, holding me at arm's length. His new seriousness momentarily terrified me.

"I'll be over in the morning to get you, Sharon, and we'll choose the plants. We'll be together all day, but I can't be with you tomorrow night. The house is having a special dinner party and I must attend. It's limited to members so I can't invite you, but I'll see you early Sunday morning. We're flying up to Maine for the day. I want you to meet some more of my close friends and I want them to meet you."

What was there to say? I wanted to spend the next night with him, but he owed me no excuses. At least I had the promise of Maine on Sunday. I was already eager at the thought. If it was to be anything like this first night. . . . Dell would be furious, but now I'd have to put Dell off anyway. Philip wasn't the type to share a woman with anybody. I felt guilty about Dell for a moment, but when Philip leaned over to kiss me goodnight, everything else was wiped from my mind. He kissed me lightly once again before closing the door behind him.

I lay in bed a long time trying to resist taking my evening pill, but my thoughts were racing and colliding. Philip, the man I worshipped, said he loved me. I still couldn't believe it. Finally I couldn't stand my own thoughts any longer and I raced into the bathroom to gulp down the pill. The doubts dulled, the pill settled, and I fell asleep.

CHAPTER 20

Early Saturday morning I awoke, bubbling over with enthusiasm for the new day. My doubts were gone with my dreams. I put on a sleeveless, hyacinth-blue sports dress. The matching shorts barely covered my bottom but they were perfect for gardening. Praying there wouldn't be anyone else up this early, I headed for the buffet. By this time I knew that my absences were always noted.

The sound of voices hit me full force the moment I opened the door. Electricity charged the room. Nearly every seat was taken. Strangers I'd never seen in the building before were scattered at the tables, all absorbed in excited talk with the more familiar residents. No one noticed my entrance except the birdlike, omniscient Grace, who paused in her conversation long enough to wave me to the empty seat beside her. I quickly picked what I thought I could swallow from the buffet—orange juice, coffee, and a small portion of eggs Benedict—and quietly slipped in next to Grace. The conversation continued without an interruption; no one bothered to introduce me to the strangers at the table. But there was something different about Grace this morning. She seemed to be purring. I knew she couldn't possibly know about Philip and me, but I began to feel uncomfortable.

I sat quietly, thankful that I was being ignored, watching the door and waiting for Philip to walk in. I wanted to see him, but hated the thought of facing him before all these people I both knew and didn't know. Then he was there, standing in the doorway carefully surveying the room, nodding as he caught eyes all over the room. Then he found me. In an instant he was behind me and before I realized what was happening he leaned down and kissed me soundly, almost missing my lips. My face grew hot and flushed. With his kiss, he had clearly and deliberately announced our relationship to the whole room. I could only sit there and smile up at him weakly.

"Why don't you squeeze a chair in with us, Philip? I'm sure your friends won't mind." I managed to keep my voice steady, but the words burned in my tight throat.

"No, darling. I'm starved and I'm going to have a small feast. I'm glad you didn't wait for me. Finish your breakfast and I'll see you in a little while."

"I can get a few errands done while you breakfast," I said, trying to keep the conversation impersonal.

"How about in an hour? I'll knock at your door. If you're not back, call for me. O.K.?"

"Of course." I appreciated his attempt at nonchalance. It was absurd, of course, but all of these people seemed to be somehow interested in Philip and me, and I wasn't imagining the hush that had settled over the room as he and I made our plans.

Philip kissed me again on the top of the head and went for his food. With a sidelong glance around the room, I noticed everyone was oblivious of me again, all except Grace. This time she broke into a broad, silly grin. I could have thrown something at her. Instead I swallowed, looked down, and picked the last bit from my plate. Before the fork reached my lips, Grace reached out and ran the tips of her waxy fingers up my arm. The long, firm fingers pressed against my flesh. I froze. Then, without a pause, Grace again picked up her conversation with the black man on her other side, but did not remove her fingers from my arm. I couldn't bear it another minute. Pushing myself away from the table, I mumbled an excuse and nearly fell over the chairs as I hastened out of the room.

CHAPTER 21

I only had one hour, and there was something I had to get done before I saw Philip again. My freedom in the building was at the mercy of those two idiotic keys issued to me by the General. I'd never expected that Philip would be keeping me so busy on this day, my first opportunity to get an extra set made.

Never in my life had I had this kind of claustrophobic feeling every time a door closed behind me. The idea had crossed my mind the day I read the building's book of regulations, but today the matter suddenly seemed urgent. Watching all the new people at the buffet, strangers in the building but clearly known to all the neighbors except me, gave me a sense of being entirely alone in the midst of a closed society. Sitting at the table, I had become more and more aware of how vulnerable I was, with my every moment dictated by these people. Even Philip, as much as I adored him, was hemming me in, leaving me with no time for decisions of my own. If I was ever to have the reassurance of a second set of keys which they didn't know about, I really had

115

to get them now while I had the chance. I was going to get them—to hell with the General and all his silly rules.

I opened the door a fraction. I preferred to avoid running into Philip and making up a lot of excuses. I peeked toward his door, then heard behind me the noise of the elevator opening. I ducked behind my door, leaving it open a crack. It had to be Philip in the elevator. Once he was safely inside his apartment I could slip out. But no, the steps were lighter than his. I waited until they passed, then peeked again. It was Grace. She was way up at the very end of my hall. She stopped, and I started to pop my head inside again, but she didn't turn. She just stood there, facing the wall. She glanced back once over her shoulder, but didn't notice that my door was slightly open.

"Come on, Grace, *move*," I thought impatiently. I had no time to spare. She seemed to be nervous about my possibly seeing her. But why would I care what she was doing?

When I dared look out again she was leaning down, doing something to the wall. I could see her hand feeling around at the bottom of the corner. Suddenly the wall began to slide, leaving an opening as wide as a narrow door. It had to lead to the other side of the building, where I had imagined there were other efficiency apartments. But if that were the case, there would be no need for a secret door. Then I thought of Romano. Perhaps that hall was where his mental patients lived, and the door was concealed to keep people like me from stumbling in there by mistake. I'd never noticed the outline of the door, but that was because the wall was covered in blue flocked paper. The cracks were lost in the pattern, unless you knew where to look.

Grace quickly stepped through the opening and the wall closed behind her. The second she was gone I went to the elevator.

It didn't take long by bus to reach the five-and-dime store, where I quickly found the right corner of the basement and a little, wizened old man who luckily was without customers.

Taking the keys off the small ring, I thrust them out at him.

"Could you make me one of each of these?"

He looked the keys over carefully, turning them around in his small, grimy hands.

"Lady, these keys is for some special kinda locks. I ain't sure I can make them so they will work."

"Try anyway, please. Take your time. I'll pay extra, but please, please try to make them right."

"I'll try. I ain't got none these colors though."

"Just make them like regular keys. I don't want them to look like these."

After nearly an hour's tedious work, the man handed me four keys. Grabbing them out of his hand and dropping money on the counter, I squeezed through the people now lined up behind me and raced around the store buying a number of small items as ostensible reasons for my trip to town.

It was nearly eleven when I got back to the apartment. I needed a safe place for the new keys, and decided on the medicine cabinet. When I had more time, perhaps I could find a more suitable place. Slipping the keys down behind a box of after-bath powder in the medicine cabinet, I ran the comb through my hair, washed my face, and put on some fresh lipstick. I took my morning pill, to help me regain control, and as soon as my breath became even I rushed down the hall.

Philip greeted me at his door, covering his annoyance with his most charming smile. "Well, it's about time. We'd better get this gardening done. I have an early appointment tonight, you know. Besides, I had another surprise for you and now I'm not sure I'll be able to get it all done. Your storage delivery will be here today." He was clearly trying to control himself, but beneath his smile I could see that same excitement that had radiated from all the others this morning.

I wanted to cry. He had gone to a lot of trouble, and probably much expense, to have the storage company give me special service, and I had done a disloyal and distrusting thing behind his back. I couldn't speak. Philip spoke for me.

"Here, here, none of that. The truck won't be here for at least an hour. It's after eleven now. You must have needed whatever you bought pretty badly to have rushed off so early for it—and this morning, of all days. Well, we'll just have to hurry a bit with the plants, that's all. And I did want to spend a leisurely day with you, Sharon, watching your home begin to bloom, feasting on seeing you make it come alive."

His generosity made me hate myself. "Oh, Philip, I just can't believe you do such impossibly wonderful things. I hate being thoughtless, but shopping took longer than I thought and then I couldn't get a cab. I tried my best to hurry. I'm sorry. You've been so good to me."

"Let's forget it, honey. How about a cool drink before we start? I've been busy. I have all the plants selected. I'm sure you'll like them. I've chosen ones that don't need much care. Of course, you're welcome to any exotics you want, but you'd need Grace to help you with them, and I know how you'd like that."

Pulling me along with him, he handed me a cold, tall glass of tea laced with mint and brandy. It was delicious, but there was no time to sit and drink it. Glass in hand, he led me to his garden, a forest of color and greens. The area was far larger than I'd imagined, covering most of the roof in front. Rock gardens, ferneries, and clumps of flowering bushes with mossy flowers carpeted every inch. Rock paths wound in and out between small, heavy-leaved trees. Each plant and tree had a tiny marker announcing its name and country of origin. Grace must have had to work very hard to keep this place so luxuriant.

Philip gave me no time to browse. A dolly was standing on the path. Picking up the handle, he pushed it before him, stopping every so often to reach for a small pot of greens or flowering plants. I couldn't identify many of them, but they were all thick and fragrant. When the dolly was full, Philip stopped and said we'd have to come back for the rest. I followed meekly behind him, still carrying my drink. He took the plants to my balcony, placed them carefully, and stood back to study the effect. After five trips, he was satisfied I had enough. My own roof garden was almost a tiny version of his own. Inside, in the living room, he placed a large gardenia plant, a bamboo tree, and a pot of what looked like oversized violets. He had chosen just the plants the apartment needed. Standing back, he looked over his handiwork. He didn't look proud, only satisfied that the job was completed.

"We'll wait until your things arrive from storage. I'll help you with them and then I must go." He sat in the large chair, impatiently looking at his watch. This seemed as if it might be my only chance to ask him a few of the questions that were bothering me.

"Philip, who were all those people in the buffet this morning? You seemed to know all of them so intimately."

He looked me over, as though weighing whether or not to answer before he spoke: "They're members of our other chapters. Corintha told you about them, I'm sure. You've just forgotten."

"Maybe. But what kind of chapters? Is it some kind of organization?"

"Well, sort of, a social organization. Each chapter devotes itself to entertaining the others in some particular way. Our chapter entertains through taste, as you could tell by our dinner party. The others use sound, touch, sight, and so on. Plus there's the House of Games. The chapters are all located in different parts of the world. That's why we travel so much. That's all. . . . I wish that damned storage van would hurry up."

"What's the House of Games?"

"I'll tell you about it some other time. They just entertain with games, that's about it."

It all sounded so innocent, but why in the world would entertaining create such excitement in all these sophisticated people? Philip's description didn't at all fit the status and personalities of the people I knew in the building.

Philip stood up angrily. "I'm going to call them and see what's happened. This is absolutely deplorable." The words were no sooner out of his mouth than the phone rang. It was the General calling to announce that the storage van was at the back entry.

Philip brought everything up to the apartment himself. I never saw the delivery men. Not even the General intruded. I tried to help, but without even a screwdriver, I couldn't open the boxes. There seemed to be more boxes than I remembered, and they didn't even contain my clothes. Philip told me simply to sit still until he brought up the trunk. At least then I could get busy putting clothes away. On the last trip he brought the manifest for me to sign and took it back down with the dolly from the van. He returned at last with hammer and screwdriver and opened the boxes. Pictures, china, glasses, silver, a vivid Indian rug, books, the memories I'd almost forgotten. With every item he unpacked, my life was being made whole again.

During all this time, Philip would eat or drink nothing. I had my lunch and a couple of Pepsis to quench my thirst. It was a long day and it wasn't until after five that all the boxes were unpacked. Philip allowed me to help dump the trash, but he wouldn't let me unload a single thing but my clothes. For some reason he insisted on placing every piece of bric-a-brac himself, even deciding where the china and silver should go. There was nothing I could think of that he'd have to place in the bathroom, but all the time I was on edge that he would discover something that had to go in the medicine chest. I breathed a sigh of relief when it was all done.

At last Philip sat down on the sofa and looked at his watch. "I must be going. It's nearly seven and I have to shower and shave. Now, I insist you get to bed early tonight because I'm going to call you early in the morning. You remember, of course, we're flying to Maine. Wear something for sailing or tennis and bring a bathing suit. I suggest soft-soled shoes. It will be a busy day."

"Philip, you'll be worn out. You shouldn't have done so much. I could have done it. Can't you get out of the dinner party? I'm not tired, but you certainly must be."

"This has been nothing for me, Sharon. But I want you wide awake for our outing tomorrow. And of course I can't miss the dinner tonight. You know that. I explained how important it is to me. I'd rather be here with you, but you must realize I do have some obligations in which I can't include you. I won't stay late."

He kissed me lingeringly, tipping my chin up with his finger to hold me close, then rushed off down the hall. Though Philip had done most of the work, it had been an exhausting day, especially because I had felt on tenterhooks the whole time he was there.

As I turned back to the apartment, the warm glow I'd felt waking up that morning returned. It was home now. It was vibrant with colors placed just where they should be. All my own things, clothes to choose from. At least it looked as if I finally belonged here. Everywhere I looked I could see something of myself, placed around the room by Philip's loving hands. He was right. I was exhausted. A hot bath and bed. No more could be done tonight. And at last, contented with the apartment, I forgot all about the keys.

Flopping on the couch, with hardly a breath left in me, I remembered I'd forgotten to take my pills again since morning. No wonder I was so tired. Those pills always gave me energy. Recalling the doctor's warning about experiencing a bad reaction if I didn't keep to my schedule, I had taken them quite seriously. Now I felt a sharp pain in my chest. Dr. Romano had been right. My God, I thought, and stumbled into the bathroom to grab and swallow a pill. The pain subsided almost instantly. Could it have been my vivid imagination? I started back to put my morning's purchases away when I remembered, with a shock, that I hadn't even called

Dell to break our date for Sunday. Philip had absorbed me so completely that nothing else had mattered. I felt worse than miserable. Dialing Dell's office number, I let it ring until I was convinced he wasn't there. Then I tried his home, and was about to hang up when a sleepy voice answered, grumbling:

"Yes, who is it? What do you want?"

"Hello, Dell? It's Sharon."

"Sharon?"

"Yes. You do remember me I hope?" I laughed uneasily.

"Oh, Sharon, sorry, I was asleep. Came home early for a change and I must have slipped off. What time is it?"

"About seven."

"My God, I'm expected somewhere at eight. It's a damned good thing you woke me. I was good for the night. By the way, I got that letter off to your ex-husband. I was going to call you about tomorrow. What time will you be ready?"

"Dell, it's about tomorrow that I called. I'm afraid I can't make it. I—"

He cut me off with sarcasm. "You're in that deep with your cabal already, huh? You can't even take one day off?"

How could I answer him? I didn't want him to know that Philip had given me all the plants I needed, or that Philip and I were spending the day together. I couldn't lie convincingly, but I wanted to stop him from hating my home more than he did already. Somehow, his goodwill seemed extremely important. Dell's friendship meant more to me than I had realized.

"Yesterday"—I developed my story as I went along—"another girl moved away and left the most beautiful plants you've ever seen. She couldn't take them with her, and she was about to throw them away when I saw them. So now I've got almost more than I can use. But you were right, they do wonders for the apartment. And my things came from storage, too. They just got here. I'm up to my neck in packing boxes. It's a mess! I've just got to get this stuff put away! I'm stumbling over everything—plus I'm afraid there might be mildew or bugs in these crates. I won't have time next week when I go to work and I can't live with it like this. But once I get the place cleaned up, it'll be like coming home at last. Just having my clothes here makes me feel better already."

When I finished I was afraid I had spoken too quickly, too easily. The lie wasn't easy, but the truth would have hurt him more. Someday I'd tell him the truth. When he spoke again I was listening intently for the inflections in his voice.

"Okay, then how about going out somewhere for dinner? You'll be tired and it'll save you from cooking."

"I'd better not make any commitments, Dell. I don't know how long the unpacking will take, and if I'm in the middle I won't want to stop. My clothes have been packed for so long they all need pressing or washing and I want to get it all behind me. Why don't you let me cook you dinner one night this week as soon as I'm settled?"

"All right, if you'd rather. Well, I'd better cut this short. I'm due way out in Maryland and I don't want to be late. Why don't you give me a call when you find the time?"

He hung up abruptly. He hadn't believed a word I'd said.

The evening was long, even with all the lights on and the television going full blast. I turned it off and tried to read, but it was impossible to concentrate. Finally, turning out the lamp, I lay in bed staring up at the ceiling. Tired as I was, I couldn't fall asleep. It was after midnight, but I could hear the elevator running constantly. There had to be many guests in tonight. The occupants of the building wouldn't keep the elevator that busy. Hours passed and I still couldn't sleep.

The keys! In my guilt over Dell, I'd forgotten to move them to a safer place. Slipping out of bed, I turned on the lamp, hurried into the bathroom, and grabbed the keys from the nearly empty shelf. Momentarily it amused me to realize there hadn't been anything in writing about duplicating keys, and I laughed to think the whole tribe of perfectionists had actually overlooked something.

Every spot I could think of in the apartment was either too obvious or too hard to get to if I ever needed the keys in a hurry. Philip had placed everything so precisely I was afraid to rearrange anything. Then I remembered the makeup case I had stored in the bottom of the closet, with two other bags piled on top of it. It was tucked away behind the other cases and held all the elaborate makeup I didn't use any more. For some reason I hadn't thrown it away, and now it was the perfect invisible hiding place. Philip was too lordly to stoop to examining my personal junk.

Getting down on my knees, I pulled the larger cases out to get to the small one. My hand had just touched the case when I heard a low moan. I froze. It came again, a long, deep sob. I crouched closer to the wall. It had to be coming from Philip's bedroom! With my ear to the wall, not moving a muscle, I heard it again. It wasn't a woman's cry. It was Philip. He was moaning, deep in his throat, then wailing loud and high. Somehow I managed to drop the keys into the case and close it. The sound of the latch clicking was much too loud. Still I dared not move. I couldn't go to him. He would have hated me for that! What had happened to him after he left me? Something too terrible to bear—it had to have been at the dinner party! But how could it have been?

Shaking and stiff from the tension of my crouched position, I thrust the cases back against the wall, falling sidewise against the corner wall as I did. It was fiery hot! I recoiled to the middle of the floor. Then, carefully, with the tips of my fingers, I investigated the wall. It was scorching hot, from the floor up at least a foot. Rising awkwardly to tiptoes, while roughly pushing the clothes aside, I found that the wall was hot as far as I could reach. Strangely, the heat didn't warm the closet, but the closet was large and the air conditioning vent was blasting. Then I remembered—the incinerator room was at the back of the building near the trash chutes, and the kitchens were also at the back. Such heat couldn't possibly have been generated by hot-water pipes. The only thing it could have been was Cheena's kiln. This wall had to be part of its flue to the roof. But why in the world would Cheena have been using her kiln at this ungodly hour? Possibly she couldn't sleep either, and work was her outlet, as crying was Philip's.

With Philip in the next room consumed in misery and Cheena's kiln raging below, I went back to bed. The sobbing had stopped, but I kept seeing Philip, hearing him wracked with pain as he tossed in his bed. I would have to be very careful how I acted when I saw him in the morning. I didn't dare let him even suspect I'd heard him wailing as though something awful was tearing him apart. What was it about the dinner party that had brought out such intense emotion, as well as such excited anticipation?

Falling back against the pillows, my thoughts in tumult, I trembled and perspired and, still wide awake, watched the sky begin to lighten. At last sleep came, but I dreamed of Philip being consumed in flames and screaming out to me for help.

CHAPTER 22

When Philip knocked at my door early Sunday morning I was already packed, dressed, and pacing the room waiting for him.

"Good morning, good morning, my sweet love." He kissed me warmly. I clung to him, afraid to look into his face, afraid I'd find ravages of pain from the night before; but he jauntily pushed me aside to pick up the beach bag. Nothing about his manner testified to the sounds I'd heard coming from his apartment the night before. He was his usual self, exhilarated and alive.

"We're off to the bounding Maine," he sang lustily as we waited at the back elevator. "Wait 'till you meet these people! Absolutely the wildest spirits you'll ever see. I love them! Being with them is electrifying, better than anything you can imagine."

I tried to quiz him about his friends, wanting to be at least prepared for their scrutiny. They meant so much to Philip, I had to make them like me—at least, to approve of me.

126

"Oh, *no*, you've got to see what I mean. It wouldn't be fair to tell you ahead of time. Just be yourself. I want them to know you just as you are."

We drove to a small airport in Virginia. Philip piloted the plane, while I sat beside him in the only other seat. He was deep in his own thoughts, yet every so often a smile crept over his face as though he were already enjoying whatever lay ahead. If this day was especially for my pleasure, he was taking a peculiar way of showing it. For the first time I felt distant from Philip. Instead of feeling that we were soaring alone, away from the world, I felt like a piece of cargo. Finally, after a painfully silent few hours, Philip brought the small plane down in a clearing that was nearly hidden by huge trees. As soon as we touched ground a large black Lincoln came speeding alongside the plane, to stop just beside the wing. A big man, dressed only in cutoff shorts, ran toward us from the car, waving wildly to Philip, who bounded out of the plane to hug him.

On closer view, the man was a boy who couldn't have been more than sixteen. He and Philip were already in a wrestling match, tussling each other to the ground, where they sat, laughing wildly. Then they got up, dusting themselves off.

"Sharon, this is Jet Harman," Philip managed between breaths as I climbed down from the plane by myself. "How do you like this sample of the next generation? All these young devils are dynamos, each one—but you'll see. Come on, girl, we've got a big day ahead of us."

I tried to study Jet as he shepherded us into the car. There certainly was something special about him even at first glance. Young as he was, the muscles of his body were as firm and strong as a grown man's, his shiny, bronzed skin very beautiful. He kept flipping his sun-bleached hair out of his eyes, a princely arrogance showing in the fluid toss of his head. But there was also an intensity in his eyes—a worldly-wise attitude that made me feel not quite at ease near him.

He drove like a madman, swinging the heavy Lincoln around sharp curves as though he merely willed the car to follow his directions.

Philip and the boy chattered across me about people, places, everything, but I wasn't included and they didn't seem to care. What they said wasn't important, but I had the strangest feeling that although their conversation seemed perfectly commonplace, they were speaking in a code which they, but not I, could understand. Every so often, Jet would interject something for my benefit, or ask me a polite question. But he had the air of an adroit inquisitor who couldn't care less what I said, but who was evaluating something about me just the same.

We sped along the twisting road as though the curves didn't exist. The dense trees broke abruptly; ahead lay a broad span of lawn, with a glistening, sprawling white house set far back on a promontory overlooking a bay.

The car had barely stopped when Philip sprang out, pulling me with him. We ran up a path toward a crowd of people, all young. Soon we were in the middle of the crowd, when a heavy but tall and solid older woman bounded toward us with the same energy as the young ones. Philip threw his arms around her, lifting her off the ground. He finally let her down, as I edged closer, anxious to take part in all this attention, wanting Philip now to include me. With a boisterous swoop of his arm he pulled me to his side.

"Helga, this is Sharon. Isn't she perfect? Sharon will be getting her workout today, but this lady can measure up to anything."

The wondrous Helga nodded to Philip: "I'm sure she will." She spoke warmly in harsh, deep-throated, broken English. "You are welcome, most, Mrs. Crane. Philip does not underestimate you. Please to participate in everything. We are happy to have you."

She knew my last name and Philip hadn't mentioned it. He must have written or called her about me. She made me

nervous, this heavy-boned, powerful woman. She wasn't rich
or social, or a member of the intelligentsia, like most of Philip's friends, but she was despot of her domain, whatever this
place was. Dressed in shirt and mannish black trousers, she
had the stance of a sergeant major. The grin she bestowed
on me was voracious, and she held my hand in a powerful
grip, rubbing her strong fingers along my arm as Grace had
done. Looking at Philip, she commanded affectionately, "Go
on, you children. Make the fun. I'm happy to have you, but
work I must do."

Throughout the day I was to meet the whole community
of young people. None was older than twenty, none younger
than fifteen. Each was especially gifted. Many were foreign
born, but in two ways they were all alike: all were from
wealthy homes—that much was quite apparent from their assured attitudes—and they all exuded health and vigor, and
seemed unimpressed with their own intelligence. They almost seemed to be a younger edition of the group in the
cooperative back in Washington.

Were they also sizing me up as Philip's prospective wife? I
could hardly believe that his choice of a woman was so important that all his friends had to give their approval. Was I
being judged on my worthiness to be a queen bee in their
hive?

"Come on, Sharon," Philip called above the clamor of the
young people. "We're going sailing first. Honey, you'll love
it. It's choppy out there, but you'll be in good hands. Come
on, let's not waste a minute of this glorious day."

Laughing, he pulled me by the hand down the side of the
cliff onto a small dock, to the loveliest little craft I had ever
seen. It shone like moonlight on the crests of the choppy water. A strange hand reached up from below to help me onto
the deck. I grasped it while Philip was thrusting me onto the
little boat from behind. His hands left me, and I heard a
board creak, felt him step away. Before I had a chance to get
my balance, the hand that held mine was pulling me for-

ward, and I tumbled into the arms of the boy waiting below. He grabbed me to him, against a body like Philip's—tall, magnificently muscled, with that same animal magnetism all the young men possessed. His coloring was completely the opposite of Philip's, but they were both built like steel. This boy could not have been more than eighteen. With a cool, precise, yet somehow sensuous voice he welcomed me: "Hello, beautiful Sharon. I'm Rudolph. And Rudolph is going to give you his approval, whether you're a good sailor or not."

He had me pinned to him, with one arm wrapped about me so tightly I couldn't move. His blond hair blew in the wind and his hands began to move. In seconds they had reconnoitered my body, probing, holding, seeking out. Then they were under my clothes, hard fingers rubbing my bare breasts, then up between my legs. I twisted and turned to get loose, but every move made it even worse. To my horror I realized that I was about to have an orgasm. Jerking away at last, I turned and saw Philip, who was just climbing down into the boat. His face was glowing, but with excitement, not anger. Could he have been aroused by Rudolph's behavior? Or had he gone back to the end of the dock to fetch something, and not seen anything of my struggle?

Now Rudolph and Philip were embracing, greeting each other and making plans for the day. I ducked under the boom and scrambled to the prow of the bobbing boat, crouching against the rail. I couldn't wait to tell Philip what had happened, but now was not the time. Philip and Rudolph were racing the boat through the choppy water, skimming neatly through giant waves, laughing. I was close to tears, but Philip didn't notice.

Furious at being ignored, I decided to ignore them too, and I paid no attention to anything they said until I heard Philip's voice rise in an angry bellow: "What in hell do you think you're doing?"

My first thought was that Rudolph must have bragged to Philip about me. But though I had to strain to hear even bits of what they were saying, it certainly had nothing to do with me.

"Philip, old man, you just don't have my vision. My God, the whole world is there for the taking."

"That's stupid and you know it. You've been with us . . . enough to know you can't get away with it. Why should you even want to?"

"Christ, man, you must be . . . You won't be around anyway . . . but I'm ambitious . . . too smart not to . . . "

"But you can't want any more money. Power? For what?"

"Maybe I want all of it."

"You've had to make contacts . . . the House of Games. How did you get away with it?"

"Don't worry, I'm covered. You've only your own limited responsibility for me. If you . . . "

"Are you threatening me?"

"Big brother, you can bet your ass I'm covered. I used your name. You see—I can do it any time I want."

The boat swung around, and the wind swept the rest of their conversation away from me. They didn't seem to care whether I overheard or not, but I stopped listening and just wished that this endless sail would come to an end.

Finally they moored the boat, and Philip returned all his attention to me, carefully helping me up to the pier, hugging me to him as we made our way back to land and the other youngsters. He looked at me closely.

"Come on, Sharon, how about a swim? We'll meet Rudolph down on the sand after he puts the boat up."

I studied Philip's face. It was completely composed. How could he have allowed what Rudolph had done to me? By now I had decided that he must have been watching. He had to have seen it. He should have been angry, but he wasn't. And whatever their argument, it was apparently over. But there was also something sinister about Rudolph that even Philip seemed to be worried about.

What could I say? If I complained about Rudolph, Philip

might even turn on me. I had to have this episode out with him, but right now, at that moment, I was actually afraid. I decided to keep quiet for the moment. I was too far away from home.

Dutifully I followed, but the promise of the day was gone. We swam, but Rudolph was hardly even polite. He was busy with his younger friends. Philip kept urging me on, racing me, jumping waves, tussling in the water. He stayed close by my side every moment now.

After swimming, he wanted us both to try the trampoline, then tennis, then we graduated to rougher, more strenuous games. I was ready to drop, but one or another of the group just wouldn't let me. They had the energy of the sun.

Finally a bell pealed and Philip grabbed me. "Come on, dear. You're pushing too hard. I don't want you tiring yourself. The kids are used to this kind of pace."

He was talking as though the workout had been my idea. I swallowed my anger and followed him without resistance as he led me up the steep incline to the side of the cliff. Behind us the games continued.

At the top of the cliff was a welcome sight. Large, soft lounge chairs had been placed around a cleared, inviting promontory. The broad expanse of water lapped far below. It was nearly dusk, and more than beautiful, peaceful and quiet. At least for the moment I was relieved. At last we were alone. Philip became himself again, taking my hand in his, and kissing me gently. Again I wanted to bring up the episode with Rudolph, but I was so glad to be on good terms again with Philip that I couldn't bear to break the spell of the evening. We sat in silence for a few minutes, then Philip spoke.

"We'll have to go soon. They'll be serving dinner. But I wanted you to myself for a few minutes, just the two of us alone in this beautiful place."

"It is lovely," I replied, vaguely aware that being alone with Philip had changed my attitude about the day. I thought back to his behavior since our arrival. It didn't seem to matter to him that I couldn't share his enthusiasm for his friends. I had never seen him like this before. Never had he been anything but perfect in my eyes. It was unnerving. But I still had to know what this place and these people meant to him and why he had allowed me to go through such treatment. I still didn't dare complain about Rudolph. By now I knew that somehow he'd manage to twist the episode, either laughing at me for being so bothered by a young man's infatuation, or blaming me, not Rudolph, for what had happened.

"Philip," I tried instead, "do all these people live here? Who are they?"

"They're just good friends of mine, Sharon. I knew you'd like them as much as I do. They're all so wonderfully gifted, so full of life."

"Please don't evade me, Philip. I want to know whether they all live here."

"Of course they do. You can see that yourself. I'm not evading you. Why should I? They're here with Helga for the summer. It's a marvelous place. What in the world is so strange about that?"

"Nothing. Nothing." I was defeated. This was all he was going to tell me.

"We'll be dining shortly," he said coldly. His eyes were veiled as he looked over the sea. We sat there in uncomfortable silence for a long while. Our first disagreement, and I didn't even know what it was about.

At last, as I lay stiffly on the lounge, Philip sprang to his feet as though nothing at all had bothered either of us. He leaned across and kissed me passionately. I responded at once. His power over me was so strong that confusion, doubts, and anger died at his touch. Holding out both hands, he lifted me from the lounge, held me softly to him, and kissed me again.

"Sweetheart, we'll have to hurry to get ready for dinner,"

he said. "I'm starved. You must be, too. Change, and I'll meet you as soon as you're ready."

Philip had said nothing about dressing for dinner before we left home. My swimsuit was all he'd told me to bring. Yet he appeared later dressed in fresh clothing, a coat and tie. I felt like a frump in my wilted sports dress and tennis shoes. Philip didn't even notice as he rushed me along a wide hallway to a closed double door. At least a hundred young people were seated inside, all dressed as if they were dining at a chic Washington restaurant. They looked strangely formal for a group who, less than an hour before, had been bouncing around like Olympic athletes. They now sat at long tables presided over by Helga. Philip and I were accorded the head table with Helga and Rudolph, where my informal clothes were very conspicuous.

Dinner was painfully slow, each course served formally by silent waiters, each portion small but delicious. Throughout the meal Philip divided his attention between Rudolph and me. There was no female-to-male arrangement in the seating and Philip separated me from Rudolph. For that at least I was grateful. With me he seemed dutifully solicitous, but the eagerness with which he turned back and animatedly shared something with Rudolph was unnerving.

When the endless meal was over, so was the day. All the young people melted away as soon as the last course was over, courteously but quickly passing me by. As they drifted out of the dining hall, Philip went for my bag, while I waited for him alone in the large entry hall. The young diners were racing past me as though I didn't even exist. A few seemed intent on their conversations, but most were silently rushing away to other areas of the huge house. Rudolph was with Philip when they returned, whispering as they walked. As they reached me, their conversation instantly stopped. Rudolph escorted us to the door, gave Philip a brief adieu, and strode off toward the back of the building. He hadn't said a word to me, but Philip didn't comment on his protégé's rudeness.

The only person left in the hallway was Helga. I would never forget that face, those strong, heavy-boned jaws grinning ravenously. She had been everywhere at once, always supervising, always assessing everyone. Her goodbye to Philip was almost as effusive as her welcome had been. She, at least, smiled at me, clasping my hand tightly in a goodbye shake.

I was so glad to be on our way back to the airport that Jet's demon driving was nearly a relief. I climbed into the plane immediately, but Philip didn't join me. What now, I thought desperately. Looking out the windshield, I saw him and Jet dragging two large packing cases from the trunk of the car. These they stored in the cargo space behind my seat. Then Philip jumped into his seat, waved to Jet, and soon we were high in a darkening sky. I sank back into my seat, trying to unwind. The day had been awful, but I would keep my thoughts to myself as long as I could. I was too depressed and exhausted even to think straight. Philip's own energy was astounding. I could never match it, even if I took twice as many almond pills. Almost everyone Philip knew had that amazing stamina. I looked up at him. He knew how I'd reacted. That's what angered me most of all. Finally, it was all too much. I fell asleep.

I was awakened by the slight bump of our landing at the Virginia airport. Groggy and stiff, I could hardly remember where I was. My muscles ached as I unwound from the cramped position in the plane and staggered into Philip's car. I curled up in the corner of the seat, aware only that Philip and another man were transferring the two large crates to the car. Slipping into the driver's seat, Philip pulled me close to him and quietly drove back into the sleeping city. The moment he parked in the building's garage, Philip hopped out with all the vigor he'd had in Maine. I felt I'd never manage another step, but he left me in the car while he went to get a dolly, calling out behind him, "Honey, why don't you go on up? I'll be quite awhile putting these crates away. I'll check on you to say goodnight."

"No, please Philip, I'd rather wait for you. I'm awake now. It was just more exercise than I've had in years. I must have slept all the way home. Please let me stay with you." Some persistent curiosity was stronger than my exhaustion.

"If you insist. But I have to get these lobsters into the freezer. It may take some time. I can get it done faster if I do it alone."

Funny, the idea of these people eating frozen lobsters when they prided themselves on the quality of their food.

"Please Philip, I won't bother you. I can hold the doors open for you. I don't want to go up alone."

Philip never gave in gracefully. "Well, come on then," he snapped. "But you'll have to wait in the kitchen while I unload these things. You can't go into the freezer. It's too cold."

He pushed the crates onto the elevator, then through the sterile hallways to the kitchen. I followed, meekly but eagerly, about to get my first glimpse of a new part of the building. Philip stopped before the only door on the floor. A combination lock was set high in the middle of the door, and I watched the numbers that Philip spun to open it. Fluorescent light flooded the room automatically when the door opened. Again I followed him inside.

The room we entered was tiled in spotless white and equipped with massive steel sinks, ovens, stoves, and several huge chopping blocks. Tall white cabinets stood in rows at the far end. Even the floor glistened white, and every few feet there was a large drain hole in the floor. In the left wall was what looked like an extra-large elevator, with the same kind of keyhole all the elevators in the building had. Huge deep carts were lined up beside this door. I pictured cooks racing with hot foods on those carts to place them with exquisite care on the lowered dais.

The ceiling was high. Below it was a network of pipes. One large pipe led down and opened up over a large table near the center of the room. That had to be the way they aerated those fabulous aromas into the banquet hall. For all the strangeness of the room, it was the size of the ovens that overwhelmed me. Whole cows, kicking, could have been shoved into them with ease.

Philip bustled through the long room, silent and intent. He was still annoyed with me, so I followed him as quietly as I could. We hurried through another door into a second kitchen which was a duplicate of the first, only smaller. Philip moved on through this kitchen without stopping. As we neared a third door at the end of the room, he turned to look at me. His eyes searched me up and down. I tried to appear indifferent and weary. Still frowning, he turned away abruptly and twirled another combination lock set at shoulder level in the door. Again I memorized the numbers. The idea of penetrating even a fraction of the secrets of this building excited me. The excitement overcame my fatigue.

Philip opened the door wide and pushed the dolly through. He didn't have to urge me to follow. The third kitchen was a replica of the second, but there was only one chopping block and one table, each bigger than the others. Again, a pipe opened up over the table.

We came to the next door. Philip thrust out his arm to hold me back. Now he was clearly furious, but trying to keep his temper from boiling over. He spoke sharply: "You'll have to wait out here, Sharon. This is the freezer. Sit on that stool. I may be some time."

Obviously, I had no choice. He turned back to look me over again and then started fiddling with another combination lock. This time it was harder for me to see what he was doing, but still my eyes took pictures. Such secrecy was titillating, reminding me of those nights my parents went upstairs early, sometimes even before "Sing Along With Mitch."

I couldn't see beyond the opened door. It stayed dark inside as Philip pulled the dolly through and closed the door behind him. Then a light shone through the small frosted window.

When Philip finally returned, he seemed immensely relieved, more like his usual self. He took my arm and moved me swiftly back through each of the rooms, turning out the lights and carefully inspecting each door to be sure it was locked .

When we reached my apartment Philip paused. "Darling, forgive my impatience. I think I'm tired. Too much work. We're both exhausted, so I think it's best to leave you alone tonight. But I'll never be too tired to tell you I love you. I do love you, Sharon."

That did it. "I know, Philip," I murmured. But I couldn't forget the day. Why had he taken me to such a place at all? It was so strange, so different from the lovely Georgetown party we'd attended. Even aside from the awful moments with Rudolph, I had been on display the entire day—just as I usually was in this building. I didn't mind it so much here; it somehow seemed rather natural for people to be curious about a new neighbor. But with those children it was altogether different. If Philip loved me so much, why had he put me through such embarrassment, such physical punishment, such instant and unexplained changes of mood? The spellbinding fascination I had felt for him was bruised. I looked up at him and wondered how soon, if ever, such bruises would heal.

CHAPTER 23

It was the first of October. Already. Two months had slipped by so quickly. All of those two months had belonged to Philip, and we had done everything he wanted. And everything he wanted seemed to take place at the spur of the moment, all of it exotic and exciting: the opening of an opera in Milan, a party on a yacht anchored off the coast of Africa, a safari in Kenya, a week in a villa high in the Andes, two weeks deep in the Sahara desert. Philip was showing me off, but not as he had on the trip to Maine. He seemed to be trying to make up for that. He was the perfect lover, even more. We were so busy it soon seemed that terrible trip had never happened. I belonged to him again.

At first I was self-conscious at the fuss his friends made, but the lightning pace of these trips left me little time for shyness. I was happy just being with Philip and not being taken for granted. His friends were all pleasant, idiosyncratic only in the money and effort they spent searching out their pleasures.

My work in the doctor's office didn't suffer. Romano assured me that he had hired a girl to fill in whenever I was away, but somehow I always missed her. She kept a very clean desk. And I had never seen Dr. Romano so cheerful as when I saw him in between my jaunts with Philip.

Philip was almost overly solicitous. He fussed over me constantly: stay out of the sun, eat and drink only what I say, take your pills. I was almost glad for it. My skin was radiant as never before; never before had I felt so wonderfully vigorous, so alive, so pampered. So snug and well loved.

Right after the trip to Maine I managed to meet Dell at the drugstore a few times. Afterward I would race to the stores on Connecticut Avenue, hoping that the big dress boxes I brought back to the office would serve as an obvious excuse for why I wasn't eating in the buffet. I thought I was getting away with it until one day I walked into the office to find Dr. Romano waiting for me. He greeted me curtly.

"Philip has been calling you. He is most anxious to get in touch with you. I am late for an appointment myself. I only waited to speak to you. Mrs. Crane, in the future, please don't take more than an hour for lunch. We don't expect much from you, and we've been quite lenient, as you well know. But we do feel entitled to a little consideration from you in return."

Without giving me a chance to respond, he turned and left. He'd made himself clear. He knew where I had gone; probably he also knew who I'd been with. His anger was controlled, but he didn't hide it. I began going to the buffet again, and soon Philip had me under his spell again. In the two wonderful months that followed, I thanked Dr. Romano for propelling me back into Philip's arms.

During all those hectic weeks, Philip left me only once. He called the office on a Thursday and asked me to meet him early in the buffet. When I arrived he was quiet and humble, which of course was very out of character for him.

"Honey, I have to take a trip this weekend without you. It's important or you know I wouldn't go." He squeezed my hand. "I'm leaving tomorrow, but I'll try to be back Sunday, Monday at the latest. I'll call you the minute I get in. While I'm away please rest. I've been overtiring you, and you've been such a love to let me, but take this opportunity to relax. This coming weekend you'll be glad you did."

Of course I agreed. I loved him too much to ask for an explanation; intuitively I knew he would offer me none.

He left me in the empty buffet while I was still finishing my coffee. No sooner was he gone than my thoughts spun with all the things I could do in this brief respite. Suddenly I was glad for his absence. At last I could see Dell. Love could be all-encompassing, but I still wanted my friend.

But I wasn't to see Dell. Back in the office after breakfast my head began to ache. The room spun relentlessly. I broke out in a cold sweat, my body a mass of cramps. I doubled over the desk. I don't know how long I was there, too miserable to call for help, but after what seemed like hours I became aware that someone had come in and was standing over me.

"What is the matter, Mrs. Crane?" It was Dr. Romano.

"I feel awful." Tears were drenching my face.

"You haven't missed taking your pills? That might bring on such a reaction."

"No, I haven't. I felt fine until just a little while ago. Can't you do something, for God's sake? My head is bursting."

He helped me into an examining room and checked me briefly. When he finished he seemed relieved.

"It's only the latest flu virus that's going around. You must have been exposed to it on one of your trips. It's vicious, but it doesn't last long. Get right into bed. I'll bring you some medication and food you're to eat until you recover. But you must stay in bed or the pains will return. Just take the pills and eat nothing but the food I'll have sent up to you. I'll be away for the weekend, but you'll be perfectly all right if you do as I tell you. Your neighbors will look in on you. And you can always call the General."

The doctor didn't offer to help me to my room, but no sooner had I undressed and crawled into bed than he limped in, without knocking. He carried a number of small vials which he quickly put into the freezer. Then, without a word or pause, he came and stood above me, offering a pill with a glass of water. He laid a bottle of pills on the night table.

"Take these, Mrs. Crane. When you awaken, fix yourself some of the soup I brought and take another pill. By the time you've finished these pills and the soups you should be feeling much better."

He waited until I swallowed the first pill before starting to leave. Groping for his hand, I pleaded weakly: "Please don't say anything to Philip. I don't want to spoil his weekend."

"Of course I won't, my dear. I understand. You'll be perfectly fine again before he returns. I must go." He wanted his hand back.

"Doctor . . . "

"Yes?" His patience was artificial.

"Shall I take the regular pills?"

"Of course. But of course! Take one each time you awaken. Without them your whole system could have a violent reaction. I've cautioned you before; you must listen to me. Without them the effects of the virus would be much, much worse. Never forget them, Mrs. Crane. " His white brows almost met in a deep, irritated frown.

If he said anything more I didn't hear. Within minutes I was deeply asleep.

I'd sleep, then awaken. Sometimes it was light, sometimes dark. Each time I'd grope my way to the kitchen, heat the soup and sip it as if I were in a dream. Then I'd trudge back to bed and take the next pill. Once I found the water bottle that Romano had left me, empty. As I went to the bathroom to refill it I listened for a while to hear the elevator motor, which I suddenly realized I missed. It was so terribly quiet, possibly because I knew Philip wasn't on our floor. But I had the eeriest feeling I was completely alone in the building.

There was no motor noise. Everything was silence. Suppose I did call the General. Would he answer? I didn't even know what day it was. Had I been following Romano's schedule for one day or two? I looked into the refrigerator and there were still several containers of the soup left. Maybe I could dress and go down to the street. But as I started to get into my clothes, the room began to spin. The headache crashed into my skull as though I'd been hit with a sledgehammer. It was all I could do to grab the water bottle and stumble toward the bed. Quickly I swallowed one more pill. My last thoughts before sleep overtook me followed me into my dreams. In my dream, I was being kept immobilized in a deserted building, while across the street, through brilliantly lighted windows, I could see Philip, Mrs. Byrom, and the others, all in evening clothes, eating an elegant, apparently interminable meal.

CHAPTER 24

The sound of the telephone reverberated in my ears like the blast of a siren. I awakened cursing. But as I recovered my wits I realized the headache and dizziness were completely gone. I dashed to answer the phone. It was Philip. He was back.

"Good afternoon, my big baby. What's the matter with you? Did you have to get sick just because I was away from you for a few days?"

"See what you do to me?" I teased back. "But I'm all right now. You're back and I feel just fine. Why don't you come right on over?"

He needed no coaxing. In a few minutes I was in his arms. But something had changed. He held me back at arm's length, looked me up and down, worry and anxiety clearly etched on his face. "Are you sure you're feeling all right now? Nothing else happened while I was gone?"

I reassured him, but he was still anxious. He kept moving from the couch to the chair, not seeming to know what he wanted to do or say. Instead of our usual chattering, he seemed to be finding it hard to come out with whatever was

144

on his mind. But maybe it wasn't Philip. Maybe it was I who couldn't carry my end. I was worried—about my menstrual period. During the last two months I had had a scanty period and then none. But Philip hadn't known. Despite the fact he wanted to take me to bed wherever we were, there were some places it was impossible. I kept making excuses to myself that it was because I wasn't used to the pace we were keeping; but now that he was back again in our home surroundings, I knew I had to tell him. I had been due again this past week-end and nothing had happened. I couldn't delude myself any longer. Philip hated my diaphragm and had given me a supply of birth-control pills that Dr. Press had prescribed. I couldn't imagine how they had gone wrong. But I couldn't consult Dr. Press before telling Philip—and I dreaded telling him. I was so afraid to lose him. How would he take it? How could I ever begin? At those perfect times when I'd spent a passionate night in Philip's arms, he'd lie there afterward staring at me. Not with tenderness; instead his look was un-certain and impatient. He had that look on his face now. Often at those times, when I knew he was studying me, the picture of the girl in the red dress came back, that pathetic, mesmerized creature moving down the street with Philip. What had become of her and her baby? As lovely as the girl was, Philip could not have been the father of her child. She was too uncultured for him even to notice. She simply worked in the building and her employers had assumed re-sponsibility for helping her through her pregnancy. But it was different with Philip and me. All of his friends would know that the child I carried was his.

Philip had returned on a blustery Monday and he decided we'd stay in. I was relieved, but more tremulous than if I had been awaiting a jury's life or death verdict. This would be my chance to speak the words that had been choking in my throat for weeks.

That evening I dressed and we were sprawled on one of the immense sofas before his roaring fire, sipping my now-favorite brandy. Philip was still in his silent mood. His light-blue eyes were moving over me, like icy fingers. He seemed, somehow, to know what I was afraid of putting into words. He waited. I could't stand my own silence. Finally, I couldn't hold it in any longer.

"Philip?"

"Yes, Sharon," he whispered in an unusually intense, hoarse voice.

"I'm pregnant." My voice faltered. I sat there waiting as if turned to stone, wincing to see Philip's jaw stiffen. Then he rose and stood above me, ecstatic. He lifted me high into the air. All at once he was laughing until tears ran down his cheeks. He groaned in wild, abandoned delight. He swung me around and around, then drew me to him, still laughing madly.

"Darling, you're sure? How long? Oh, my dearest, my baby. You don't know what marvelous news you've given me. Sharon, my Sharon. Our baby. Here's to him!" He grabbed up a glass and downed the brandy in a swallow, laughter spilling the drink from the sides of his lips.

I sank into his arms in tremendous relief. A rush of tears washed my own cheeks.

Later, as we still held each other, Philip became serious.

"Darling, have you seen Press yet?"

"Not yet."

"Well, you mustn't wait. I don't want anything to happen to either of you."

"I wanted you to know first."

"And I'm very happy you did, my angel. Now would you rather I made the appointment for you?"

"Of course not. I'll call him."

"You won't put it off? I want you to see him as soon as possible."

He was beginning to annoy me; I wasn't going to be irresponsible about my pregnancy.

"Of course I won't. But you should know what is bothering me."

"I know. But don't worry. We will be married. We just have to wait a little while."

"Why, Philip? I'm practically living with you now; all your friends, our friends, know it. Ever since our first date you've been parading me before everyone you know. Is this the way your crowd lives? Maybe you can face them, but I can't. If you don't want to marry me, tell me before it's too late. I won't spend the rest of my life trying to bring up your child by myself."

His words came smoothly, soothingly. "Sharon, dear, you don't understand. Give me a chance to explain. Of course we'll be married. But I can't right away. The reason why has to be kept confidential or I'll fail at what I'm doing. I'll tell you what I can. Then you'll have to have faith in me.

"You've always known that I make a lot of sudden trips. Well, I collect rareties for special clients. I'm under contract to these people. I bring them invaluable, ancient works of art from some of the most inaccessible places in the world. It's only because I have the contacts to get at these rareties before they are claimed by the countries where they're found that my services are unique. I am the only person alive who could possibly fill the contracts I've signed. It's too complicated to explain anything more. It would be dangerous for you and for me if you knew more. Please try to understand. I'll finish my commitments as quickly as I can. It will mean almost constant traveling for me for awhile, but if I know you are properly taking care of yourself I can do it without being distracted by worrying about you. Then we'll do anything you want."

"How long?"

"Only a few months. We'll be married long before the baby is born, I promise you."

"Philip, why can't we be married first?"

"Because there's a clause in every contract that I remain single until I fulfill the agreement."

Suddenly I was incredulous. "What?"

"It's not crazy, Sharon. I have to perform delicate negotiations under very hazardous conditions and I have to be a free agent to do it. You don't understand, but that's all I can tell you."

"I'm to take you on trust?"

"Yes."

CHAPTER 25

I was no sooner sitting at my desk the next morning than Philip sauntered in.

"Hi, Sharon. Come on, we're going to see Press."

"For God's sake, Philip, I told you I'd see him."

"Now, honey, don't try to talk me out of it. I want to be with you when you see him. Does that bother you so much?" His concern was aggravating.

"Of course not, Philip. But Dr. Romano isn't here yet. There's no one to cover the phones."

"You've left them before. You know Rome won't care."

What could I say?

"O. K., but let me get my bag. Dr. Press probably isn't even in yet either."

"Come on, Sharon. You know I'd check first."

Of course.

The short, corseted Dr. Baldwin Press waddled into his waiting room as soon as we entered. He was obviously prepared for my visit. Philip must have called him early that morning, or even the night before. The doctor waved me into his examining room. He never talked much, but a little bedside manner would have been appreciated. Instead, he told me brusquely to strip down.

He was a small man, not more than five feet tall, but compact and solidly built. His head seemed overly large, with thick, curly hair dangling like black snakes over his low forehead. The very thought of those hands touching me made me shudder. But he wasn't interested in me yet. He was intent on reading a folder. It looked like my medical record, but Dr. Romano was the only physician I'd consulted so far. Maybe it was a duplicate, but why in the world would these doctors share my medical records unless they worked as a team and all expected to be treating me.

The doctor looked up at last and mechanically waved me onto the examining table. "I see you were slightly anemic when you were first checked. It is better now."

"Will that cause me any problems, doctor?"

"No, no, no." His thoughts were a mile away, and I wished he were too. The examination seemed unending. He prodded as though I were a piece of machinery and he an engineer. The only noise he made was sucking his lips. Never had I seen such lack of professional manner, but at least he was efficient.

At last he motioned for me to get dressed. I felt so dirty, I didn't want to put my clothes back on until I could bathe away the doctor's touch. But that would have to wait.

When I had dressed, he ushered me back to where Philip sat waiting. Talking directly to Philip, the little doctor gave him all the instructions: I was to double the number of almond pills I was already taking, plus two others he prescribed. He told Philip to be certain the little lady came back to him every Monday for an injection. He didn't bother to explain anything to me, only that it was essential for my safety and the baby's that I follow his instructions implicitly.

Before Philip and I got out the door, Press grabbed my hand, holding me back. He pursed his lips, and then warned me: "There may be some side effects from the injections. If you feel anything unusual, even drowsiness, go immediately to bed and stay there. Rome or I will see that you are cared for." He abruptly closed the door behind us before I could ask any questions.

I immediately turned on Philip. "Philip, I've always been in perfect health. Why all these precautions? I can't imagine myself in bed for so long. I feel fine. What's the matter with me, anyway? Press didn't tell me a thing. The way you were conferring between you, he acted as if you were the pregnant one, not me."

"Don't worry, Press is like that. I'll go right downstairs now and have these prescriptions filled for you. After this, you'll just have to be sure you don't run out. And you heard what he said about the injections. If I'm not here, you must not forget them."

Philip acted as if I deserved no explanation of all the instructions Press had given. I wondered how he could have understood it all so much better than I had. Unless he had been through all this before. . . . I shuddered at the implications of my thought. It just couldn't be. This was no time for suspicious thoughts. I had to trust Philip, particularly now. But I couldn't help answering with a touch of sarcasm.

"Of course I won't forget the damn pills or the injections either. But I'd certainly like to know at least what they are."

"Nothing but the usual things they give pregnant women or he'd have told you. Now stop worrying, Sharon. My friends are all interested in our child. And in you. This is quite an event to them as well as to us."

Philip was trying to be efficient and helpful, but somehow I had expected him to be more emotional about becoming a father.

Philip returned so soon, Pavel must have had the prescriptions already filled when Philip reached the laboratory. He brought the first pill to me at my desk, with a glass of water, and watched as I swallowed it. Setting down the glass, he

BETTY E. ULLMAN

pulled me to my feet, drew me to him, and kissed me hard and long. Releasing me just as quickly, he vanished before I could say a word.

I sank back into the chair. Suddenly I couldn't move. Everything was crashing in on me. Sounds, colors, shapes, all were swirling in a blur. My head dropped to the desk.

Someone was roughly shaking my shoulder. It was Dr. Romano.

"Mrs. Crane, wake up. You've slept through the day. I've been calling for hours. Press spoke to me about your condition. The medication must be having the side effects he warned you about. I'm going to help you to bed."

That was fine with me. I was barely aware of his leading me to my room. The next time I woke I was in my own bed. The small lamp burned beside me. Beneath it lay a large, white envelope with "Mrs. Crane" scrawled in a flourishing hand. "IMPORTANT" was in large letters across the front. It wasn't sealed. My fingers trembled as I withdrew the letter to read it. My eyes blurred. I tried to concentrate on one word at a time:

Mrs. Crane:

My husband, Dr. Romano, and Dr. Press have asked that I prepare these instructions for you. They must be followed carefully. Minor complications have arisen in your pregnancy because of certain factors in your constitution. Unless properly counteracted during this early stage, the life of yourself and your child will be endangered. However, with proper care and medication, you should be able to resume a relatively active life within a short time.

You may be feeling quite well when you awaken, but you are *not* to leave your bed. Do *not* leave the bed unless someone is with you. You will find a tray on a cart beside you. This is your dinner. After you have eaten, take your medication, also on your tray.

Mr. Hawk has been informed of your condition. He has been waiting impatiently to see you, but he expresses deep regrets that he could no longer delay his departure for a busi-

ness appointment. He will contact you immediately upon his
return.

Your position as receptionist has been filled, but you will
continue to draw your salary. You are *not* to come to the office
under any circumstances.

Wilhelmena Romano, R.N.

The letter was as cold as her heart.

The cart was where the letter said it would be, covered
with silver dishes. I was as hungry as I was tired. With every
mouthful the headache and fuzziness diminished, and the
more I ate, the sleepier I became. I saw the small paper cup;
this time there were three large pills inside. I swallowed them
down with the coffee. My pains dissolved almost at once, but
slowly my strength began seeping away again. I became
aware only of the messy tray filled with empty dishes as I
sank into deep sleep.

Each time I woke, the cart stood replenished beside my
bed. For all I knew, days or weeks might have passed. Sometimes when I was conscious I was aware that someone else
was in the room. I'd try to speak but could only grunt. Whoever was there did all the talking, but I could only see lips
moving. I couldn't decipher the words. Sometimes I recognized Cheena Wescott or Grace. Even Mrs. Byrom stood
watch. They talked at me as though I were an invalid, or a
blithering idiot.

Sentences like: "Your name is Sharon Crane." "Do you
know who I am?" "Are you still sleepy?" "Would you like to
see Philip?"

All I could do was stare at them through half-closed eyes.

Finally Philip came. At the sight of him relief flooded me.
But his expression, as he leaned over the bed, was so bland,
so curiously like all the others, I couldn't speak even to him.
He said nothing. Just leaned down and watched me, then
walked away. Romano and Press were with him. I could only
catch scattered words of sentences as they huddled by the
door.

" . . . transfer her . . . "

"Impossible."

"The mind hasn't responded yet. Can't you see . . . "

"What else then?"

" . . . Cheena or Grace . . . "

" . . . not Corintha's fault . . . "

"Not mine!"

"Not to be foreseen."

"Couldn't diagnose . . . "

" . . . have to . . . all of us I expect . . . "

"Too late . . . "

"You know the date is settled."

Obviously I wasn't responding to whatever they were giving me. I must have something far more serious than they'd thought. Now they were all trying to do something for me. They seemed so worried. Their voices faded away and again I was asleep, in my psychedelic whirlpool.

Once Cheena came in as I was eating.

"Well, thank God. I finally found you awake. How about sitting up awhile and chatting with me? And you don't need that dessert. You're fatter than a pig."

At that I began to cry and couldn't stop myself. I didn't care what Cheena thought. The tears felt wonderful.

Cheena seemed to understand. She smiled down at me, but it was an artificial smile, which frightened me even more. "Don't worry, Sharon. You're all right now. I'll be over to take you out soon. There's an exercise room downstairs. We'll get rid of some of that fat for you. Wouldn't you like that?"

Funny, I thought, Cheena could talk to me easily and intelligently, unlike the others. After that she came often and lingered for hours, and all the while now, as long as Cheena was with me, I managed to stay awake, if not fully alert. After awhile I realized my medication must have been changed. I no longer woke only at mealtimes. Cheena and I spent hours talking, and she told me all about herself. She began to take me down to the exercise room every day and put me through a thousand routines. I had gained at least twenty pounds and gradually the blubber firmed into shape again. After a workout we'd snack at the buffet, Cheena always selecting the food I was to eat, bringing a special tray to me at the table. The dining room was always deserted while we were there, but I had no idea of the time and wasn't sufficiently alert to put any incidentals into clear perspective. I knew enough to be worried about the baby, but Cheena reassured me over and over that the exercises I was doing were all good for the child.

Although most of the time it was difficult to think, there were beginning to be moments when everything seemed clear. Those times were the worst. I was being kept drugged because of my illness, but I was getting stronger every day—surely it was time to let me come out of it. I didn't like being in a fog, but what I really worried about was what the drugs might do to the baby. Surely Dr. Press knew what he was doing—but what if the baby was affected? Maybe she—I always thought of her as a little girl—maybe she would even become retarded. I kept trying to talk to someone about my fears, but no one would take me seriously. Except Cheena, and yet even her reassurances sometimes seemed false.

Sitting bundled at my window one chilly day, I casually remarked, "I'm getting cell fever, cooped up in this place for so long, Cheena. One of these days I'm going to escape."

Cheena didn't appreciate my joke.

"I'll take you to my place, then. That will be a change. Would you like that?"

"It would be heaven, Cheena. Anything would, after this jail."

Cheena's eyes focused on me through the large black-rimmed glasses she wore when she was alone with me. They magnified her thick, black lashes, exaggerated the slant of her eyes. The high cheekbones, lush mouth, and sensuous eyes were stunning. She gave me so much of her time, yet she talked mostly of men, going over and over her romantic episodes. She almost made me feel as if I were living them with her. I wondered why she didn't give her men more of her time instead of cooping herself up with an invalid. Cheena never once mentioned names, or places, or hints that would give their identities away. Just enough to tantalize my curiosity.

She dropped in uncannily on those evenigs when I was most restless, when my thoughts dwelt constantly on Philip. I mostly recalled the lovable things about him, putting out of my mind his recent neglect and unresponsiveness. Cheena would appear then and interrupt my confusion with tales of her conquests. They were a wonderful elixir. She could have any man she wanted. That was what bored her. She didn't want easy men.

Cheena wasn't the only one who dropped in to see me during those long evenings. One night Grace came knocking. I was even glad to see her. She started visiting regularly, usually on nights when no one else was there.

Grace was really an enigma to me. She didn't treat me as a friend, or even as Philip's possession. She wasn't sisterly, or motherly, nor was she interested in my views of whatever she talked about. And her talk was all but incoherent—her gardens, her perfect health, people I didn't know. She seemed to be reminiscing, but not for my benefit. All I could see in her was some kind of anxious greed. She kept coming too close to me as she babbled on, watching, inspecting me with an expression I couldn't fathom. She had a terribly hungry look but somehow I didn't ever think she was a lesbian.

I couldn't stop her. She was constantly rubbing her fingers on my arm, my hand, even touching the skin of my face. It was so unnerving I wanted to thrash away from her touch, but she was too adroit for me. She would usually approach me when I was half drowsing, lulled by the monotony of her monologues.

One night Mrs. Byrom would visit, then came the doctors' wives. None, except Cheena or Grace, stayed very long and

none of them came together. Philip kept the busy schedule
he'd cautioned me about. They were short trips, none longer
than a week, but when he'd come to visit I could feel he was
itching to leave again. He talked of nothing but the next trip.
He never apologized for his absences. Cheena tried to make
excuses for him but they didn't help. October and November
were lonely months.

One evening Cheena saved me again. She finally came
through on the promise I thought she'd forgotten.

"Sharon, how would you like to get out of this hole for a little while? Come on down to my place tonight."

I was ready before she finished the invitation.

Entering Cheena's apartment was like entering a monas-
tery. Luxuriously designed and nearly bare, it enhanced
Cheena's exotic beauty.

She hurried me through a maze of large rooms, all done in
dark gray. Though the furnishings were sparse and severe,
in every wall were niches of all sizes and shapes, and in them
hidden lights displayed Cheena's works: Magnificent figu-
rines, unique bowls, urns etched with figures. All the statues
were grotesquely posed, with ecstatic expressions of either
pain or joy. But I had no chance to examine any of them
closely. Cheena was hurrying through the tour, as though
she'd had second thoughts about having brought me there.

We finally returned to the largest room. In the middle of
the floor was a mass of huge, black suede pillows. Cheena
sprawled on the soft, enveloping pillows and crooked her
finger for me to join her. The surroundings soon began to
hypnotize me, and I began to have the strange sensation that
I should get up and leave. The place suited Cheena, but not
me. Suddenly Cheena got up, walked over to the one bare
wall, and pulled aside a section of it to display a cabinet the
length of the room. The shelves inside were laden with exquisite, translucent bone china, softly lighted by a panel of
lights at the back. She had somehow created an unusual,
fragile luminescence tinged with pink.

"I've made these for our neighbors with some differences in design," she murmured. That was all she said. She daintily tapped her finger on one of the standing plates, then quickly drew her finger back. She slid the wall closed again and locked it. She acted as though she had been burned, came and sat down beside me in a sullen and silent mood I'd never seen before.

I had to ask: "Cheena, those are magnificent. Don't you ever show or sell them? I know Philip has some of your pieces, but these things belong in museums for the whole world to enjoy. You could be famous for what I see right here."

She seemed bored. She had probably heard praise like mine so many times before.

"I never sell them. I give them away to special people. The satisfaction—well, you probably wouldn't understand, so please don't try. Would you like to see how I make them?"

I was very interested and a little nervous for some reason. Visiting Cheena's kiln seemed like a very special, significant event. I started to untangle myself from the pillows, when Cheena sat down again.

"I'm expecting an important call"—her smile told me it was from one of her men—"so we'll have to wait a few minutes. Are you comfortable? Why don't you stretch out again for a while?"

At that moment, the phone rang and her attitude changed from impatience to enthusiasm. "Here, you watch the TV for a few minutes. I'll take the call in the other room." She pushed a button; a cabinet slid open, revealing a huge, sleek machine. She flicked it on on her way out, and an image appeared instantly.

The channel was showing *Sesame Street*. I went over to change stations, and discovered that the dials and switches were more complicated than usual. I pushed buttons and nothing happened. Then I tried several of the switches. *Sesame Street* quickly disappeared, but I was stunned by what replaced it.

It was, it had to be, a closed-circuit channel, and it had to be televising from this very building. On the screen were about ten of my neighbors—Grace, Schine, the Ahnesbachs, Pavel, and others, all kneeling on cushions around a shallow pit in the middle of a brightly lit room. They were shouting, gesturing wildly, riveted on what was happening before them.

In the pit were at least a dozen big snakes—snakes and rats. The rats' tails had been clipped, so that each tail was a different length, and the participants were prodding the snakes with sticks, urging them to swallow the terrified rats. In a second, I took in the game's meaning: a sick game of survival for the rats, and each of the gamblers was laughing, roaring, as his snake caught and devoured someone else's rat. Revolting! I fought back nausea as I punched wildly at the buttons to remove the loathsome spectacle. God, suppose Cheena caught me watching this! The screen blackened again, then another picture appeared.

As the focus sharpened, I realized that this was even worse. The quality of the picture was different, as if it had been taped. It had to have been. Nothing like this was going on in the building or the people I'd just seen would have been there. A large audience of formally clad people—no one I recognized from the cooperative—were seated around a stage, and familiar words came from the set: "Ho! Let the doors be lock'd. Treachery! I seek it out. It is here, Hamlet: Hamlet, thou art slain. . . ."

This performance, however, was a far cry from any production of *Hamlet* I had ever seen, for all the actors were nude, except for helmets and adornments necessary to the actors' roles. Bodies lay strewn all over the stage, which was slimy with blood—the incestuous Queen, the vicious King, Laertes, and the noble Hamlet. But the blood had gushed from very real wounds and the anguish of those poisoned was too horrible to be play-acting. Hamlet expired in an agony no actor could ever have been able to portray. Before my eyes he truly breathed his last, and the fascinated on-lookers hunched forward in their seats, their faces enraptured by the spectacle of slaughter they had witnessed. It was like certain pornographic films I had heard of, but on a grand and awful scale.

My shock and repulsion were so great that I was paralyzed into inaction. Released by the sound of applause from the screen, I quickly turned back to the control panel and jabbed wildly at the nearest button. I had to get *Sesame Street* back before Cheena came in. I remembered the first switch, touched it, and sighed in relief to see Big Bird back on the screen. I sank into the cushions, trembling, but I needn't have hurried. Cheena's conversation seemed endless, and I was almost asleep by the time she came back into the room. By that time, though, I had made some sense of what I'd seen. Remembering Philip's words of long ago, I began to understand that I had accidentally seen a sample of the entertainment provided by the chapter concerned with the sense of sight. I was numb with fear.

But all Cheena saw was a drowsing girl. She closed the cabinet and it was, for the moment, all over.

She came and stood over me. I prayed she wouldn't notice my excitement, or my heavy breathing. "I think it's getting too late to make our little trip now," she said. "Sorry I was so long, hope you weren't bored."

"Oh, no!" Suddenly my voice was overly loud. "I've been dying to see where you work. Let's go now. I've never had the nerve to ask you, but I'm fascinated. Have been since I saw those incredibly lovely things you gave Philip."

Even that didn't seem to reassure her, but she smiled.

"We'll have to hurry, then. I don't take many people down to my workshop. I like its privacy. I don't want anyone else's thoughts bombarding my own vibrations. My ideas must flow freely there. I suppose you find that absurd."

Of course I said I didn't; though I did.

Without another word, Cheena led me to the back elevator, helping me along whenever I groggily fell behind. We finally reached the lower basement. She rushed me through a long, winding, dark tunnel until at last we came upon a massive steel door. Another combination lock was set high in the door.

Cheena twisted a complex combination. I watched the numbers. Cheena shot a glance back at me once, but I had quickly fixed my eyes in a blank stare at the far wall down the corridor. Cheena continued with the lock.

The door did not swing out. It rather grunted. Stepping over a high sill, Cheena reached her hand back to save me from stumbling in the dim light and pulled the door closed behind us. I felt lost in a black pit. Suddenly there was light and the whishing sound of cold conditioned air sweeping in from all corners of the room.

Cheena led me into a tremendous stone cavern. Over to one side in the floor was what looked like a large trap door and another large drain like the one in the kitchen. The place was cold and damp. I tried to hide the shiver that ran down my spine. Cheena noticed and tried to explain.

"It seems cold down here, I know, but you can't imagine how hot these furnaces make it. And the air gets terribly stale when the door is closed. There's a complicated system for ventilating the place, but I'd fry down here without the air conditioning."

She took my hand and pulled me toward the massive stone structures that dominated the center of the room. They stood at least ten feet tall and were even wider than high. A stack rose from each of them and disappeared into the ceiling. Directly before us were two iron doors, so large we both could have stepped through them without bending. I couldn't imagine Cheena budging them. Beside the ovens was an open hearth Cheena explained was used for some of the finer metal work. That too had a wide venting chimney above it.

We spent almost an hour while Cheena told me all about how she molded different figures in different techniques. She forgot time. She glowed in telling of the background of her most cherished treasures. Then suddenly she caught herself. Her words stopped mid-sentence, as though she suddenly remembered I was there.

She cut herself short and, without another word, hastily escorted me back through the outer door. But I turned around for a final look. The whole area around the furnaces was barren and spotless, reminding me of nothing but the antiseptic kitchens. Another shiver ran through me. But Cheena must have thought it was the cold.

"Here, I'm keeping you so long and you must be tired. I forgot myself. Rude of me, but there are so few people I care to talk to about my work. We'd better go up. I do like you, Sharon. You're different from the other girls who've lived here. Mindless, shallow bitches. You're refreshing. Come, we'd better go."

Her green, slanting eyes narrowed until she looked like an Oriental cat. I caught the glint of tears in her eyes. I couldn't fathom Cheena at all. She spoke of the others as mindless bitches. But at this point I was almost mindless myself. Had she brought me down here to help me hasten the recovery of my alertness, or had she been testing me? And why should I have gotten the impression I was being tested? Something about the whole episode hadn't rung sincere. Only in those moments when Cheena had been carried away by her own enthusiasm had she seemed close to me. I longed to ask her whether she ever shared in the sport I had seen on the television screen, or if she had ever seen that hideous production of *Hamlet*. But if I confronted her with my knowledge of her depravity, I would probably lose the only friend I seemed to have—except for Philip, of course.

CHAPTER 26

I was deposited again in my apartment, feeling depressed, unnerved by what I had seen. The General brought my supper tray late because they had expected me in the buffet and I had been too exhausted to try to get there. I thanked him as he placed the tray on the table and, with a quick, pained smile, looked at me questioningly, then hurried on out of the room.

Somehow, for once, the food didn't tempt me. Thoughts of those huge kilns were eating at me. They left the impression not of beauty but of evil.

I didn't want the neighbors to know I wasn't eating, so I flushed all the food down the toilet. I made a pot of fresh coffee and then there was nothing I wanted to do but get some sleep. I lay in bed courting sleep but for once it evaded me. Clearly, it was the food I had been served that had made sleep so easy for me before. I lay awake and listened to the tiny motor of the clock, all sounds magnified. I listened and tried to concentrate until every car or bus passing on the street was familiar. An unfamiliar sound came from the hall. It couldn't have been Philip. He was in Africa on another of his assignments. The very lightest tread on the thick carpet. I crept to the door and put my ear against it. The opening and closing of the door down the hall could barely be heard. It had to be Philip!

I carefully crept into the closet to listen at the wall. There were sounds, quiet and slow. I could hardly make them out, but somebody was in Philip's apartment, in his bedroom.

How long I stayed there I couldn't know, but I finally gave up and crawled back to bed to cry. I lay there weeping far into the night, until at last I couldn't stand it any longer. I slid out of bed. It was four in the morning. I had to know. I hadn't heard Philip's door close, or the sound of the elevator. He had to be in his apartment, probably asleep.

It was difficult to move quietly, I felt so encumbered. The baby inside me seemed so large, but I managed to get into my robe and slippers. As I moved around the room I suddenly realized my head was fully clear for the first time in ages. Visiting with Cheena the day before had probably helped, but the biggest change had been my not eating the dinner provided for me. These brief moments of clarity and long hours of fuzziness were wearing me down. Why couldn't they see I was suffering from these "side effects"? Or was that what they wanted? To keep me quiet to protect the baby inside me? I could hardly believe that I was being helped despite the care of all the doctors I had in attendance.

But the business at hand was setting my mind at rest that Philip wasn't with another woman. I took my keys, which were right where I'd left them in my bag. Cautiously I opened my own door and gently pulled it to behind me. I left it unlocked. I might have to scurry back inside at a moment's notice.

I slowly slid one foot ahead of the other toward Philip's door. Almost sighing in relief, I caught myself as I reached it. Carefully, slowly, I leaned my ear against his door. At first there was nothing. I listened. Waited. I was ready to leave, fully satisfied that whoever had been there was long gone, when I heard something. Voices. Very low. Could it be the

TV or radio? I listened longer, but the sounds were so faint. Then they grew louder, more like footsteps coming near the door. "My God! He can't find me here like this," I thought, holding my hand to my mouth to keep from crying out aloud. I looked both ways wondering what I could do. My own apartment seemed miles away. Then I remembered Grace's special entrance.

I scampered, this time on tiptoes, nearly tripping, but I made it to the corner where the corridor turned. Quickly I felt down by the floor board. My fingers were almost numb. But at last I found it, a small, nearly invisible dent in the wall and a tiny button. I pressed it hard. The wall instantly, silently, slid aside and I slipped through as soon as it was wide enough. It closed, of itself, right behind me.

For a moment I thought it was pitch black in there, but it was only the contrast from the brighter corridor I'd just left. There were tiny bulbs along the ceiling, many feet apart. As soon as my eyes adjusted to the change I could find my way and get out through the other end. I still didn't know what was on this hall—perhaps the rooms of Dr. Romano's patients, perhaps other efficiency apartments. Maybe that was why it was so dark—to keep the mental patients calm. I decided to wait a few more minutes before trying to get to the other end. I wanted to make it without any of them hearing me. If they did, anything could happen. They might all become frenzied, a screaming madhouse that would bring all the doctors running up here.

It didn't take long before I could make out the corridor. On my right was nothing but an unbroken wall of dark, rough wood. But the left side was lined with doors, all only about six feet apart. Each door seemed to have an opening at about eye level, just large enough for someone on the outside to look in and see everything behind the door. I walked to the first door and tried to peer inside. It was completely dark, but I could hear deep breathing. It was occupied. I looked down for the doorknob. There wasn't any, only a large keyhole. I rushed along, trying to peer into each of the rooms. It wasn't until I reached the fourth one that I could see anything, but all along the corridor I could hear breathing, grunts, groans coming from inside. In the fourth cubicle a small bulb had been left lit.

At first all I could see was what appeared to be a dirty mattress on the floor at one side of a deep, narrow room. Someone was lying on it, someone or something, large and huddled against the wall, covered by a dark blanket. At the far end in front of me was what appeared to be a trough, not very high off the floor. In one corner there seemed to be something like a pile of trash.

I thought I heard a mouse scurrying across the room, but it was only the thing on the mattress thrashing around. The blanket fell aside. Beneath it was a figure that looked like a woman, with a mass of tangled, shining red hair. She was wearing a sack-like garment, but her back was to me and she was in such a knotted position I couldn't even be sure it was a human being. Then she turned over again, and I could see that she was pregnant.

I tore my eyes away from the cell. These poor, miserable creatures. The idea of a human being, much less a mentally sick one, being cooped up here in this miserable cell, or stall, or whatever it was, was insupportable. I had heard stories of how cruelly the mentally ill were sometimes treated, but I'd never imagined anything like this. And she was pregnant too.

My mouth was parched, my skin dripping wet. I was petrified, glued to that spot. My hands, holding onto iron bars at the sides of the opening, were like marble. I couldn't tear them away. The thing inside heaved and rolled into another knot, pulling the dark blanket back over its head. The movement released me. I had to get out of here. I didn't dare stay another minute or I would have gone mad with what I was thinking. That would be the end of me, and no matter how I had to fight it, I wasn't going to let them beat me at any game.

I had to get out the other end of the building regardless of the cold. I passed more doors, but I didn't stop. Finally, after what seemed a century, I did reach the door at the end. It was locked and bolted. I quickly threw the bolt, and inserted my key. It didn't work. I tried and tried again. My hands were getting sore. Nothing happened. I had to retreat. I'd never counted on having to go back the way I'd gotten in here. Suppose that wall wouldn't open! How was I going to get out? Who was ever going to find me in here? And what would they do to me if they did find me?

I ran heedlessly back to the hall's other end. Slapping my hands against the wall which had allowed me in, I searched all around it for a knob. Nothing. Then I took a deep breath, and, as I did, I realized that the stench in this whole area was overpowering. I'd been too intense even to notice it before. I had to get out. I had to calm down. Figure this thing out. . . . I'd gotten in by pushing that inconspicuous button on the other side. Getting out had to work the same way. Trembling all over, I explored the corner of the wall. Starting at the bottom, I found nothing. Again I broke out in cold sweat. My fingers traveled on up the wall. There it was! The indentation. I pushed madly. The door slid aside with no sound at all. I was through it faster than I could breathe. Kicking off my slippers, I grabbed them up and ran all the way back to my door.

Once inside I slid to the floor, the door closed and locked behind me. I crouched there until my body was getting stiff from the tightened muscles. I had to get up, relax. Painfully, sickeningly, I crossed the room, weaving like a drunk. I grabbed the almond pills and swallowed down three as fast as the water could get them past my parched throat. I stood there leaning over the sink, barely holding myself upright, and the effect came as swiftly as usual, like knockout drops. I had to get back to bed. Dropping my robe somewhere along the way, I climbed back in the bed and was asleep in no more time than it took to close my eyes.

CHAPTER 27

Morning brought a new kind of fatigue. The tray had been brought to my room again, but I pushed it aside. I'd go down to the buffet by myself and manage to eat whatever the others were eating. I spent a long time deciding whether to chance taking the other pills I'd been given, but the only way to find out their effect was the process of elimination. I dressed carefully for the buffet. No sooner had I reached my door than someone knocked. Thinking it was Cheena, I swung the door open wide. Grace was standing there, her eyes lowered, a broad grin spread over her face.

"Thought I'd surprise you this morning, Sharon."

I wanted to smile, but the smile I managed looked insincere, I knew.

"You need to get out of this room more often. So here I am. And I see you're all ready. Must have been mental telepathy."

Grace started my mind racing. I knew she wasn't telepathic—but perhaps my room was bugged. Maybe there were even cameras watching me.

Or perhaps this was my imagination. If I were being watched on camera, surely Grace would have known about my excursion to the mental ward the night before.

They were all there breakfasting. Before I could make a move, Grace spoke up: "Now you go right over there and sit beside the General. I don't want you overdoing yourself. I'll bring you your tray."

I was foiled again. If Grace wanted to doctor my food, there was nothing to stop her. But I meekly did as I was told. I hadn't the strength to revolt, not then.

The General was the first to lean over the table to look me directly in the eye.

"My dear child, you look upset and drawn. Have you been going to Dr. Press while Philip is away?"

"Yes," I replied. "He's been coming up to my room twice a week with my shots. They seem to make me drowsy, though. And the exercises I take only help my figure; they don't give me energy. Otherwise I feel perfectly fine."

Apparently satisfied, the General sat back and resumed his conversation with Pavel, sitting beside him.

Grace wanted to make herself heard. In a loud voice that cut them both off, she announced to the table: "I'm going to give Sharon an outing today. I want her to see my domain. I've been so busy taking care of Philip's garden I neglect my own. In fact, last night after I'd gotten ready for bed I remembered that Philip's plants hadn't been watered. Heaven knows what time it was when I went up there. But I've been promising to show Sharon my treasures and today I am putting everything else aside and keeping that promise."

"Will it take long?" I asked, starting to tremble again. Was Grace going to take me to that dreadful place again? "I'm really supposed to rest and I'm trying to be a conscientious patient."

"Sharon, dear, this will be therapy for you, help you rest better tonight."

I was afraid to be alone with Grace. And today, while I was

able to think almost clearly, I wanted to try sorting things out. But I couldn't put her off.

As I pushed the food around my plate, I considered her remark about Philip. I knew that she did have a key, and was in charge of his plants. Maybe it *had* been she in the apartment. Grace couldn't have been in his bedroom, but I might have heard her puttering outside. The other possibility was frightening. If Grace was deliberately covering up for Philip, it meant they *were* watching me. I preferred to believe her.

The moment I set down my empty coffee cup, Grace excused us both to the rest of the group at the table.

"Come along, Sharon. It's getting late." She smiled at the General and the architect, and at Cheena, who barely looked up.

Grace didn't even give me time to fold my napkin. She hurried me out, down the corridor to the back elevators. When we reached the top floor she brushed me aside while she dug for a key in her purse and unlocked a door on the side of the corridor at the back of the building. I was beginning to smile to myself when I noticed there wasn't a combination lock, but the door Grace opened led only into a vestibule. There it was, another door with the inevitable combination lock high in its center. Grace was doubly careful as she touched the dials, cupping her hand around the lock to hide the numbers while she twirled it around. Then, with both hands, she tugged at the door until it opened just wide enough for us to slip through. The first step over the sill was mine.

The whole place was brightly lighted. Aisles of plants were potted under a glass roof. There were greenhouses all over the vast roof, and plants tall as trees and others so tiny they could hardly be seen under so much foliage.

Suddenly I heard a pounding on the door we had just come through. Grace looked furious, but nearly fell over herself to get back to open it. It was Dr. Press and, sotto voce, he was apparently ripping into Grace. Her face was red when she turned to me again.

"Come, Sharon dear, it seems I'm urgently needed and we'll have to postpone our little venture until some other time."

Dr. Press was holding the door wide open, looking exasperated. Grace made as if to usher me back through the door, reaching out both hands to guide me. But instead of helping me, she pressed one hand against my back and ground the other into my stomach. She was trying to feel the baby! I jerked away, bolted through the door with Grace at my heels, defiantly babbling something about the baby to Press.

Once again out in the hall, Press slammed the door behind us and Grace stalked off toward the back elevator without another word. Dr. Press had taken over.

"Come, Mrs. Crane. We can't have you overdoing it." The two of us waddled like two fat ducks back to my room.

"Now into bed, if you please." In his hand was a syringe.

"Can't I undress first?"

"You needn't bother. This takes effect slowly. You'll have time." Without another word, he pushed up my sleeve and I received the shot. Then, instead of leaving the room, he went to the couch and sat down, waving me into the dressing room.

As I changed into a gown I could feel the effects of the drug again gradually erasing my powers to think. But I did have time to wonder who at our table had told Dr. Press that Grace was going to take me to her domain. They didn't want me in there. It certainly was verboten and Grace was in trouble for making the attempt. But Grace—if only Press had gotten between the two of us. The memory of her covetously grasping my stomach nearly made me faint. But whatever Press had shot into me was quickly taking over now and I barely managed to stumble into bed. I was aware only that he was standing over me and then he must have gone, because I knew no more.

CHAPTER 28

Looking down at myself, I noticed my stomach pressing tight against my nightgown. The strenuous exercises I'd done with Cheena had restored my figure, but I had no clothes to wear out on the streets, even if I could manage to make it that far. And even though Philip's trips home were infrequent, I hated the prospect of his seeing me in bursting seams.

There was a knock at the door. I recognized it. It wasn't timid like Grace's, nor heavy like the doctors.' It was Cheena. She stood in the door holding out a huge dress box. Laughing, I reached out to grasp the box and hug my friend.

"Well, come in, come on in. How in hell did you know what I was thinking this time?"

"I'm a telepath, old girl. Just a witch like my dear old grannie. But my grannie wouldn't have had to read minds to tell what you were thinking of yourself yesterday in that dress splitting at the seams, and Philip coming home any day. In the robe you don't show so much, but in dresses, my dear, it's absolutely disgusting!" She laughed, then helped me tear the box open and pull out three lovely maternity dresses. One was prettier than the other, all chosen to compliment my coloring and best features.

"They are perfect. Cheena, how can I ever thank you enough. They make me feel better already. But they must have cost a fortune. I insist on paying you."

"Consider it a gift to the expectant mother from the baby's aunt. Seeing you look so pretty is payment enough."

"Don't be silly, Cheena. But I've just remembered. I haven't gotten any checks from James these last months or, at least, I don't remember where I put them if they did come. But as soon as I find them, I'll have them cashed and pay you."

"Well, don't fret it. You know there's no hurry. And remember, if there's one thing I don't want for, it's money." She shrugged and backed toward the door.

"Cheena, you're not leaving so soon?"

"In case you haven't noticed, my dear, it's after two. You've slept the day away. Not all of us can afford that luxury. I have an important appointment. You know I have to keep my 'special appointments.'" She winked and disappeared.

I bathed, put on Philip's favorite perfume, and slipped into the prettiest of the new dresses. It was perfect, hyacinth blue, angora wool, and it flared out very full. Around the high collar was a braid of matching leather and the same wool material. In it I hardly seemed pregnant. It made my eyes glow almost the same blue. Philip would be here soon. For the first time in months I'd be able to meet him as a real woman, not a stupefied slob confined to her bed. He'd be able to take me out again, be proud as he once was. My pulses were racing. I could barely wait.

Exactly at seven he was at the door. I knew it was he, even before he knocked. The moment we were face to face he gathered me in his arms.

"Sharon, my darling girl, I've missed you so much."

It was as though the past few months had never been. He was the Philip I'd fallen in love with.

"We're dining in my apartment." He took me right down

the hall and sat me at his table. We ate a sumptuous meal. But there was something different about him. It was as though he were playing a game. All through the meal he seemed to avoid everything personal between us. Instead he kept the conversation on books we'd read, and new films he'd seen.

Afterward we sat before the fire and sipped brandy while Philip, in a curious monotone, told me about flying from country to country. But it was all a whirl in my head. I didn't care where he'd been. All I wanted to know was when these constant trips would end. But I couldn't broach the subject. To Philip it would have sounded like harping on our marriage. He was deftly avoiding that. He kept talking about the pressure he was under to deliver on the contracts. I felt guilty knowing I was the cause of his new, taut look. At last he stopped talking of business and looked deep into my face, as though he were examining the depths of my feeling. I kept my face carefully blank.

"Darling, I'm afraid I've some bad news for you. I wanted to take you out tonight for an evening on the town, but I checked first with both Rome and Press to be sure they didn't think it would strain you. And they both agree that you'd better stay in for a while longer. The weather is vicious and they're afraid you'd catch cold. You've been confined for so long now your resistance to viruses is low in bad weather. And you know how I'd worry if anything happened to you or my baby."

Afterwards he was almost his old loving self on the sofa before the fire, but not entirely. Several times his thoughts drifted away. I traced the line of his jaw with my fingers, lying on the sofa with him sprawled below me on the floor watching the fire, but he barely noticed my touch.

"Philip, how long will you be home this time? I'd like to cook dinner for you one night. I'm tired of doing nothing by myself."

"What did you say, Sharon?"

"Never mind."

"Sorry, honey, I've got so much on my mind. Trying to rush these damned consignments is getting them all fouled up."

"I just wanted to cook dinner for you one night."

"I don't know when it can be, sweetheart. I've got to attend a dinner party tomorrow night. I can see several of my customers and try to cancel some of my commitments. Then I'll have to be off again Sunday."

"I won't see you before you go."

"Of course, darling. I'll see you Sunday."

"What about tomorrow?"

"Tomorrow's taken, love." His "love" was abrupt, but he reached over and kissed me, and at least the hurt went away.

CHAPTER 29

Saturday I woke to another cold, dreary day. The sky was gray, threatening more snow. The wind howled outside. Inside, the monotonous voice on the radio droned, " . . . gales up to twenty-five miles or more . . . " and "at least four inches by evening." Even the weather was conspiring to keep me inside. Nothing to do during the long day ahead but wait for Sunday, when Philip might give me some of his precious time. Then he'd be gone again.

To hell with what the weatherman predicted. My stomach was already twice as big as I'd expected it to be in these few months. I didn't care what the damned doctors said, my baby wanted an outing as badly as her mother did. A few hours outside and I'd be as peaceful as anybody's lamb for the rest of my pregnancy.

As I dressed carefully, I wondered where I would go. Possibly Dell would have lunch with me. And I would tell him everything. With nervous fingers I dialed his office number. It rang until finally I had to give up. I tried his home number. An answering service picked up.

"Mr. Singleton is not at home. Is there any message?"

"Are you sure he isn't there?"

"Yes, Miss. Would you like him to call you when he returns?"

"Damn! Don't you know when he'll be back?"

"He's away for the weekend. He left no message. But he goes skiing most weekends and usually comes back late Sunday."

I thanked the operator, told her there was no message, then wearily pushed the phone back to the other end of the table.

Five minutes later the phone rang. Philip's voice came through as though from a dream.

"Sharon, honey, I'm sorry I was short with you last night. I've been so damned tired trying to get everything settled in a hurry, I took it out on you."

"Oh, Philip, I understand, I'm the selfish one. I'm trying to be patient, honestly. But sometimes I slip too. I miss you so much. Can't you come over today? Just for a little while? For lunch? I promise not to try to hold you here. I do understand what you must be going through."

"Sharon, darling, I can't! I just can't today. As it is, I had to excuse myself from a meeting to call you. I must get back. Trust me, dear, or I don't see how I'm going to be able to keep this up. I'll call you again later, I promise. If things go well I might manage to get through in time to see you today. You know there's nothing I want more, but I simply can't promise you what time it will be. I love you."

"I'll be here, Philip." I couldn't think of anything else to say. I knew I was making everything worse by pressuring him. Yet his promise to call whenever he had the moment kept me waiting inside the apartment again all day. And with every dragging minute my anger grew.

Frustrated, fermenting, I flopped down in the chair and turned the radio on loud. Here I was all dressed, determined to go out, with nowhere to go. Now I couldn't even leave the phone in case I missed Philip's call. He was so unpredictable and he was always able to make me shoulder the guilt, no matter what went wrong.

The long day dragged on wearily. I had more energy than I'd had in months, but it only got on my nerves because I couldn't spend it. I tried cleaning the apartment, then went to work again on myself. I treated my skin and hair with everything I had available, then took several of the routine pills, dozed in fits. And waited. And still there was no call. He had to go to the dinner tonight and he had to be ready by seven. It was five already. That left very little time for him to see me. I was becoming desperate.

There wasn't a sound in the hall. The elevator began humming constantly as it had on other days before big dinner parties, but never did it open on the eleventh floor. I was well acquainted with the tiny click and squeak its doors made when they opened. Each time I heard the elevator I hurried to the door and held my breath again to listen. Each time I dragged back disappointed, my breathing once again shallow and tense.

Seven o'clock. Sitting in the dark. No supper. For the last two hours I hadn't moved from the spot. I changed into my gown and robe, tears spilling as I hung away the lovely dress I'd worn all day. The telephone rang like an alarm. I jumped to answer.

"Sharon, darling," Philip was panting, "I've been pushing like mad. The damned meeting just ended. It went all day. Couldn't even manage a break to call you. I'm absolutely bushed, but I think everything is finally going our way. After this next trip we'll have easy sailing."

He didn't give me a chance to say a word, just went on as though all I needed was his enthusiasm.

"I must get ready for the dinner now, honey. I'm already late. But, darling, believe me, it is all worth it."

"Will I . . . ?"

"I'll call you in the morning as soon as I get up. See you before I leave. Please, Sharon, for my sake, do exactly what the doctors tell you. If anything happened to my babies I don't know what I'd do. Remember, I love you. If you could only understand that I, and all my friends, are doing everything for your sake." He did sound tired, and was searching for the right words to reassure me. With a huskily whispered "I love you," he hung up, leaving me holding a dead phone, disappointed, but wanting to believe him.

I spent the evening staring dully at television, watching shows that didn't answer the questions that kept spinning through my head.

Around midnight the elevator started running again and I tried to imagine how many guests were leaving. Philip might be coming up any time and there wouldn't be any sign except that tiny click-screech of the elevator doors. I didn't want him to hear me or he'd know I was still awake and waiting. But I had to know. Despite all the assurances he'd given me, I was afraid my possessiveness was chasing him away.

At last the click came. I sprang from the couch and hurried to press against the hall door. Cold sweat wet my face and hands, yet the rest of my body was hot, my mouth dry. Momentarily I was relieved, then I gritted my teeth to keep from sobbing. Philip was not alone! The voice in the hall was deep and throaty. A moment later Philip's door opened and closed, disturbing the silence. I leaned against my door, stunned. It wasn't Philip's voice I'd heard, or another man's. I know a woman's sexy voice when I hear it.

I hurried over to the closet and, pushing my clothes aside, leaned down against the wall, pressing my ear to it. I pressed harder, but heard nothing. Immobile, I crouched there waiting. I had to know. They might still be in the living room, but eventually they'd come to bed. My muscles grew stiff, sore with the unusual exertion. I waited until my legs gave way and then, with a loud thud, I fell against the wall. It was scorching again. Reaching out, I gingerly tried to touch it once more, and recoiled.

Head spinning, I found myself heading for the bathroom to take a pill. I hadn't eaten since lunch; now it was past midnight and I'd not taken even half the day's ration of pills! I wouldn't take them. To hell with their damned filthy pills! To hell with Philip! My baby and I were all that counted now. If Philip wasn't in love with me, why these months of masquerading, why all the care lavished on me by his friends?

I went back to the closet and found my tennis shoes. Awkwardly I put them on. Then, with a strength I had thought was lost, I squeezed into my now-tight jeans and a loose shirt, tossing my robe and gown onto a chair.

Dressed, I felt more alive, determined to do something—anything—to defy them. But it hit me again as I moved to the door. Where was I going? Even if I managed to make it out of the building, who could I go to? Dell was away. I knew nobody else. Where could I go now in the middle of the night? The police would think I was crazy. I had only wild, unsubstantiated suspicions to tell. And the way I looked, who would ever believe me or take me in? No doubt Philip would only find me and bring me back.

I could go to a hotel. But I needed money. I tried to remember—I should have had plenty left. I'd spent nothing for months. I went for my pocketbook and found my wallet. It was empty. No identification, not even a dime for a telephone call. I searched frantically in every drawer, suitcase, cabinet, even under the sofa pillows. Nothing. This had to be deliberate. But I was going anyway. First, though, I had to have some kind of proof. The first thing I thought of was the kiln. If I knew what they were burning there, in the middle of the night, I might at least know something of what these dinners were all about.

Turning off the lights, I crept into the hallway carrying nothing but keys and a flashlight. Now the stillness was reassuring. I glanced toward Philip's door. I had to pass it to reach the back elevator. At least he couldn't hear the elevator from inside his apartment—I never had when I spent time there. Clutching the keys deep in my pocket so they wouldn't rattle, I tiptoed until I was at the end of the long corridor. Thank God I still had the key to bring the elevator up. At last it stopped and the doors slid open and closed behind me.

The descent to the basement was interminable. When the doors opened wide enough to slip through I scurried into the network of tunnels through which Cheena had led me. I didn't remember all of these doors and turns, but I was certain I'd find the way. All the doors had designating signs. The first sign the flashlight found was "heating equipment." I kept going, down one tunnel, turning, down another. At last the way became familiar, widening and inclining. Now I knew I was going in the right direction. At last I saw the massive door facing me at the end of the tunnel. I flashed the light to the bottom. There it was: Kiln. Wiping damp fingers against my pants leg, I twisted the dial, trying to remember which of the combinations unlocked this door. All of the combinations I had memorized swam together in my mind. I couldn't remember! Damn! I stood back to breathe. Dammit, do it, I told myself. You've come this far. Standing tall before the door, I made myself visualize Cheena twisting the dial.

The tumblers fell into place. The door swung open at the barest touch and I hopped over the sill. Once inside, there was smothering darkness, pierced only by the feeble beam of my flashlight. I pulled the door in until it was almost completely closed, then traced the flashlight beam across the walls until it hit the light switch. I'd have to chance the glow it would cast into the tunnel; I was banking on the unlikelihood of any of them coming down here at three o'clock in the morning.

The room wasn't as hot as I'd expected. The dozen or more air conditioners were blasting cold air. Turning toward the largest of the stone structures, I felt another blast of the intense heat it was creating. The room was much different than when I'd first seen it. Now there was a pile of indistinguishable objects heaped between myself and the furnace.

And beside the pile of articles was a line of large, corrugated cans standing close together.

My hand reached out to touch the pile. It was clothing. And picture frames with snapshots of strangers. And books. And a cheap-looking assortment of ornaments that might have decorated some girl's apartment. And a huge, framed print. And shoes. At least a dozen pairs. I couldn't figure out why they'd be burning all these personal belongings at such a strange hour. Why now, after their party, of all times? I lifted one of the shoes—a flashy red, high-heeled sandal, almost new. It revived a hazy memory. I dropped it quickly as though it would contaminate me. But I couldn't stop there. I forced myself to go back into the pile and started rummaging through the clothes more thoroughly. The smell of cheap perfume still clung to them. There were dresses, large, flapping, and flamboyant. And underwear, lacy and frilly, bargain-basement catches. Scads of junk jewelry were cast in with everything else. Suddenly my eye caught something that triggered a distinct memory: a red dress with large white polka dots. The dress I'd seen on that girl in the corridor, the girl who was the only visitor who looked like a patient, the girl I'd seen with Philip that night I moved in. They had to be her things. The garishness of it all fit her.

I felt as though the dress was burning my hand. I dropped it and backed away. But I couldn't leave it there. It had been deep in the pile. Left where I dropped it, it would be a red flag announcing the pile had been disturbed. I'd have to shove it back. Holding my breath to block the smell of the girl that lingered over everything, I feverishly stuffed the dress into the bottom of the mound.

Shaken, I started back to the door, but as I moved I sensed something still left undone. Ransacking that girl's belongings had made me nauseous, but it hadn't told me very much. This was the only chance I'd have. The corrugated cans called to me. I had nearly forgotten them. Taking a deep breath, I went to the can nearest the furnace and grabbed the lid to yank it off. It wouldn't budge. It was almost unbearably hot where I stood, but I was determined. In this can had to be something that would enlighten me. Flashing the light closer, I saw the lid had been screwed onto the can, hermetically sealing it. I put the flashlight down and, using both hands, managed to turn the lid until it came loose. It was much heavier than it looked, but I pulled with every ounce of energy I could muster until it was half off the can.

An awful stench blasted out. It was dizzying, but I fought the compulsion to retch, grabbed the flashlight, and beamed its light into the can.

It was filled with bones. Long, thin bones, some with dried flesh clinging to them. There were many, all shapes and sizes. Among them was the entire skeleton of a human hand, sinews and some flesh holding it together. I dropped the flashlight, swayed where I stood, leaning back against the second can. I jumped away as if it had bitten me. It took all my willpower to push the lid back on the first can and twist it until it was tight. Then, running back to the wall, I hung on, grabbed at the switch, and shut off the lights. With the beam of the flashlight darting around the room, I forced myself to survey the darkness again before leaving. Somehow I remembered to twirl the dial of the lock to cover my intrusion, but I couldn't cover my throbbing panic. My mind was too clouded, too quailing to allow me to wander further into any unknown parts of the building. I was almost to the point of collapsing where I stood, but I could never let them find me out of my room, and God knows I couldn't be found here. At least my own apartment offered the safety of being where I was supposed to be if anyone questioned me. As soon as the door was locked behind me, I fell onto the sofa in exhaustion, and fear.

Sleep dropped over me instantly, as though my mind could take no more. Next thing I knew it was hours later. I didn't feel drugged, yet lay sprawled on the sofa still dressed in jeans and shirt, without energy to move. It must have been those pills and shots, I thought, as I tried to sit up. I'd been wrong. They were having a cumulative effect. Although I hadn't taken them for a few hours, they still had a hold over me. I allowed myself to slip back to sleep. Something gruesome was hovering at the edge of my thoughts, and I didn't want to wake up and face remembering what it was.

CHAPTER 30

I slept all night in my shirt and jeans, waking to the sound of the telephone.

"Good morning, my darling." Philip's voice was cheerful, as if everything were normal. "How about having lunch with me?"

"What time is it?"

"Nearly noon. Don't tell me you were still asleep?"

"I'm awake; not dressed, though. Give me time for a shower. Just a few minutes. Want me to call you?" I didn't know how unnatural I was sounding. I couldn't keep the tremor out of my voice.

"No," he murmured in his deep, throaty way. "Why don't you come on over as soon as you're dressed. Or wear your robe. Just hurry, darling. I've a plane to catch, and I want to spend as much time with you as I can before leaving."

I hung up the phone, and as I did, the grotesque sights of the night before flooded my mind. But I couldn't think of them now. I had to behave normally, at least until Philip left again. That was the important thing, to keep him from being suspicious until I could be alone again.

I bounded off the sofa, tore off the jeans and shirt, showered and dressed, being sure to pick the dress I hoped would most please him. I made up my pale face meticulously, despite trembling fingers. And at last, just before leaving, I reluctantly swallowed two almond pills, praying they'd make me appear calm.

Philip was all smiles, leading me over to the couch and sitting beside me. In front of each of us was a tall, frosted glass of juice, laced with coconut and honey. As I sank back against the cushioning leather, his eyes devoured me, especially the bulge where our baby lay. I could feel my skin flush.

"What's wrong with me, Philip?" I laughed nervously. "Can't a lady sleep late without a reason?"

His laughter was not light, though I wished it were. "Of course, sleepy head. Can't a man stare at his love so he'll be able to remember every part of her wherever he may be?" He laughed again and seemed to relax a little. "I've had a very successful few days and I thought you'd be happy to hear it. This next trip will take several weeks, possibly even longer, but it means the end of most of my commitments. Aren't you even pleased? Sometimes I can't quite understand you."

It was difficult to keep my face smooth. Even if Philip and I had simply been two lovers who had to be separated for a time, it would have been outrageous of him to expect me to understand and remain patient, satisfied with his spare time. But there was obviously much more involved in our situation, and he was barely taking the trouble to conceal it all from me. He was contemptuous of my intelligence, and I had to play my part, acting as if I were perfectly content and stupidly shallow.

"Philip, I'm sorry. I want everything about you to be etched in my memory, too, so it can help me through those long days until I'm with you again. When you're away the time passes quickly, because you're so busy. But for me the time drags and all I want to do is sleep. But I'll be your good little girl. I'll do anything you want. Just knowing you'll be thinking of me makes everything all right. I'll do anything they tell me, as long as I have sweet dreams of you to hold me, no matter how long it takes you to come back."

My simpering seemed to satisfy him. We finished our drinks and Philip went out to the kitchen to serve the lunch he'd prepared. Smiling, he placed the first covered dish before me and lifted the lid. It was a plate of spare ribs—but there were five of them, and they were carefully arranged in a fan-like design, just like the outspread fingers of a human hand.

I dropped my napkin; he picked it up and held it without a word before handing it back to me. My heart nearly pounded aloud and my hand brushed his glass, almost knocking it over. I pressed my fork against the plate to keep the trembling of my hands from showing. Philip's eyes weighed every move I made. When he told me he'd have to be leaving in another hour, it was all I could do to keep the relief from my face. I sighed, and finally wept, and that seemed to be the right reaction. His goodbye kiss was long and ardent.

I was alone again, drained of all sensation. For the first time, Philip had extracted no promises from me, no admonitions to take my pills, no lectures on obeying the doctors and staying in bed as they told me. These last few hours we'd shared had seemed almost as if we were acting on a stage. In a few minutes he'd be on his way to the airport and I would have a little more freedom. How did I feel about him now?

Whenever I was with Philip, everything about him, his strength, his beauty, his hypnotic blue eyes, had been able to erase everything else from my mind. Even today it had been almost impossible to do any independent thinking whenever he looked at me. Yet here, alone again, the shock of my recent adventure overcame me. Philip was an ogre; he would swallow my whole will with his charm if he could. But it was too late now. I couldn't forget the kiln . . . those bones. I had to face the fact of that memory. What could they have been but human bones and flesh? What were they doing there? Worst of all—what had they to do with this place? With Cheena? With me! A sudden vision appeared before me—Cheena's china, fragile and glowing with that almost miraculous pink light. I swayed for a moment before my mind refused to accept the awful possibility. But I could never get the sight or the awful stench of that can out of my mind, no matter what they did to me or how they tried to distract me. Now I wondered frantically if they knew I'd been down there. They seemed to know every other move I'd made. Was that why Philip had so unexpectedly intervened today, acting the ardent lover again only to find out how much I'd seen or understood? Now, I was terrified.

It was Sunday. Dell was out of town. Even the weather was against me—cold and wet, snow slushy and wind howling. But I was going to get my baby and me out of the building. Now! Today!

CHAPTER 31

Racing around the apartment, gathering my warmest wool dress, heavy boots, a wool scarf and coat, I was ready and waiting at the door for the moment I heard Philip leave. There was no need to take my purse, only the keys. For some reason they had allowed me to keep them—probably so I could get to the buffet. I jammed them into my coat pocket so they wouldn't jangle, and waited. I was still feeling the effects of the drugs, but I could think clearly enough to know what I had to do.

I didn't have to wait long. Philip's door opened and I heard him slam it shut. Then came the sound of the elevator and its doors sliding open and shut. I slipped into my coat and started down the hall toward the back elevator, the opposite direction from where Philip had gone. As I came to his door I was surprised to find that when he'd slammed his door it had not caught and was now standing partly open. Maybe this was the chance I'd been hoping for. There might be a way out the other end of the building through his apartment. It was the most logical thing for him to be able to go either way he wanted.

189

Just as I stepped inside Philip's door, I heard a loud beeping. Certain it was an alarm, I had turned and was almost out the door when I realized that the beeping was coming from Philip's television set. It was huge, exactly like Cheena's, and it was beeping loudly and on the big screen was a written notice:

A SPECIAL MEETING IS TO BE HELD IN THE BOARD ROOM IMMEDIATELY.

In another second the beeping stopped and the notice disappeared. In its place on the screen I could see a large room, which had to be their board room.

I stood before the screen, hypnotized. One by one I saw them filing into the room, the people I'd known as neighbors, eaten and talked with. The people who had welcomed me to their city, and into their home.

Without a word each person took a seat around the long, V-shaped table. The room itself was stark, furnished simply in dark brown rugs and leather chairs. Bright lights shone into every face and before each person at the table was a small tape recorder.

The faces were somber. The acoustics were excellent. I could hear even whispered comments, but in the main only a few people were speaking to their neighbors.

A gavel fell.

"The meeting is in order." The sonorous voice came loud and clear. Whoever was at the head of the table was out of range of the camera. All the others sat back in their chairs, waiting. Only one person moved. Corintha Byrom was clutching and twisting her handkerchief. There was dead silence.

"We are here to discuss the scheduled item, which has caused us so much trouble. This creature has not responded properly to our normal processing and last night she managed to accomplish something that will require deviations on the parts of many of you who have been most directly involved with her schedule.

"Those of you who have not been directly involved with this creature will also take heed. The entire chapter may be in jeopardy. As you well know, our schedules are mandatory, as are those of our other chapters. This type of situation is so embarrassing that the entire chapter could become victims in the House of Games." A muffled gasp went up from the group. The speaker's voice was now ironic. "I see I need not warn you further. But let me make the danger clear."

In a voice pitched even lower than before, the leader went on. "Ladies and gentlemen, you have all carefully read, signed, and are bound by your contracts, which also include specific responsibilities to the House of Games. As you are all aware, they entertain far less frequently than the other chapters. But—and he drew the word out softly, menacingly— "they are equipped to eliminate either individuals or entire chapters whenever it becomes necessary.

"I am of the opinion," the leader announced, "that our current episode would affect the entire chapter, and so I want all of you to appreciate the situation. Fortunately, the next scheduled creature responded instantly and we were able to eliminate the need for the preliminary stages in the apartment. She is now progressing most satisfactorily, housed in the west side of the building with the others. Our entertainment schedule will not be delayed nor hampered by this deviation. However"—and the word rang ominously through the room—"we must discuss the present untenable situation to determine where we have erred in order to prevent such a thing from ever occurring again. We will also assign certain new duties to some of you which may even preclude your attending some of our other chapters' festivities."

The faces around the room were tense, all of them. Some were chewing at their lips, others sitting stiffly. Everyone of them seemed terrified at the mere mention of the House of Games, but not one voice was raised, not one body moved.

They were all paying strict attention to every word.

"We will interrogate those here who have been involved. First, we will hear from Mrs. Byrom. Mrs. Byrom, why was it you selected a potential creature from a first-class section of an airplane instead of a more likely source?"

Corintha Byrom's voice could be heard clearly though she spoke so softly her words quivered: "The creature I sat beside on the plane was clearly unaccustomed to first class. I could see she was young and naive from all her actions. I began taping the moment we began to speak. I questioned her thoroughly. All of you heard the tapes before she was first brought here for your inspection. You could see she was unsophisticated and extremely lovely, perfect for our purposes. When you listened to the tapes, you all agreed that there was nothing about her to indicate possible problems, most particularly in the absence of any connections with anyone who might be interested in her whereabouts."

The flustered woman peered around the room into the eyes of all who sat there, trying to read their expressions. But as she reached the head of the table, she cast her eyes down and continued.

"This creature was more helpless than many I've brought in. I am sure Philip will also testify to every word I say."

As Corintha Byrom hesitated, the voice at the head of the room cut her off. "We will next hear from Dr. Romano. The doctors were all given the opportunity to examine the creature thoroughly. Dr. Romano . . .

The rabbity man leaned toward the table, his hands clenched. "I gave her the most thorough of examinations. I certainly didn't detect any abnormalities to preclude the effects of our drugs. Nor did any of the physiological tests show anything. We had no way of foreseeing that she would be immune to anything. None of us. You realize that."

The leader agreed. "Yes, true. She responded remarkably well to some of the treatments. Others, no. I have no explanation. She was tested thoroughly. The flavoring, though, is having impressive results. Unusually gratifying despite the other problems. We will now continue with Mrs. Romano's activities in this matter."

Romano dropped back in his chair as if exhausted by his brief testimony.

"Mrs. Romano, you were primarily responsible for allowing the creature to become rather well acquainted with a Mr. Wendell Singleton, whom she has been meeting frequently. Will you please explain why it was not made mandatory that she use the buffet for all meals except those in her apartment?"

"She must have met him before she started working in our office."

"Even if she did, the meetings continued after that. Why did you not stop them instantly?"

"I tried; we both tried. But she wasn't responding to the drugs, nor the initial hypnosis, and she was too independent to follow orders, no matter how strongly they were put to her."

"This outside contact is a most serious problem. She has seen him and has been calling both his home and his office. It will have to be remedied. However, I believe I have a plan that will end this contact. If not, Mrs. Romano, you may even be in jeopardy within the chapter under your contract. For your sake, I hope my plan is effective."

Mrs. Romano, too, sank back in her seat.

"And now we will hear from Mr. Hawk." The leader's voice filled the room, though he was speaking in no more than a conversational monotone.

"Mr. Hawk, why did you take this creature with you to social events after the initial sex act? You have always been successful at effecting immediate conception. Why was it necessary to entertain this creature afterwards?"

Philip sat straight and defiant. His voice was assured, as cold and as calm as that of the leader. He was not defending himself. He sounded dangerously insolent.

"It was time for me to test Rudolph again and this was the perfect specimen to use. This one has been far more alert than the others and I felt that if Rudolph could demonstrate satisfactorily with her, he was doing well. It will still be some time before he becomes eligible for my type of position, but as I am best able to judge his capabilities, I wish them to be completely accomplished before recommending him for an actual situation."

Philip's fluency was making his neighbors more tense. Grace lifted her hand to stifle a nervous giggle. Several pairs of eyes turned toward her at the interruption. Philip looked down the table at her, visibly annoyed, but he went on: "Then, after that trip, she regressed in her attitude toward me. I almost lost control over her. The drugs weren't working properly and hypnosis wasn't as effective as it should have been. I wanted to be certain she was missing her menstrual periods. She didn't confide in me. Even hypnosis couldn't bring her out. I therefore kept her with me as constantly as possible, using her at least every third night to determine whether or not she had conceived. I was fairly certain it had happened, but I wasn't positive until she confessed. As you know, I had to practically force her to go to Dr. Press, and then had to constantly follow up on her abiding by his directions. It has become a nuisance, except that we had the good fortune to find an instantly receptive creature for the next occasion. It was possible to get her to conceive within a few days after she began working in Romano's office. If not, I'm afraid it would have become almost impossible for me to continue my schedule without interruption."

The sonorous voice rose once again. This time he directed his questions to Cheena.

"Miss Wescott, you have conducted yourself improperly. You have allowed the creature into a private domain. Your kiln."

"Yes, I did. I took her to the kiln to quiet her down. It has been a challenge to do what all your drugs haven't accomplished. If I hadn't, she would have insisted on getting outside the building. It was the only thing I could do to divert her and so I did it."

"Do you realize the monitors caught her in your kiln room at three o'clock this morning? Do you realize what it means if she is still capable of reasoning?"

"How could she have gotten down there? The combination lock was on."

"She unlocked it by herself. The monitors picked that up. I would also like you to explain how she is capable of unlocking that door."

"But it couldn't have meant anything to her. She'd seen it before."

"Not under the conditions that existed last night."

"I'm sure she didn't comprehend. . . ."

"That remains to be seen. If she did, Miss Wescott, you have committed a serious infraction of your contract. We will have to make a decision depending on the repercussions of this episode."

"I did nothing to—"

"That will be all, Miss Wescott. At the moment you aren't being judged. We will now hear from Dr. Pavel. It has been expected of you, Dr. Pavel, to be sufficiently superior in pharmacology to be able to meet any challenge required of you. Can you offer any explanation as to why your drugs have not worked properly on this one creature?"

Pavel was almost smiling, but it was a nervous twitch. He started to rise, but then sat back in his chair, his long, thin fingers forming a steeple at his lips.

"I spent many uncomfortable hours, to the point of missing many precious social engagements, trying to reconstruct my formulae to meet this situation. I shall continue to experiment, but I must be extremely careful, as you all know, to keep the fetus from becoming improperly affected. As far as I know, to date, the fetus is growing beautifully, better than any we've produced so far. This situation may be a blessing in disguise. We might have a more exciting product to entertain our guests than ever before." He breathed shallowly, awaiting his reprimand if it was to come.

"I do hope you are correct. However, you will be constantly and closely involved until this one is completed, and you, in particular, may be called upon at any time to resolve problems as they arise."

Pavel relaxed his posture. He was not to be charged, not yet, but he, too, was being warned that his performance had been imperfect.

"And now, Miss St. John. Why did you offer to take the creature to your domain? You were not assigned her surveillance."

Grace's mouth dropped open. But she quickly recovered herself.

"This one is stimulating me. She is better than our other young ladies—quicker, more resistant and more responsive at the same time. It should thrill all of you to be aware of her as a human being. Then, when the time comes, imagine the supreme ecstasy of knowing what we've accomplished."

"You may be correct in your hypothesis, Miss St. John. I, too, rather relish this situation despite the problems we are encountering. I, myself, will become involved in the steps taken from now on. You, Miss St. John, were stopped just in time to prevent your exposing more of our domain to the creature. You will not do it again, regardless of your enthusiasm. As for you and the other members, there will be a different method of approach from now on. Mrs. Byrom, you and others will be called upon to massage the fat from the body, as the creature will have to be kept unconscious as much as possible and we certainly cannot have fat on the body." With that, the voice abruptly adjourned the meeting. Corintha Byrom grimaced. She cast her eyes down, but remained stoic and stiff as she left with the others. No one stopped to exchange reactions. In a few minutes the room was empty.

As soon as I saw them filing out, I realized my mistake. Surely some of them would be coming directly to my apartment. I raced out of Philip's apartment, taking care that the door closed behind me. I knew a lot more now, but I was scared to death. I didn't have time to worry about that now. Despite my clumsiness, I sprinted back to my own apartment, slammed the door behind me. Quickly I threw the coat to the bottom of the closet, shook off the boots, and pulled off the scarf. Everything followed the coat onto the closet floor. Then, tiptoeing back into the dressing closet, I put on my slippers. I used valuable time to calm my breathing. Then, wiping all expression from my face, I shuffled to the door. Dr. Schine was standing there as if he visited every night. Yet he had never come near my apartment before. Hand extended, his red, wet lips parted in a broad smile, he bid me good afternoon with a grandiloquent flourish. The beard was down to his chest and his eyes looked up from under the heavy black brows.

"May I come in, Mrs. Crane? I have something for you. I've not been very neighborly, I'm afraid. With my busy schedule, I've neglected hospitality. Now, my dear child, with your Philip away so often, I hope you'll allow me to atone in a small way."

I couldn't refuse to invite him in, so I stood aside for him to enter.

"Aren't you dressed rather warmly for this hot room?" He grinned, but his eyes burned over me.

"Oh, I put this on after Philip left. I felt so down, and cold. It's just a chill, I guess. It will wear off. Your dropping by has already cheered me up. Sit down awhile. I'll bring you some tea, or would you prefer coffee? It is an honor to have you call."

"No, no, my child," he cooed. "Nothing for me." He moved gracefully to a stiff, armless chair. All this time he had kept his hairy hands behind his back, but when he sat he brought them out and folded them over his bulging stomach.

They held a large, beautifully scrolled golden box. It looked a little ridiculous held so daintily in those thick, pudgy fingers. His kidney-shaped ring—which I now recognized as the carving of a fetus—hovered above the box.

"May this make some amend for my most unpardonable discourtesy. I've brought you a small sample of an exquisite delicacy I've created for which I admit I'm justly praised."

All I could think to say was, "How nice of you."

"You may not have learned of this in your short residency here, but I am quite the master at concocting the most unusual and delightful candies. Who would look at me and believe that my elaborate laboratory is devoted nearly entirely to confections, but, as you know, my dear, we are all rather eccentric and fanatic about indulging ourselves in our talents. I happen to revel in the candies I concoct."

His precious candies were destined for the toilet bowl the moment he was gone. But for the moment, I poured on some sugar. "I'm sure you have many talents, Doctor. But if your candy is as special as everything else created by your friends, I'm sure it will be the best candy in the world."

The gross man seemed to have a sweet tooth. He ate it up.

"Even for modesty's sake I will not disagree with you, my dear. It is the best. Here, I must see you try one. I glory in observing the expression of one who tries my candy for the first time."

He lifted the lovely box with both hands. It was smaller than it looked at first. It couldn't have held more than a half pound of candy. I waited for him to move his fat hands and bestow his precious gift. He pulled himself up from the chair, his two-pointed beard bobbing, and daintily lifted the lid. I wasn't going to be able to get out of taking one. There was no excuse that he'd accept. Each piece was small, looking no different from other miniature chocolates, but when I lifted one in my fingers, it was lighter than it looked. It would have been insulting to pop it into my mouth with the great doctor breathing over me. I had to move my hand deliberately as he obviously expected. As I did, his tongue slid out between his teeth and lips, savoring his creation as if it were in his own mouth. That it was delicious was no surprise. The smooth chocolate melted slowly and blended with the oddly flavored filling. I was aware only of the desire to hold on to the taste as long as I could. I also prayed it would have no other effect.

Dr. Schine sat back to enjoy my savoring the aftertaste. To my alarm, I found myself craving another piece. I knew that my craving had been artificially created. I knew it after only one piece, yet I couldn't restrain myself. The doctor needn't have worried. I kept eating, greedy for more and more. I wasn't listening to his polite conversation, only grabbing for another and another piece. When Schine left my apartment I didn't even see him go. But he must have locked the door and turned out the light, because the next thing I knew I was alone and the room was completely dark. I didn't know where I was. My mouth was parched and gritty. Sprawled out on the sofa with one leg dangling on the floor, I felt the afghan tucked in up to my neck. It was hot. My head was swimming. With both hands, I yanked the cover off and breathed deeply, trying to sit up. As I dragged myself up the heat lessened and I could almost feel the blood beginning to pump again through my veins. My eyes began to focus, and the smothering blackness turned back into dark outlines, familiar furnishings.

The longer I sat there in the dark, the stronger I felt. But I was lost. It was hard to think clearly. Light would help. I grasped at the lamp, managed to turn it on, and then caught a glimpse of the clock. It was nearly eight. I had been lost in that blackness for hours. Looking down at the coffee table, I saw the small box. It was still there, nearly full. I was almost certain I'd already eaten more than half its contents while Schine was there, but now I was elated to find there was enough left to gorge on for the rest of the evening. I tried to move, but found my body resisting. There was a loud crash beside me. The light went out. I scrambled for the lamp by the bed and saw what had happened. The afghan had caught in the cord of the lamp beside the couch and had slowly dragged it off the table.

Moving heavily, holding onto furniture to keep myself upright, I managed to pick up the lamp and replace the bulb. Then I stumbled around the room turning on every light in the apartment. Nothing had changed. Only the gold box proved that Dr. Shine had been there.

My willpower had brought me to a standstill. I was able to keep from eating the candy, but I couldn't quite bring myself to flush it out of reach either. I turned on the TV set, but none of the news of the world was as fascinating as that small gold box in the center of the coffee table. It glittered there, defying me. I had to resist. Schine had arrived in the early afternoon. Whatever those candies contained had kept me unconscious for hours. It was night now, but I wasn't going to let that stop me. Once again I started drunkenly for the coat closet.

My muscles tightened again; my forehead broke out in sweat. There was another soft tapping at the door. At first I couldn't believe it. Not Dr. Schine back again!

It was Cheena. She stood there beaming.

"Hello, Sharon. I just had to stop by and see how our two babies are getting along. Sorry I couldn't come sooner. I've been so busy. I'm ashamed of myself. Aren't you going to ask me in?"

"Oh, of course," I stammered.

"What's the matter? You look dreadful." She followed me into the room.

"Don't know. I fell asleep and when I woke up I felt awful."

"Did you call Rome?"

"No, I didn't think to."

"I'll do it then. He should see you."

"No, please. If I don't feel better by morning, I'll call him."

"The baby? Has it been bothering you? It's all right, isn't it?"

"I felt so rotten I haven't had a chance to think about the baby. But she's still there kicking like mad."

Cheena draped herself in a casual pose on the couch. She noticed the candy box.

"Well, I see you've been honored with the great doctor's greatest gift. He only bestows it on a very favored few, you know. Mind if I have a piece? He gave me a box once, but I committed the cardinal sin—I didn't gush properly. But they are absolutely delicious, and I've never been too fond of sweets."

Cheena popped piece after piece into her mouth. She'd allow one to melt, savor it as long as she could, just as I had done. Then she'd take another. They weren't having any effect on her, except to make her greedy for more. Without a pause in what she was saying, she lifted the box and held it out to me. My hand drew back in hesitation, but Cheena had been eating so naturally, I felt like a neurotic fool.

"You've been staying in too much, Sharon. Now that Philip is away for awhile, why don't we go to the Kennedy Center or a movie tomorrow night? You need to get out of this room. You've been cooping yourself up too much. Oh, I know, you've been waiting around just in case you have some word from your precious Philip, but that's silly. He can call back."

"I really haven't," I said with some agitation, trying to steer Cheena away from the way Philip had been treating me. Here at last was my chance to get out of the building. Cheena had always treated me differently from the others. Maybe she had been trying to help me all along, was trying to help me now. Words exploded from my lips.

"I'd love to go with you. I've been cooped up here for so long. I don't care where we go, but please, let's go."

"Of course, Sharon, of course. I didn't think it was that important. We'll go to the Kennedy. It's a musical and it got a very good review. I'll pick you up tomorrow at six. We'll have dinner first."

All the time we'd been talking, Cheena was handing me the candy box, and I kept eating the chocolates right along with her.

CHAPTER 32

I never got to the Kennedy Center or to dinner with Cheena. For a long, hazy time I woke fitfully, only conscious that someone was spoonfeeding me. Blurred features hovered above me. My limbs were numb. The spoon was pushed between my lips and I swallowed obediently. Waves of heat would crush down on me after they'd left and I'd sink deeper into that dreamless, deadly stupor. I tried to move my head, change position, but all I could do was focus my eyes on a small area of ceiling. When my eyes managed to look down, they saw nothing but my body covered by a heavy blanket. I couldn't raise my hands to touch my face. Even half-conscious, I was aware that I had to do something, but I kept losing the battle to stay awake.

One night I awoke shivering. The room was freezing. The blankets had slipped to the floor and the balcony doors had been left open. Someone had forgotten to close them. Or had that someone purposely tried to help me? The cold air was bringing me out of the doped coma that held me helpless. I breathed heavily, deeply, each gulp of air further clearing my fogged brain. At last, with all the energy I could muster, I pushed myself into a sitting position, sliding my feet over the side of the bed onto the cold floor. I looked down at myself. I was a naked, shapeless mass, swollen all over with fat. And my belly was huge. Thank God my baby still appeared to be all right. But what were all these drugs doing to the helpless child inside me? Almost in answer to my thoughts, I felt her kicking to tell me she was alive and awake. Whatever else she was, she was mine. Philip, that conscienceless monster, would never be her father. I had to save her.

Trying to stand, I fell back. Then slowly, holding onto the table beside the bed, I dragged myself painfully to my feet, shivering. Slivers of recollection passed. Somebody had exercised me, massaged me, but it hadn't had much effect. They had no faces, but I vaguely remembered pushing away hands that tried to manipulate my arms and legs.

Still shivering, I had to decide if I should retrieve the blanket and wrap it around myself. But I was afraid its warmth would bring back the drugged feeling. I tried flexing my toes, then my legs, my fingers, my arms. Then, still holding to the table, I slid my legs apart and took my first, awkward step. The next step, with the support of the table, was much harder, but I made it. It gave me the strength of will to go on.

The only sound I could hear was the wind howling outside. I looked down for my watch; of course, it had been removed. But the electric clock was still keeping time. Four o'clock. It would be dark outside for several more hours. The only light in the room came from the lamp beside the bed. They left it on for whoever came after dark. It must have been Cheena who had left the balcony door open. Grace would never have been so careless, and she would certainly never have wanted to help me.

I was wasting valuable moments. I couldn't guess when any one of them might be coming back. If I had any luck they'd think I was still drugged and wouldn't bother until morning.

Luck was with me. Shuffling like a fat Chaplin, I made it into the dressing room, put on my robe, and pushed my feet into fur-lined boots. By this time I was nearly comfortable; at least the icy blast from the window wasn't freezing my naked body. But I still wasn't fully awake. I wrapped my coat over the robe, then trudged to the balcony and threw the doors open wide. I couldn't stand there too long, but I stayed long enough to be certain the relief from the drug would last until I'd escaped somehow. Darkness was a blessing. Philip was probably still away, but I would move about carefully just in case, particularly if I had to pass his door once I was out of this room.

My pocketbook was still on the table where I usually dropped it. I tore through it, looking for the keys. I couldn't find them. I rummaged deeper, then turned the bag upside down and shook it frantically. Everything but the keys fell out. Tears in my eyes, I turned the bag upright again and ripped open the lining. Still no keys. Charge cards, pictures, money, any kind of identification, all were gone. Then I remembered the second set. These people would never give me credit for having had that much forethought. Even I'd forgotten about them.

Fighting another attack of dizziness, I dropped to the floor and burrowed down to the floor of the closet, looking for the makeup case. Finally yanking it out, I fumbled with the catches until at last they opened. I reached down into the pocket. The keys were still there! They felt like tiny, slippery chips of ice in my bloated fingers. I hugged them to my breast, then quickly snapped the case closed and shoved it back against the wall with my foot. I even took the time to replace the two other cases in front of it. Now everything looked exactly as it had before.

The key still fit the apartment door. In an instant I was in the hall, pulling the door closed and quickly locking it. The elevator behind me led to the main lobby. I had to try. Creeping slowly, sensitive to any sound, I reached the elevator. I knew it responded only to the master key. Fingers trembling, I fit the proper key into the hole. It didn't fit! They must have changed the lock: this way was barred.

I made myself believe there would be some other way. The back elevator—it might carry me to freedom. I had to try it, even if I just consumed more precious time. I reached the back elevator at the end of the second hallway. That key didn't fit either. They'd changed them all.

There had to be a stairway. There were several doors; I tried to remember what they were. Certain ones led to Grace's horticultural domain, which was useless—the roof was enclosed in thick glass walls. I'd been uncomfortably aware of that even in my one short glimpse. I thought of the stalls I'd accidentally discovered. But even if I could have brought myself to go in there again, I'd already satisfied myself that there was no exit to be found there.

That was all—except for one recessed space on this corridor. There had to be a door there. I slopped my way back, careless of the noise I was making. Yes, there was a door, tightly fitted into the wall, probably used only in emergencies. Well, this was an emergency. It didn't matter where the door led; I had to try it. It opened without a sound to the master key. A stairway wound down. The walls gleamed like a tunnel of snow, everything tiled in white. The stair treads were covered with resilient flooring, white as the tile. No one would hear me coming regardless of where this led. I was dubious, but I couldn't let myself be caught again. Such a strange stairway had to have a destination, and no matter what the maze, I would find it.

There was a landing at each floor. I counted as I went: one, two, three, four, five. I dared not stop even for breath. If I could only reach the ground floor, I might be able to find an exit to the street. Every muscle ached. My legs pumped like unoiled pistons. I had started from the eleventh floor. Six to go. I made it to the fourth-floor landing so exhausted I knew I couldn't take another step. Pains were now knifing through my legs. As dangerous as it might prove, I had to take a few minutes to sit down on the steps. But I didn't dare sit too long. Even if I heard someone coming, there was nowhere to escape. And the stairwell was stuffy. Before I started feeling sleepy again I made myself push on.

At last I was down to the third floor, but as I reached the landing, my heart nearly stopped. The stairway ended. I'd have to leave its relative protection and take my chances in more open areas. There was only one door and my key fitted the lock.

I opened the door very slowly, trying to adjust my eyes to whatever light would be on the other side. I listened for a minute straining to hear if anyone was on the other side, and then pushed it just wide enough to get through. I was afraid to go on, but I had nowhere else to go. The only retreat would be back up to my own apartment, and anything I might find here would be better than that.

My eyes flew open when I discovered where I was. Of all places! It was the first kitchen. Why would such a special stairway lead from my floor directly down to the kitchens? Putting that thought from my mind, I tried to reason out my next move.

Perhaps I could get out through the banquet hall. But those doors were sure to be locked, and something told me my keys weren't going to fit. I'd seen Philip use a heavy black key for special places, and this was no doubt one of them. But I had to try. If I only knew what time it was. I couldn't afford to flounder around running into dead ends, getting lost, retracing steps. Everything would be lost the moment any one of them saw me. I pushed open the door and slipped into the dining hall. It was a huge, dark cavern looming almost endlessly. The uncovered tables and chairs were like skeletons set out in a weird panorama between me and the reception-room door.

I managed to cross the room, carefully avoiding anything that was in the way. Relieved that I had stumbled over nothing, I hurried up the steps to the main entry, the key already in my hand. I jabbed it into the lock. It wouldn't fit. Heedlessly I shook the tremendous doors, pushed against them with all my strength. It was like attacking a lead wall. Turning back on the landing, I stared again across the vast room. I would have to go back through the kitchen. This time I was more careless in crossing the dining room. Time could be running out. I had no idea how long it had taken me to get this far, but it seemed like hours. At last I reached the kitchen door. It had swung back behind me and locked. Then I remembered. This door had a combination lock—and I knew the combination! Then, in my panic, my mind went blank. Suddenly, like clouds parting, my memory cleared and the vision of Philip standing before that door flashed before me. I could see him reaching up and the combination he spun as clearly as though he were standing there again now. Wasting no more time, I twirled the high dial, my fingers wet and slippery with sweat. It worked. The kitchen door swung open easily and silently. I stepped through and pulled it closed behind me.

Once inside the kitchen I rapidly considered which way might offer the best chance of leading me out. There was the door which had opened from the stairway, and the large, imposing door that led to the second kitchen. Aside from those there was only one that might lead to the hall. Nearly running now, I had the key out in front of me again. Trembling, fumbling, in real panic, I jabbed it into the lock. It wouldn't turn! It wouldn't work! I slid down to the floor, beat my fists against the wall in frustration and despair. But I couldn't give up. I would try anything before admitting it was hopeless. Anything!

I ran across the room to the door to the second kitchen. Perhaps in there would be another exit. The door came silently toward me with no effort at all. I went through into the room, now dimly lit and ghostly.

Doors! Where were they! There was only one more. Directly ahead, far across the room. It was the one with another combination lock, and it led into the third kitchen.

I didn't hesitate. I went up and turned the combination lock as though I did it every day. One of these damned kitchens had to have another exit. They had to have some way to take out the garbage and trash. There was no sense in trying the wide elevator-like doors in the second kitchen; I knew they led only to the ramps where they filled the dais.

In the third kitchen the stillness was like a fog hanging down over me. I could hear my own breath coming in short, spastic spurts. I forced myself to stand still and breathe deeply before going on. Scanning every wall, I saw that there was only one other single door—directly ahead—the door to the freezer. If there was a way out, it had to be through there. It was my last hope.

The last combination lock stared down at me, daring me to keep on. This was the place where Philip had stored the lobsters he'd brought back from Maine. I concentrated on recalling the combination I had so casually fixed in my memory, and again my desperation paid off. The tumblers clicked, the door released and opened a crack. Pulling it open, I hesitated on the threshold. I sensed something terribly revolting in the darkness that lay ahead. It wasn't the cold. The wave of frigid air hit me, but it felt good on my feverish body. This time I looked behind me and decided I'd better leave the door open. If there was no other way out of here, I didn't want my baby to die in this freezing tomb.

I found the light switch on the wall and turned it on. The light was even dimmer than in the kitchens, but my eyes soon became accustomed to the difference. I took one cautious sliding step ahead and then another, becoming aware of things hanging in rows from the ceiling on both sides ahead of me. They had to be the butchered and dressed meats. Hurtling along now as fast as I could move through the narrow aisle, I cringed at the thought of one of the stiff carcasses touching me. It was like running through a nightmare, my bloated body moving in slow motion, and the end of the room seemed very far away, as if seen through the wrong end of a telescope. I was aware only of all kinds of shapes, no doubt some of them beef, but most of them far heavier, shorter, larger, or grotesquely different in some way from what any normal butcher would stock.

I stopped running. Although my first impulse had been to get clear of the carcasses, I realized an exit could just possibly be on either side rather than at the far end. I had to hesitate long enough to look through each row of hanging shapes, to search the side walls. At first there was nothing but unbroken shadow, except for some areas lined with shelves and stacked with crates and boxes. I wasn't about to investigate their contents and there was certainly no door behind them.

As I neared the center of the room I could see a wooden chopping block. It was larger than a bed and stood high on thick legs. Over it hung a large light, like the type used in a hospital operating room. The floor underneath sloped toward a drain hole nearly as large as the chopping block. Carefully I threaded my way around the table, noticing every detail, even to the size of the faucet and the hose which they most likely used to wash away the fats and entrails when they butchered. So this was their method of disposal. Anything could disappear down that huge well. It was all diabolically efficient, but it certainly offered no escape hatch for me.

Backing away from the table, I became sharply aware that something beside me had a hideously different shape, reaching almost to the floor. I couldn't help myself. I had to look up. It was a horrible, gigantic snake, inches thick and hanging down from a hook many feet above my head. Dead and skinned, but its head and eyes, left intact, were glaring down at me. Bile rose in my mouth. Turning like a shot, I abandoned all caution and began to run. I ran until there, dead ahead, was something else, something I'd almost known would be there, something so awful my heart nearly stopped. Right in my path, hanging all by itself, was a human body, butchered and hung like all the rest of the meats. A woman's body. My legs went slack. I nearly fell. I backed up until my back touched the table. I couldn't move. It couldn't be, and yet I'd seen it. It was in shadow, but I had to be sure. I had to force myself to go close enough to be certain. I'd have to move past it. Somehow, without even looking, I knew now that there wouldn't be another door beyond that body, but I had to take that one last chance. I had to make myself see beyond that body, into the darkness. They must have brought this thing in through some other entrance. They couldn't have carted it through the kitchens or the halls. Or was that why the stairway I'd descended had been so sterile! Step by cautious step I put one foot before the other, my eyes glued on the dark shadows beyond the body. As I came to within a yard of the awful thing hanging there, nothing I could control could keep me from looking straight at it. It was ghastly. My agonized imagination was playing tricks. It seemed as though it was swinging out toward me, beckoning me on.

The thing was hanging by its ankles from a hook. It was headless, but the arms were still intact, tied up to the hook. It had been mutilated, split from the crotch to the headless neck. Flaps of stretched loose flesh hung down from the belly, and it had been eviscerated just like the other meats. Its skin, though dry, glistened in the dim lights as though it had been completely shaved and treated in some manner. The whole body had been so carefully prepared, but what had they done with the head? In one of those boxes along the wall, or down the wash drain? And had there also been a baby under that drooping flap of skin? Was that what they had wanted from that poor corpse, or was it, too, hidden in this unbelievably vile place? This time I felt the bile swell into my mouth. Clapping my hand over my mouth, I backed away. I couldn't go past that body, I couldn't.

Some inner strength carried me on. I tore my eyes away from the body and managed to look beyond it. I could see

the far wall. There was no door, only one more wall of
shelves, laden with those peculiar containers. No way out.

I backed away again, mesmerized by the hanging body. I
dared not dwell on what it could mean; I told myself that it
had nothing to do with me, but I knew I was lying. My hands
found the chopping block behind me. I turned and the vomit
gushed from my mouth. Doubling down I managed to dis-
gorge the mess near the hole in the floor. Then, thinking
only of covering my tracks, I turned on the faucet and
washed away the mess. The running water reverberated in
the silence and some of it splashed over my boots as I washed
away everything that could give away the fact that I'd been
here in this room.

Back in the first kitchen I faced the facts of what I'd
learned. There was only one path left to me, and that was
back up the white staircase to my own floor. I was awake and
could think clearly. If the next person to come to my room
was a woman, I would try to overpower her at the door to the
elevator and take her keys.

I tugged at the door to the stairwell, then remembered to
unlock it. Time was running out. My absence was sure to be
discovered. I started up the stairwell. There at the next landing something moved! It was coming toward me, racing as
fast as I was. We both came to an instant halt. Standing there
at the top of the stairs was Cheena. She glared at me like a
wild woman, both of us panting, as though she'd been trying
to find me as desperately as I was trying to escape. Neither of
us moved. I was too stunned. Then, cautiously, Cheena lifted
one foot to come on toward me. I pressed back against the
wall. Here was my first battle. Cheena crouched catlike,
ready to spring. Then she stopped again. Her hand went up
and, with her finger to her lips, she whispered: "Sharon, I
want to help you. Take it easy. You'll never get out this way."

"I'm not going back. I'll fight you first."

"There's a better way. Come on; come back with me. I'll
help you, but not that way. You'll only get caught. You can't

imagine what they're capable of. Death itself would be better. Please believe me. You've got to believe me. I know."

"Why should you help me? You're only trying to get me back so they won't blame you for my getting out."

"How do you think you ever woke from that drug in the first place? The windows were open. Don't you remember? They didn't open by themselves. You've got to trust me, Sharon. We daren't waste a minute. I'll have to explain later. Who else do you think would help you now? Not Philip. He's already involved with the next one. Come on, time is running out. We'll have to wait for the next chance. What's the matter with you? Can't you see what a spot I've already put myself in? I'm your only chance. What do you think will happen to you and to me, too, if they find out I've helped you even this far?"

I was so weary. I didn't dare move and yet what else could I do? In one thing Cheena was right. Time was running out. It might already be too late. I had to trust her. At least she hadn't given the alarm. With leaden steps I dragged myself up toward Cheena as she edged down carefully to reach me. The moment our hands touched I collapsed. With superhuman strength, Cheena half-carried my blubbery mass back up the interminable stairs. At each landing we'd stop to listen while I rested. Several times we heard sounds of activity in the halls, so we didn't dare try to make it to the back elevator even though Cheena had a key for it. She kept muttering to herself as though ordering them to disappear, to allow us to make it back before anyone found my room empty.

Each time it was quiet we agonizingly made our way up another level. At long last we made it to the top. Cheena motioned me to be quiet, then opened the door to the hall. After a survey in both directions, she locked her hand around my wrist and, with her finger up for silence, led me out into the corridor. Almost heedless of noise then, she rushed me on; trembling as much as I, she unlocked the door and thrust me inside. She barked orders as soon as she caught her breath.

"Get those damned clothes off! Quick! I'll put them away. Thank God you had sense enough to close the windows. It's warmed up again. They'd know about both of us if it was cold in here."

"Did I close the windows?" I couldn't remember. If I hadn't, then somebody else did, and they already knew. But I didn't want to suggest that to Cheena. I was too weary even to think about it. All I wanted to do was fall into bed and forget everything.

Cheena bustled around the room putting my coat, boots, and gown away. Then she came over and roughly tucked the covers in around me.

"Don't move a muscle. You've got to trust me. Close your eyes. They can't find you awake. I'm going to give you something to put you back under, but as soon as it's safe, I'll open the windows again and you'll come out of it. Quick. Lie back. Don't dare move. For God's sake. It's almost morning. Someone will be in here any minute."

She was nearly hysterical trying to fight back her panic.

"Why should you be helping me?" was all I could think to ask, but I couldn't speak. Someone was already at the door. I looked down at Cheena's hand. She was holding a hypodermic she'd grabbed up from the bedside table. She heard the sound too. Pushing me back against the pillow, tearing at the blankets to cover me to my neck again, she thrust the syringe into her pocket without ever having had a chance to use it. Standing over me, somehow forcing her face into repose, she slowly backed to the chair. I forced my eyes to stay shut and, with every effort at my command, made myself lie still.

I could hear the door open and close, but whoever it was didn't relock it. As weary as I was, my every nerve was on edge and alert. A slight scent wafted through the room, one that wasn't familiar. The soft tread of feet quickly moved nearer. Then they were standing over me and I was amazed at my own ability to act, to hold my body still, keeping my eyes closed without a flutter, controlling my breathing so it had the evenness of sleep.

Dr. Ahnesbach's voice was the first I heard.

"The skin seems flushed. Look, Sylvia, she seems to be coming out of it."

The odd scent preceded her and I could hear her breathing when the woman leaned over me.

"She is. The skin is definitely flushed. What's been going on here, Cheena? Has she been out of this bed?" Her voice grated.

"She has. She came out of it last night. I let her up for awhile." Cheena's voice was controlled but defiant. "Too much of this stuff and it'll ruin everything. She's back under now."

Dr. Ahnesbach was the examiner.

"You must have walked her. Where?"

"Around the room, of course."

"You opened the windows?"

"Yes, I did. I had to. How else do you think I could have made her walk?"

"She could still ask questions?"

"Naturally. But she was so groggy she didn't know what she was asking, much less what I answered. I know what I'm doing."

"We're not so sure about that. . . . " His voice trailed away. The doctor continued bombarding Cheena with questions, his wife interrupting with her own whenever he paused.

"What signs were there before you allowed her to come out of it?"

"How much did you give her this time?"

"Did she offer any resistance?"

Cheena was a superb actress. She played her part perfectly, not too cowering, not too defensive.

"She made a feeble attempt. She's too far gone. Of course

her mind has deteriorated from all these drugs. If we don't ease up, we're going to ruin this one, after all the preparations and the propaganda about this event. What's going to happen if we go on as we have? Do you want all of us to be sport at the House of Games?"

The Ahnesbachs were silent for once. Then the doctor spoke.

"Yes, I've warned Rome already. We're all in danger if this fetus absorbs too much. It will be ruined. You're right. And all this fat would be a catastrophe too. Disastrous. I think we should keep her sedated, however. But lightly. Cheena, you're certain you know how to handle it? If not, you'd better say so right now. There's no penalty for suggesting someone else take over for you. Sylvia could manage. I have no reservations at all about my wife's competence. This one has certainly been more trouble than anything I've seen. She'd better be worth it."

"We had to go on with it once the process started," reminded his spouse.

"Yes, yes. I know. But everything has gone wrong almost from the beginning. Everybody has handled her wrong. Even I wasn't aware of all the mistakes until our meeting. But I was suspicious. Too many of our members were deluded, to say the least. In the first place, Corintha should have taken her measure better. And Rome certainly should have detected the extent of her immunity. And Philip should have been much more observant. I certainly credited him with more perception about all types of women. Now we've become too involved with her to drop her. It's a damned nuisance. And, as you say, it might even be very dangerous for all of us if this one proves to be a failure. I, for one, am furious to be in this position."

The surgeon's deep voice was threatening, but he hesitated and paced the room. He wasn't convinced of Cheena's competence, but he didn't suspect her loyalty.

"Oliver! Come here!" Sylvia barked loudly from the other

end of the room. They didn't seem concerned about waking
me, probably because Cheena had told them my mind had so
deteriorated it didn't matter if I overheard.

The footsteps retreated. Fuzzily, through half-slitted eyes,
I could see their backs: hers tall, the knobs of her hair stick-
ing out like oversized earphones, his back slouched as he listened to whatever it was she found so important to tell him.
Cheena stood frozen in her position near the bed.

The telephone screamed for attention.

"Sylvia, get that!" ordered Ahnesbach. "Cheena, stay
where you are. Sylvia will handle it."

They'd discovered something. I could feel the change in
their attitude, which was suddenly charged with viciousness.

Slyvia lifted the receiver.

"Hello. . . ." Her voice had turned sweet, simpering, sick-
ening. Somehow she managed to sound like a young girl.
"Oh, Mr. Singleton. I'm so sorry, but Sharon isn't here. She's
away for the holidays. With the wedding so close now, she's
always rushing around just like mad."

Pause. Dell had to be asking questions. So they wanted him
to think I was getting married. The way Sylvia put it, he must
have been told that lie before. I was away for the holidays. It
had to be Christmastime. I'd been lying here for nearly a
month.

"I'm an old friend of Sharon's. Just got into town. I'm staying with her until I find a job. She's been so wonderful
. . . .Well, you know, she's out so much these days, that's
why you haven't been able to reach her. Maybe the maid took
your message. I didn't. . . . Oh, I'm sure she got it. But you
know Sharie. She's been in such a state. So many parties. Getting her trousseau. You men don't have any idea what we
girls have to do."

Another pause. Sylvia cast one look back toward her husband, then answered Dell again in the honeyed drawl.

"Oh, I'll be here for awhile, but I'm going back to California soon if I don't find something. Yes, you'll probably see

the lights on. If you do, it'll probably be me. . . . Sharie isn't home very much. I don't like being alone unless all the lights are blazing. Oh, no, I'm keeping busy all the time what with all these parties being given for her. All these new people I've been meeting! We're having a ball. And Philip is so devoted to her. She's the luckiest girl alive. It was so nice of him to let her send for me just so she'd have one old friend to exchange girl talk and last-minute butterflies with. . . ."

How she was going on, explaining everything away so Dell would never call again. He must have called before. He'd left messages. He hadn't given up when I hadn't returned his calls, but the way Sylvia was going on, he'd certainly never try again. She was making sure of that.

"Well, I certainly will. I'll give her your very best. I know she'll be pleased that you thought about her. Forgive her for being so neglectful and impolite, but I'm sure you understand. The holidays, the wedding and all. These people live such busy, interesting lives. It's got us both in an absolute tizzy. I'm not used to it. They're all so glamorous."

She even languished over a sexy "goodbye," then lifted her arm and slowly replaced the phone on the receiver, patting it. In a pantomimed gesture she announced to her husband she had finished with that intruder for good.

I wanted to rip off her hair knobs. Then I realized what this all meant to me—the telephone was still working. It had never occurred to me that they'd take my charge accounts but leave the telephone! The moment they left me alone I'd call Dell, or the police.

"I think I'd better take this thing out," Sylvia said, reaching down and pulling the wire from the wall.

"Cheena, you can leave. We'll take over until Grace comes." Dr. Ahnesbach's words were oozingly soft; I preferred him screaming.

"Fine, I've had enough of this dump." The high pitch in Cheena's voice was the touch that gave her away. She was frightened—more than frightened, terrified. As the doctor and his wife stood sentry beside the bed, Cheena stormed out of the room, slamming the door deliberately behind her.

I lay there petrified, still not daring to move a muscle, yet every nerve screaming to dash after Cheena. Perhaps now they would examine me more closely. All they'd done so far was give me a cursory glance, but that wouldn't satisfy them now. Something else had happened.

Instead of coming toward me, Dr. Ahnesbach turned and slumped into the big chair. His wife walked around him and sat on the couch.

"Is she awake?" Sylvia's voice was back to its normal, whiny tone.

"Doesn't matter if she is or not. She's been under long enough this time to cloud her mind completely." The doctor was very sure of himself.

"None of the others had to be kept under this long. The other way worked beautifully. They were at least functional enough to care for themselves."

"But they had different mentalities. This one's intellect was far superior. The others were carefully chosen. And you heard them at the meeting. She has immunities nobody could have detected."

"Do you think there's any possibility she's still lucid?"

"No chance."

"Then you tell me what she was doing outside this place with Cheena?"

"What makes you think they were?"

"Her boots are wet."

"Wet!"

"Wet. That's what I said. The first thing I did when we came in was check the closets. The boots caught my eye. Must have been thrown in there in a hurry. They looked wet, so I felt them and they were. I think we'd better take this up with our friends."

"After what happened to you, you must relish that satisfaction."

"Oh, shut up, Oliver. I never held it against Cheena. But what she's done this time is far worse than my minor transgression."

Abruptly I was the center of conversation again.

"Now, what are we going to do about this one?"

"Nothing."

"Nothing!" She was getting very loud.

"Yes, nothing. What's the matter with you, anyway? Do you think we can go on with those dosages and not ruin her baby? After all the priming this one has taken, we're not going to throw it away. But just look at her. We must get her moving around again or she'll be nothing but fat."

"What if she tries to get out again?"

"How could she? Without Cheena's help." He turned on his wife. "You can't prove it was Cheena who informed on you. You've made it an obsession that she did, and you know it. I'm sick of it. I will give them the facts. Are you certain you know what this means before we go to them? If you're proven to be malicious and can't support your accusations, it would be your second offense. You'd better be damned sure you have facts."

"I am certain. Of all people, I should know the consequences. I'm not stupid, Oliver. Shall we wait for Grace?"

"It isn't necessary." His voice dropped to a low growl. "Grace will bring her breakfast, but she doesn't need constant watching."

"What if she tries to get up?"

"What harm can it do? It needs the exercise."

They left the room and my performance was over. But I still lay motionless, paralyzed with fear. He had referred to me as "it." I was no longer a person. I was something they no longer considered human. And he hadn't cared whether or not I could comprehend what he was saying.

CHAPTER 33

In the end it was Ahnesbach who gave me the courage to move. I wouldn't lie there like the creature he took me for. I got to my feet, but my head spun, and I stood still for a moment, naked again and shivering. Holding onto furniture, I managed to get to the closet and reached for the robe and slippers. Just clothing my heavy, grotesque body gave me some comfort. Now at least nobody could think of me as "it." "I am Sharon Crane, I am Sharon Crane," I kept repeating to myself. Then I remembered—I had to find my keys. Standing there helplessly, looking at familiar furnishings—nothing out of place—I couldn't remember what I had done with them.

Then, in a clear moment, I remembered. I'd had my coat on. Cheena had only had time to hang the coat away. Besides, none of them even suspected yet that I might have that other set. I went to the closet. My throat clogged as I reached into first one pocket—nothing—then the other. The keys were there.

But now I would have to find another hiding place. My

221

coat would be the first place they'd look if Cheena broke down and told them how she'd found me. And Grace was due any minute with my breakfast. I had to work fast. The food would probably be drugged, and they'd force me to eat. To give myself courage, I reminded myself that I wasn't in any immediate danger. They'd do anything but kill me, or I'd have been dead by now. They were waiting for the baby. If this was Christmastime, it wouldn't arrive for four months.

There was only one place to hide the keys, and that was back in the makeup case. At least I'd be able to remember where I'd put them. It was no easy task to get down on the closet floor and pull out the case. I sweated with the effort of forcing my drugged, cumbersome body to react as I wanted it to. I had just replaced the last bag in front of the makeup case when I heard Grace opening the door. I could never make it out of the closet in time! Furiously dragging myself, I managed two faltering steps, made it into the bathroom, and quietly pulled the door closed behind me. There I waited, my skin now cold and clammy, pulses throbbing. Taking long breaths, I listened intently for footsteps in the bedroom. Grace must have gone over to the bed. A quiet moment, then she was coming toward the bathroom door. She pushed it open.

"Oh, I'm sorry."

"Grace . . . good you came. I made it in here, but . . . a-fraid you have to help me. I can't . . . " I spoke in a deliberately disjointed voice.

Smiling at my incapacity, Grace helped me back to bed, fawning all the way. Her fingers on my arm were pincers testing the flabbiness. I managed a show of a simpleton's gratitude and dropped against the pillows. My eyes caught the clock. Five after nine. Maybe they kept a schedule. If I could only keep my wits about me while I was awake, I might be able to learn when to expect them.

Grace was standing over me, silent. Assured I wasn't going to resist, she went into the kitchen, and in a moment was back with the breakfast tray. Setting it down on the night table, she lifted the napkin and tucked it under my chin, fingering me, taking her time. It was all I could do to bear her touch, but I had to convince Grace I was muddled.

Grace lifted a bowl and spoon-fed me. Turtle soup. Delicious, but surely drugged. But there was no alternative. I had to eat it, with Grace cooing inanely all the while. Just as I was finishing the last of several dishes, two more visitors entered.

It was the doctors, Press and Romano. They walked quickly over to the bed, neither of them even acknowledging Grace's presence. She moved away quickly, carrying the tray toward the door.

"Did she speak?" Romano called to her as she left.

"Nothing intelligible."

"We may as well get this over with," he mumbled as he leaned down to inspect my face. I could feel his quick, asthmatic breathing repulsively close, daring me to give myself away.

I clenched my teeth waiting for whatever was to come next. My eyes stayed closed. It wasn't difficult; I was starting to feel sleepy, warm, and comfortable. The effect of this new drug was different. I felt only relaxed, not spinning in space, and I stayed aware of what was going on around me.

Dr. Romano lifted my eyelid. His ghostly white face hovered above mine as he pointed a light into my eye. Then, moving in beside Romano was the smaller shape of the obstetrician. Most of their examination was conducted in silence, but as they backed away, their conference began.

"Too much fat. It's abominable." Romano's voice.

"I warned him about that long before the meeting. She needed constant exercise. How long has it been this time?"

"About a month."

"Do you think the mind could still be functional?"

"It should have . . ." Romano used some medical terms, but I knew what he meant. I wasn't their first patient, but I was the first to give them such problems. The others must have gone into a permanent stupor long before this stage of their pregnancy. I construed, from the little I could understand, that they had used a combination of drugs and some sort of hypnotic suggestion and it had always accomplished their purposes almost instantly.

Probably my treatment at the sanitorium had given me whatever immunity I had. For all those months in California I had practically existed on tranquillizers, mood elevators, and sleeping pills. But this meant I had to maintain the masquerade. Somehow I had to prove my submission, constantly, with every move I made, awake or asleep. My life depended on it.

Drowsiness was pulling at me, but I had to stay awake long enough to hear everything they might say. They walked away from the bed but didn't lower their voices, and I could hear and comprehend nearly every word. This situation was more than serious to them. They had discovered something in that examination. It was almost as if their lives, not mine, depended on it.

"Christ, Press, this confirms it," bleated Romano. "Our tests aren't infallible! Don't you realize the enormity of all this? She's putting us all to absolutely mortifying inconvenience, not to mention destroying our schedule for the apartment."

"Well, we're managing, aren't we? We've devised alternatives. You may underestimate your own brilliance, my friend, but don't forget that the next one is progressing perfectly well. Underestimate yourself if you want, but I won't put myself in the position of accepting the major blame. No one in particular was blamed at the meeting. It would certainly have been made clear if we were to . . . Cheena is the only one who seems to have committed a deliberate error and I can't even guess what will be done about that."

Romano wasn't satisfied.

"But that fat. We've got to get it off her, but her mind revives every time the medications are reduced."

"Rome, her regression has been progressive. I've noticed a

great difference now when she's awake. So have the others.
She just responded slower, that's all."

"Slower, my ass. There've been too blasted many coinci-
dences for me to accept that stupid theory!"

"Wait just one minute, Rome. Fact one: we've got to get
the fat off; fact two: she's got to be in constant motion to do
it, and fact three: for your information, it would take every
one of us to keep up a routine of that sort, and that is out of
the question. Any more strength in Raoul's prescriptions
would taint her or the fetus or both. I recommend a lobotomy."

"A lobotomy!" Romano's voice was low, aghast. "Who the
hell could perform a lobotomy with the results we must
have? Ahnesbach? He's good for nothing but amputations.
He'd butcher the head. We'd be ruined for sure. For Christ's
sake, don't even mention lobotomy. The others would think
you were slipping so far they might put the blame on you."

"What the hell does your ingenious intuition tell us to do,
then?"

"Let her move about the room by herself. She can't get out.
You know how the others reacted. Like caged animals, restless. We can inject heavy doses of the stimulate to the basal
ganglia and cerebellum to keep her physically active while
our current drug continues to debilitate the cortex and the
hypothalamus."

"You think it will work?"

"Of course. Don't you remember the lab tests?"

"But her system resists and reacts differently. You said so
yourself."

"Different, yes, but she's sunk too far in the past month."

"She got down to the kiln, didn't she?"

"What of it? It meant nothing to her."

"Suppose it did?"

"You never saw any evidence that it did."

"How could I? You made the decision. He went along with
it."

"But Philip certainly confirmed our suspicions. He

checked her reactions further than either of us. He isn't inept."

"Well, it's done now." Press dropped the argument. They left, and sleep dropped over me like a smothering pillow.

I woke soon afterwards. It was still the middle of the morning. My mind was completely clear for some reason. Then I noticed: the room was cool. The windows were closed, and there was no thermostat in the apartment, so it must have been deliberately lowered from somewhere else. This time I wasn't going to make another rash move for freedom. I had to do some thinking while I had the chance. This new drug they'd given me wasn't as strong as what I'd been having for a long time. Obviously they had other plans to control me.

Suddenly I thought of Corintha Byrom and my fear was replaced by bitterness. I'd almost come to rely on the woman as a substitute mother. Her betrayal was in some ways more wrenching than Philip's. Philip had been a Prince Charming, every girl's dream but never quite believable. But Corintha Byrom—tears ran down my cheeks, and I clumsily wiped them away. I couldn't let them find traces of tears. It would mean that I could still feel emotions.

I lay back against the pillows, swallowing the sobs, making myself try to be objective about all of them. I had to think of them as people, not as superhumans. If I remembered that they were only human, I might be able to pit myself against them.

I went to the balcony and stood in the doorway, breathing in the fresh air. The sun was shining, as if there were still a real world outside, and it gave me the courage to try to analyze everything I'd heard.

They'd spoken as if I were part of a series of women. Whatever was happening to me had happened to other women, and still others were to follow. I recalled the glazed look of the girl in the red dress. That was what I was supposed to become, but what would they do with me then— after I produced the baby? The body in the freezer—I

couldn't bring myself to believe the implications of what I
had seen. Thank God my body had already built up a resistance to their chemicals. Maybe their other victims had
been fresh from small towns and had never resorted to pills.
Corintha Byrom had screened me for my loneliness and susceptibility, but had I told Corintha or any of them about the
long and intensive psychiatric interval? I was sure I hadn't.

I closed the windows and came back inside. They would be
returning soon now, and would immediately guess my secret
if the room was well aired. But I continued to map out my
plans. I dared not trust Cheena to help. She was in great
enough danger as it was, and she certainly wasn't going to
forfeit herself for my sake. I looked toward the building
across the street. Dell! He could help, but how? He'd never
call back again after Sylvia's sly bit of chicanery. Even if he
did, they'd taken the telephone away. What if he called and
found that the number had been disconnected? He'd assume
I'd married Philip and moved. If only I could signal him. He
used to watch for my lights. But that was just a silly game and
the chance of his looking this way deliberately now was pretty
slim. But he might still do it occasionally.

I'd heard Sylvia telling him it was she who kept the lights
on. But I could try flicking them off and on. I'd have to watch
his windows to know when he was there. If they would only
leave me alone after dark. . . .

CHAPTER 34

Someone was in the room. I woke drowsily, but naturally. One o'clock. It was Mrs. Romano with lunch. Wearing her nurse's uniform, her red hair severely pulled back, she was as competent and cold as ever. I felt a wormy aversion to Grace, but this woman was worse—like the frost of death. She handled me like a block of wood, feeding me, counting the seconds it took for me to swallow each mouthful. She said nothing, treating me like a cow she had to milk.

As soon as I finished the meal, she cleared it away briskly and strode out, spot-checking the room before she left, looking for any signs that I was moving about.

I sank back into a light sleep after the meal, but it soon wore off. I woke with the urge to get up. Bewildered, I didn't know whether to be thankful or frightened that I was reacting so strangely. This was their newest plan—to "get rid of that fat." I fought my way out of the binding covers, driven by the mania to move. Every part of me jerked constantly, as though I were wired with tight springs, until I could imagine the layers of fat literally seeping through my pores. By dark I

228

still wasn't physically tired, yet I managed to keep still long enough to fix a glance at Dell's windows. They were dark.

The room was over-heated now. Mrs. Byrom brought the evening meal at seven o'clock. She signalled me daintily to get into the bed, and I was glad to obey. The new drug had almost worn off and I was exhausted. Then, brusquely and silently, Corintha Byrom fed me, constantly glancing at her watch. Her chore couldn't be done quickly enough. Her narrow lips were pinched in distaste and her eyes avoided me. I relished the disgust I was causing her, this prig who'd probably never before stooped to feeding anything but herself.

The tedium began. For days they came. They fed me. They left. It was hell playing this game, but I had no other choice. Without a word they'd even taken the television. I was to have no mental stimulation. I was in solitary. After a few days my system started acclimating to the new drug. But it was accomplishing its purpose. The fat was melting fast. As soon as I could control my body sufficiently to open the doors, I'd rush to the balcony whenever I was alone. With each trip the drugs in my food were having less potent effects. They were now giving me more and more of the almond pills, to which I knew I was now addicted. They had little effect on my mental state, as far as I could tell, but the essence of almonds in my skin was getting stronger and stronger.

The feeders came on a regular schedule: nine o'clock, one, and seven. They'd devote fifteen minutes to feeding me, then be gone. And I'd rush to the roof garden. Dell would have to turn up sooner or later and somehow I would manage to attract his attention.

One of the doctors would drop by every few days to check on me. Luckily, they also followed a routine and I managed to be in bed after the evening meal just before they arrived. The baby was alive, it seemed large, but I was losing weight just as they had planned. They seemed satisfied now. Nothing more was said in my presence about moving me. If they did that, every hope would be gone. I could never escape from one of those locked stalls.

The feeders changed frequently. Even Dr. Pavel came occasionally. But Grace more often performed the ritual. She alone seemed to relish my helplessness and the act of feeding me. Her eyes gleamed hungrily and she never took them off me all the while she was in the room. She was the worst of all.

One day Pavel thrust the tray at me. As usual, his little mustache was twitching under the penetrating eyes. He scolded me as if I were a baby or a dog.

"Come now, Mrs. Crane. You've been coddled long enough. You are perfectly capable of feeding yourself. You're wasting our time, my dear. Eat it all up like a good girl."

He backed away and lounged on the couch. "I'll wait to take the tray. But no dawdling, I've better things to do."

I had now reached a stage where I practically didn't care about the drugs. They wore off more quickly with each day that passed. So, like a mindless pig, I gobbled up the food for Pavel's benefit. If I had convinced him of anything, he gave no sign. When he picked up the tray he only winced and hurried away.

Pavel's trial was the beginning. Now they expected me, when ordered, to feed myself. They would stay and take the tray, but I was under careful scrutiny throughout each meal.

It wasn't long before my body was back in shape, except for the huge mound where the baby slept. My baby. Now I had to face what they might be planning for her. I knew I didn't love Philip any more, but that didn't seem to affect my feelings for our daughter. I couldn't imagine what would inspire these people to torment me and my baby as they were, and to run the risk of whatever dreadful punishments were meted out by the House of Games.

One day they began testing me with little tricks and sly questions to judge whether my mind had reached the vegetable stage. I answered like a recording, repeating my responses. It was difficult to judge the correct degree of idiocy I should portray. If I appeared too mindless, they might move me out of the apartment to one of those cells. But my responses were apparently what they wanted.

For a short time the tray was brought and one of them would wait impatiently while I deliberately wolfed down everything on it. Soon they would leave the tray for whoever delivered the next meal.

A week passed. Dell's office remained dark. Then one evening after supper, my vigil ended. His lights were on. I started to rush for the light switch when the hall door opened. The huge frame of Dr. Schine filled it. He stood there in the doorway staring down at me. Those heavy-lidded eyes appeared blacker than before, large, dark shadows in a dark face. Slowly he floated toward me.

"How nice, Sharon. So good to find you up and about."

I nodded dumbly and worked my mouth until spittle ran down my chin. I made no attempt to wipe it away.

He was pleased with the trick. I fixed a vacuous expression on my face, walked toward him, and then sidled around in confused patterns. He said nothing more. He remained only long enough to check the room, rummaging here and there into the desk, through the various drawers, then left.

I had almost been caught again! My mind started racing now. I had to start putting the bits and pieces of my fragmented plans together. If I had the chance to act—there would only be one chance—I would have to be quick, decisive. As little as possible could be left to chance.

What could Dell do if he did see the flashing light and realized something was wrong? He couldn't get into the building. He wouldn't call the police on flimsy suspicions. They'd never believe him.

The keys!

I could toss them over the wall of the roof. I would signal

every night after the doctors left. Then wait to see if Dell flashed his lights in answer. I rushed over and flicked the lights. On. Off. On. Dell's lights were still on, but they stayed on. No response. So far he hadn't seen my signal.

Then, at nine o'clock, after a long, weary stand at the switch, I saw his lights go out. But they didn't come back on. He'd gone home.

CHAPTER 35

The cat-and-mouse schedule continued. They came. They left. They still dropped by to test me, but less frequently than before. Now they left the tray and picked it up regularly. Such was my routine, except for the fruitless evenings switching the lights. Each night, as I saw Dell's lights go out, I would again crawl into bed and weep with frustration. Time was passing too quickly now.

One night—it must have been mid-January from my attempts to calculate the passage of time—I was rudely awakened from a sound sleep by someone roughly shaking my arm. As I drowsily turned toward whoever it was, the bedside light went on and two steely arms yanked me into a sitting position.

"God damn it, you filthy swine, wake up! Wake up!"

By then I was fully alert. Cheena's face, close to mine, was contorted with rage. Her eyes and breath were hot. I shrank back against the pillows, but the furious madwoman wouldn't let me stay there.

"Bitch! I know your mind's not gone. Why the hell

couldn't you . . ." Her voice choked with fury, damming the words.

"Cheena, what have I done? What have I done to you? You are my only friend. I wouldn't hurt you."

"They forced me to stay with you too much, mothercoddling you. With all your sham, all your pretense, I forgot what you are, allowed myself to think of you as an equal, someone I could talk to until your mind was gone."

She slapped my face hard before she went on. I was at her mercy, not caring about the pain, anxious to know what this was all about.

"Want to know what you've cost me? If your moronic brain could only grasp the enormity of my forfeit, and all for being caught with you. They believe I was helping you. They should know me better than that. I was careless. Careless! And because of you they're going to cut off my breasts!"

Her tears of fury were splattering on my face.

"Cheena, I'm sorry," was all I could whisper.

"They think I let you try to get away. The first time they allowed for carelessness. The second time convinced them."

"The first time?"

"The time you got down to my kiln."

"You had nothing to do with that."

"I must have left the door to your apartment open. How else could you have gotten out? You still don't know what it means to me, do you? Merely leaving that door ajar."

"But I didn't know what they'd do—"

"You do comprehend everything I'm saying to you now, don't you?"

"Yes, but please don't tell them. What good will it do you to tell them?"

"Oh, don't worry about that, Sharon. They may be demons in the eyes of the world, but they are humane. All the girls before you never knew what was happening to them. They didn't understand enough to be frightened. But you will be. That will be my revenge on you. Only I'll know. You'll be aware of everything that happens. Maybe it will reach the point where you'll beg them for a lobotomy. Keep on playing your game as long as you can, sweetie. I'm amazed that you've gotten away with it this long, but your good friend Cheena isn't going to give you away. Not even now. . . ."

"But all I saw was a kiln. It didn't mean anything to me."

Cheena pinched my face between her hands, making me look up at her as she went on: "I was too damned egotistical. Plain stupid, to take you down there in the first place. You're the only one I ever considered capable of appreciating magnificence. It was stimulating, fascinating , to discover we weren't confining our activities to fools. They've all been beautiful and healthy. But so stupid. It was exciting to find someone who lifted the program to a higher level."

Suddenly her face contorted, as though she were speaking to someone a thousand miles away. The dark eyes closed and her mouth worked furiously for control.

"But I began to like you, to confuse you with things I tried for years to forget. From the very beginning I was fighting off the affinity I felt for you. When I was young, almost the same age as you, my parents died too. You must have lived with guilt for a long time, all the time I lived with hate. The weird thing was how different we'd felt toward our parents. When I first heard Corintha's tape, it shook me. I made up my mind then that before your mind went I was going to find out how you'd turned out.

"I rarely saw my father or mother all through my childhood. They kept me in schools while they went their separate ways, wherever the social whirl took them. For once, they were both coming to see me—at my graduation in Switzerland. They were driving a sports car that my father had raced at Monte Carlo. I guess the strain of the race was too much for the car. One of the axles gave out—there was a terrible accident in the Alps. When they told me, I just stood there and laughed. . . . Anyway, as you can imagine, when I heard your story from Corintha I had to know more about you, what you had become. I've been fantasizing how different my life would have been if our situations had been reversed. All my parents left me were memories of abandonment, embarrassment at the publicity about their escapades, and enough money to buy me a world, a lonesome, lousy world."

Her words had tapered off into a tearful whisper, but she regained control.

"You understood my work. Your praise was sincere. You represented a normal life I never knew. The others were different. Corintha always found them in bus stations, always on their way from small towns to big cities to make a new life with nothing but their beauty as an asset. None of us had to spend any time with them. They were completely mesmerized from the first dinner on. The first hypnosis, the first drugs, and that was all there was to it. They kept to their regimen, docile zombies. But you kept coming out of it. I was never forced to be with anybody as much as I had to be with you."

She was whispering again, but composed, half-smiling.

"Maybe I did change. Maybe I do like you. But I can't take my forfeit. I can't!"

Cheena's voice was beginning to become frightening. She was almost on the borderline of madness, her eyes darting about uneasily, her hands working , nearly tearing the sheet.

"But Cheena," I managed to interject, "why should they blame you? You were the one who caught me."

"I was supposed to be your keeper that night. I underestimated you. I took some time off to indulge myself."

"Indulge yourself?"

"I had to meet someone for a few minutes. You know. To keep an appointment. He was quick. We used Philip's apartment."

I stopped feeling sorry for her. Cheena knew the whole setup. She should have known better.

"Was it all that important?" I said angrily. "What made you take such a chance? Couldn't you have met him later?"

"For Christ's sake, after all I told you, you still can't get it through your head! You're no different. Nobody, not even you, really understands me. I need thrills. That's why I belong to the chapter, and that's why I need my kind of men, whenever I can find them. The only ones who can give me an orgasm now are so obsessed with me they endanger their marriages, their careers, their reputations, their fortunes, to be with me. They know they're putting all of it in my hands. I, Cheena Wescott, control their lives. Religious leaders, politicians, paragons of virtue. It's the risks we both take that makes my life worth living." Cheena looked off into space, her expression crafty, far away. She had forgotten about her punishment. Now she was reveling in remembering whoever she had been with that night.

"Don't the others here understand?" I asked. "Don't tell me they haven't perfected sex along with all their other pleasures."

"Sex! Christ, you are still naive." Cheena turned on me furiously, then shrugged her shoulders. "So typical, after all. No imagination. Visionless. For us there's nothing new or exciting in any form of sex. Of course some of us still indulge our sexual idiosyncracies, but that's not enough. It doesn't begin to fill the time in between, the constant craving, the need for constant thrills. How do you imagine our organization ever evolved? Jaded, amoral people bored by the jet set, even the hedonic societies, devil worship . . . all of it, just more of the same. All a dreary merry-go-round. Most of us have indulged in so many orgies, sex became as prosaic as emptying our bowels. We had to find something to keep us in constant anticipation."

She was arrogant now, belittling what she had just said she craved.

"Most of us still indulge in sex, but only to relieve ourselves. Our charter members pooled their brilliance to devise ways to achieve ultimate thrills, thrills that take us far beyond sexual orgasms. They've made it possible for us to live, knowing there's always something ahead to top all the thrills we've had before.

"It wasn't easy to be accepted, you can be sure. Once approved for membership, we had to go through elaborate conditioning until our senses reached their peak of responsiveness. Outsiders are able to attain this state of euphoria only through sex or harmful drugs. We have far more. Our state of ecstasy is with us day and night and we know it will go on and on. We've all tried men, women, children, ten at a time, banging, buggering, sadism, masochism. You name it. Why the hell do you think I joined this cabal? I was so miserably bored. I was ready for suicide. I felt I was enduring a living, boring hell. My moments of pleasure were so few. We can still enjoy our individual eccentricities, but the organization must come first. We must sublimate our baser drives to the organization's greater rewards."

For the moment, she sounded as though she were reciting a ritual speech. Then she fell silent. When she spoke again her voice was hushed.

"My men won't come near me after this. I broke a rule and so I forfeit. Can't you see their revulsion? Those men won't gamble their futures on a mutilated freak."

Her hand slapped the table. Then she looked hard into my face, drew her hand back and slapped me so hard it knocked me back against the pillows. Aghast, I had to play for time. This woman was mad. I rose slowly to a sitting position and tried to soothe her.

"But Cheena, these people can't be capable of that much cruelty. If you agreed to anything so crazy it would be against the law. It's inhuman. They won't go through with it. They're just trying to frighten you."

"Capable? They're capable of anything! That's why I joined. Each of us had to agree to allow the organization to

decide what parts of our bodies would be amputated as forfeit if we broke any rules. I was so certain I'd never commit
an infraction. So what if they cut off my little toe! It wasn't
until Sylvia Ahnesbach that I realized it could happen to me.
They cut off her ears."

"Her ears!" My hands involuntarily flew up to my own.

"She talked too much—to an outsider. Why the hell do you
think she wears that hideous wig? Those braids cover the
holes where her ears used to be. They'd have cut out her
tongue, but the parts of our bodies conditioned for our special thrills can't be amputated. Haven't you noticed that
Rome and Warden both limp? Those two were the athletes
of our little group. They've each had toes amputated. Their
transgressions were small ones, but now neither of them can
play handball, golf, or any of the other sports they used to
like. Warden was the first retribution I watched. It's a sort of
celebration for everybody but the transgressor. I was entranced. I remember that one especially because it was my
first. And Warden took it beautifully. He merely changed his
types of sport. He indulges in some fancy tricks these days.
But you wouldn't understand. Rome didn't take it so well.
His disposition can be extremely sour if anything displeases
him. He's one of the most sadistic of our lot. But he also
seems to get the greatest thrills to compensate. Sometimes,
come to think of it, I've even envied him."

Cheena continued almost gleefully, aware that her listener
was getting sick.

"Next, they cut off Pavel's balls. That horny bastard got
himself castrated! Can you believe me now? Can you?"

I wanted to scream her out of the room, but I tried to control my revulsion. The more excited Cheena got, the worse it
might be for me.

"What did Dr. Pavel do?" I asked quietly.

"That infernal eunuch! His foible was banging children,
boys or girls. He always managed to find his victims on the
outside. Finally he tried one who was verboten. He ruined a

little girl they brought here for Philip. Pavel got her pregnant. That's not his role. You see, his offspring wouldn't be the best stock. The abortion ruined Philip's schedule. So they removed Raoul's prize possession. He's adjusted beautifully, though; I'll give him that. He's another of the most avid participants in all our ceremonies—absolutely enchanted with the whole gamut." She laughed deliriously. "Philip's the only stud in this coven, baby. Nobody can take over until his successor is conditioned and ready."

I had to know one answer. "Is Philip still—"

"Studding? Of course. He is a master, never fails. And he'll go on until Rudolph's as irresistible as Philip is. He must also be infallibly fertile."

Cheena started rambling. One minute she was talking about Philip, the next she was speaking so low I couldn't hear her. Her breathing became shallow and gasping and she collapsed in a heap, head down on her arms at the side of the bed. She was tearing herself apart, and all I could do was feel compassion for her. But why? Cheena was one of these inhuman fiends. The women they impregnated—for what? What were their plans for me and my baby? Whether it was to be a monster or a creature bred genetically to some standard of perfection, it was still my child.

I scrambled out of bed to walk around the room, fastening my eyes on the dark windows across the street. I'd have to keep on with my light signals. Nothing else would work. I could never try to escape again. Not by myself.

"Cheena, why don't you just leave this place? They aren't keeping you prisoner. You can just walk out that door and never come back."

She wiped at her tears, scowling.

"Don't be a fool. They'd find me wherever I went."

"Leave the country."

"I can't leave the planet. The organization is world-wide. Who the hell do you think are the guests at our dinner parties? Each chapter competes to put on the best, most surprising entertainment to satiate all of our senses. We're discriminatory, rare, elite, but we're represented in every corner of the world by people of such power nobody even knows of our existence."

"You must have a leader. Why can't you explain everything to him? You weren't the instigator of the things I've done. You were merely a victim of circumstances. I'm sure whoever it is would know the difference if you people are really the geniuses you say you are."

"For Christ's sake, the leader of our chapter would be the first to crucify me to protect the rest of our group."

"Isn't there anyone above him?"

"Of course, at the House of Games."

"Why don't you go to him? He knows you, doesn't he? He must have power over everybody else. Tell him the truth."

"Our great leader!" Cheena threw back her head and laughed. "He's above any pleasure in power. He never exercises it except to preside over a meeting when a chapter is threatened. He established this great organization because he was bored, and the only pleasure he derives in life is the excitement the chapters provide. Listen to me? Our great leader wouldn't waste a moment's time listening to me when he could have instead the pleasure of seeing me punished."

"You could evade them. They wouldn't bother to chase you for very long."

She laughed bitterly, cutting me off. "They'd never let me go. They'd find me and take me to the House of Games."

"But if you could afford to hide somewhere, just until—"

"Afford! I've told you, I've all the money anyone could want. We all do. Why do you think any of us ever joined the organization? You could never understand what it's like to become sick of everything money can buy . . . friends, lovers, travel, jewels, anything. Money! You reach the point where you're ripe for anything that will make life give you one small challenge. They approach you when you reach that stage. You're screened thoroughly before they ever let you know what they have to offer. It's like being born again. You are among the chosen. You're invited to the Ultima Thule, guaranteed ultimate ecstasy for all your senses for the rest of your life. Anticipation, fascination, satiation.

"We compete among ourselves. That's why we travel so often. Why some of us especially resent you. You've caused us to miss some exquisite experiences that can never be repeated. You know, don't you, there are stalls on this floor on the other side of the building? Our real stock yards. This is our specialty. Don't underestimate any of us."

Cheena was finished. She drew herself up drunkenly, lurching from the chair, but she took the time to turn out the lamp. With a macabre laugh, she staggered toward the door, opened it, peered into the hall, walked out, and locked it behind her.

It was pitch dark, but I could still feel Cheena's presence crying at my side. The blackness was suffocating. I turned the dim light back on. It didn't help. It cast nothing more than an eerie glow. A ghostly vision of Cheena in an operating room somewhere in the building took shape in my mind. The room would be immaculate and stark, except for the brightly lit table, like an altar, surrounded by white-gowned doctors jockeying for the best positions. Dr. Oliver Ahnesbach was the surgeon bending over the table. The others were all assisting, intoxicated by the waiting mounds of flesh.

Eyes peered over surgical masks. The dark, sunken eyes of Dr. Schine, Dr. Press swaying on his toes as he tried to see, the Romanos, Pavel. Cheena was lying on the operating table, all in white, and, I prayed, unconscious. When it would happen, I would never know. But nothing would stop them.

CHAPTER 36

I had still underestimated them. I had thought my performance had convinced them that they could allow me to stay awake and take care of myself—but no. As soon as I'd worked off all the fat, they must have heavily sedated me again for weeks. But one day I awoke again, aware of my surroundings. My first impulse was to look down at myself. The baby seemed to have grown very little so it wasn't my delivery they had woken me for. For a second I was flooded with relief—there might still be time to escape—then I heard a voice barking at me.

"Get up! Get out of that bed, you filthy sloth. I've had enough of being masseuse to a stinking cow. It's excruciating even to touch you."

Corintha Byrom was standing over me, face red with anger and hatred. Keeping me slim had obviously been her penalty for mistaken judgment. If so, she was getting off lightly. But my figure was still slim, except the big mound where the baby lay, kicking against my insides.

"You were my first mistake!" Corintha spat. "You 've been

243

so much trouble I only wish they'd destroy you. Well, I've had enough ! You're going to walk this room until you drop or I'll . . . I'll . . . " She spluttered on, purging her fury while she had the opportunity, sure that her words were falling on ears which could grasp nothing more complicated than simple orders.

Somehow I managed to pull myself out of the bed. Mrs. Byrom didn't help, only held the robe out to me, grimacing and turning her eyes away as though the robe stank and she couldn't bear the sight of the naked thing before her.

She sank into the chair, barely watching me tread dizzily around the room. My mind was foggy but aware. I remembered to keep my expression moronic, my walk a shuffle. But Mrs. Byrom was studying me now very carefully. Her resentful eyes followed me as I moved around the room. She looked down at her watch, then back at me. She was growing impatient, but not at the chore she was now performing. I knew that expression. I'd seen it before. Corintha Byrom was experiencing that tremendous inner excitement that she and the others always wore for a week before one of their special events. Another dinner party had to be in the offing. Her lips were curved in a Mona Lisa smile; her well-groomed hands were kneading in her lap. She bubbled with expectancy. Suddenly she was getting up, leaving the room, leaving me alone. At least they weren't keeping me under constant surveillance. I recalled my plan. Perhaps their next party was this very night. If I could only stay conscious until nightfall, I might get through to Dell.

The first thing I did was look at the clock. It was nearly time for my supper. Did they still bring it and feed me? It was dark and Dell's lights were on, but I dared not try flicking mine until I was sure nobody else was coming in. I lay in the bed in turmoil, wondering exactly how I should behave. I jumped. The door was opening. In came Grace with a tray.

"Well, well, you are awake." Grace emphasized the "are" as

though she had just been told. "Now you can feed yourself again. Here now, let's see you try it."

I looked down at the tray. There was only one dish and it was filled with something pureed. There was a tablespoon beside it. I hesitated, not knowing what to do, but the hesitation was exactly what Grace was watching for. Grace put the spoon in my hand and dug the spoon into the dish, then led my hand to my mouth.

"There now, let me see you do it."

I caught on. So they thought I'd finally become like the others. That was all right with me. I'd win an Oscar for the act I'd put on. Haltingly I dug the spoon, tip down, into the mushy mess, and got a little on it. Grace helped me again, showing me what it was I was to do. Even Grace seemed a bit impatient this time. She shoved at my hand, revealing the intense excitement she, too, was experiencing. Her face always glowed, but this was something more. I dawdled, I was sloppy, spilling the greenish mixture down over the sheets, but Grace didn't seem to care. She was smiling. They'd finally accomplished what they wanted.

The minute most of the food was gone, Grace grabbed up the tray, anxious to go. Turning back to me, she said with a sigh of relief: "Now, thank goodness we can use the apartment again. Even I am getting bored to death being tied down with you. You are certainly one who will deserve your fate."

She nearly raced to the hall door. She couldn't wait to tell them that Corintha was right: I now had the mind of an animal.

The moment Grace was gone, I swung around to the windows. Dell's lights were still on. I began to cry with relief. I dashed to the light switch. It had to work. Dell had to notice. They obviously believed that at last my mind was gone and it was safe to leave me awake. But for how long? Grace's words were ominous. Apparently I was to be moved out of the apartment, and it might happen any time. I wondered where they would move me, but I knew with the cold certainty of fear that my new quarters would be in the stalls on the other side of the wall. And Dell would never find me there. No one would.

I had to make every minute count. My hand was on the switch. I heard a sound. Someone was turning the knob, using the key. I stood frozen on the spot. But as the key turned, I managed to take a few steps back into the room and stood still as if dead. I didn't have time to go any farther.

Dr. Schine was paying another visit. At first he was all solictude. Gently prodding me by the arm, he led me over near the bed. I reacted as if he weren't even there. Then he stared me full in the face and announced: "Cheena has had her operation. She had only a local anesthetic, so that she could watch us cut off her breasts. After all, we don't wish any member to miss the forfeit ceremony. I must say Miss Wescott wasn't as cooperative or brave as I would have expected of her. She screamed through the whole operation. I thought you might wish to know. "

He was carefully reading my face, watching even the movement of muscles under my skin. Luckily my shock choked me for the first few moments and by then I had recovered myself. I gazed vacantly at the knot in his tie, mumbling unintelligible syllables which, I prayed, would finally convince him I was indeed an imbecile. But Schine was thorough. He conducted one more test, one which nearly broke my nerve. He came close and removed my robe. Every nerve in me cried out at the touch, but I had to allow his huge paws to explore me. What was he going to do now? I fainted inwardly, and fought desperately not to show it. Slowly moving his huge body toward me, he lifted my hand as though to kiss it. He sniffed it. He continued sniffing up my arm until he'd reached my shoulder. I could feel the goose bumps rising but couldn't control them. It didn't seem to bother the doctor.

He was concentrating on my aroma, his nostrils flaring, his eyes closed. At last he dropped my hand and stood smiling down at me.

"M-m-m-m, coming along magnificently. I must remember to commend Pavel on you. The essence . . . permeating beautifully. . . ." It was the almond pills. I'd been taking them for months, and by now I smelled faintly of almonds all the time.

Seemingly quite satisfied, he lingered a few minutes longer over his pleasant reflections, then turned and stalked out the door.

Alone again, I grabbed up the robe and threw it around me. I was again at the door, just about to touch the switch when I heard someone else coming. I only had time to turn and start away before Romano arrived, obviously sent to verify Schine's opinion. He led me over to the bed and sat me down, turning the shade of the lamp so the light would shine directly into my face. He made a few inane remarks and then, without warning, he said distinctly: "Your friend Cheena's double mastectomy was performed last week. She's not a goddess any longer. She paid quite a price for you. Aren't you appalled, little mother, to know how your conspirator feels about you now?" He sat right beside me, glaring down into my face, a viper about to strike.

I knew what he wanted. If I could only control even the vessels through which my blood was throbbing. I forced myself to look up at him.

"Cheena?" I smiled faintly as though recalling the name, nothing more. He grabbed my arms, pulled me toward him, so close we almost embraced. He searched every inch of my face. I fixed my attention on the colorless brows above his pink eyes. Slowly his expression relaxed, and his usual egotistical self-assurance returned. He dropped my arms as though he'd been soiled by touching me and calmly walked away, locking the door behind him.

First Schine, then Romano. Schine was protecting himself by getting a second opinion. Neither had broken me. Nobody else would come. Not this night.

I rushed to the windows just in time to see Dell's lights go out. Dejected, I waited, glanced at the clock. The dinner party couldn't have been tonight. It was nearly ten o'clock. Dell had been in his office all this time, and now my chance was gone. My time was running out. I wanted to scream with despair. Instead I sank down beside the window and wept. My only hope now was to attempt it the next day, no matter who came in. Maybe the dinner party was tomorrow and it would keep them all busy. I'd had more than my share of inquisitors checking Mrs. Byrom's word. Probably no one wanted to have to stand guard duty and miss the party. But Dell would have to be in his office; he always worked on Saturday. I prayed they wouldn't move me until after tomorrow. Once I was in the windowless stalls there wouldn't be any hope.

I went onto the balcony to bask in the fresh, cold air. Tomorrow was the last chance.

CHAPTER 37

This was the day of the party. I knew it as soon as Sylvia Ahnesbach brought me my breakfast mush. She left me alone to eat, and I flushed the meal down the toilet. My food was sure to be heavily sedated today, so there would be no unexpected distractions on this special night. General Mac-Donald brought lunch. He was early, an unusual break in schedule. I lay perfectly still until he left. Lunch followed breakfast down the toilet. I was so ravenous, I realized that my craving for food was probably aggravated by the almond pills. My great fear was that they would move me out of the apartment before the day was over. But by supper time I was almost sure I was safe; for the moment they were too busy to be bothered. I would have this one more night.

The air was buzzing, electrically charged; the excitement even reached me in prison. Warden Smith came bustling in with my supper, served even earlier than lunch. He looked as if he had just come from a rejuvenation treatment. His already ruddy skin gleamed, his thick red hair had been carefully clipped, his nails freshly manicured. Leaving the tray on the coffee table, he rushed out, apparently not realizing that the table was out of the reach of a person drugged into helplessness. This had to be the night. They always dined about eight, so Warden was probably hurrying so he could dress with utmost care.

This time I left the food on the tray rather than disposing of it in the bathroom. Warden might get in trouble for his mistake, but it would further bolster their opinion of my alertness.

I went to the window. It was completely black outside. If only Dell were there! My pulse pounded. I dreaded looking up.

His lights were on! In my haste to get to the light switch I tripped over the coffee table, nearly overturning the tray. I could now hear the sound of the elevator constantly moving up and down. I wondered if I should wait until all the guests had arrived and were gathered in the huge banquet hall. If I didn't, how would Dell ever manage to get past them? They would immediately spot an outsider who hadn't been invited to the soiree.

I decided to wait, but the suspense was hard to bear. I scrambled back to the windows, dreading what I might see. But he was still in his office. Other lights on the top floors of his building began going out, until only his lights shone. He had stayed until ten the night before. He'd have to stay that late tonight. Just once he'd have to look out his window.

My mind was threshing ideas. I dove into the closet, retrieved the keys, replaced the case as it had been. I would have written a note to attach to the keys, but I had nothing to write with or on. Even my lipstick had been confiscated, and the toilet tissue was so flimsy it disintegrated almost at a touch. There had to be something else I could use to attract attention. If I was going to throw the keys over the balcony wall, Dell had to be out on the street when they fell and realize what they meant. To anyone else the keys would mean nothing.

I began pulling out the dresser drawers, searching franti-

cally for something that would help. A large scarf I'd often
worn caught my eye. It was pink and white, light enough to
show if it fell on the dark street. And Dell would recognize it.
He had admired it when I'd worn it on dates with him.

I could tie the keys in the end of the scarf. But even attached to the keys, the scarf was too lightweight. It might
catch on a tree. I found a small, unopened can of floor wax in
the kitchen, just heavy enough to weight the scarf to the
ground. It would also make a loud noise. That would help attract his attention. Noise! That would do it!

Light bulbs—they'd explode when they hit the pavement.
Quickly I unscrewed two large bulbs from a lamp. Dropped
from this height, the bulbs would have to explode.

All the while I was collecting the package, I kept running
to the windows to see whether Dell's lights were still on, then
running back to the door to listen for the elevator.

Seven o'clock. The elevators were humming.

Seven-thirty. Buzzing.

Eight o'clock. No motor noise. They had all arrived. I ran
back to the window, my precious bundle in my hand, ran
back to the lights and started flipping the light switch. From
my place at the door I could barely see the tops of Dell's windows. The lights were still on. I kept up my signal.

Off.

On.

Off.

Then Dell's lights went out. I closed my eyes, unable to
bear it. When I opened them, the lights were on again. Then
they went off. Then on. He had seen my signal! He'd seen it!
He knew! After a few minutes his lights went out and stayed
out. He was leaving the office. Now was the crucial time. He
might miss the keys if I threw them before he reached the
street. He was so practical, he might even rush off to a police
station instead of trying to storm the door to this building.
But the police wouldn't believe him. And even if they did,
those clever people downstairs would hide me away very
quickly. No, I had to intercept Dell, and my timing had to be

perfect. I watched the clock, guessing how long it would take him to get to the street. I waited exactly eight minutes. Then, rushing to the balcony, I drew my arm back and gave a lusty heave. The package went sailing up and over the balcony, scarf end trailing like a comet in the wind. Half a minute later I heard the distant pop of the bulbs. In the cold, clear, windy night the sound came to me like distant pistol shots.

Now I'd have to wait again. Wait and pray. I couldn't sit still. I couldn't stand still. Oh, God! The torture of waiting.

I heard him! It had taken less than ten minutes for him to reach the eleventh floor. I heard him at the door. Or was it Dr. Schine? Whoever it was was fumbling with the lock. That had to be Dell. None of them would have fumbled. At last the door opened and he stood there. I couldn't really believe it. Dell! He was actually here! I collapsed on the floor at his feet.

As he leaned over me, I cried: "Close the door! Close it! Quick!" Terror was in my voice. All my fear and tension had been let loose, and my whole body was suddenly shaking so badly I lost all control.

"Sharon! My God, Sharon, what have they done to you?"

"They're fiends, Dell, they're fiends. Murderers. Worse. Dear God, get me out of here, get me out! I've been drugged for months and . . . I'm going to have a baby!" Now that he was here, I was choking on my hysteria. Someone from the real world was here. After all this time, I didn't have to bear it alone. Dell lifted me, half carrying, half dragging to the sofa. I was crying, choking, laughing, shaking, curled up in a knot.

"We've got to get out of here. Shut up, Sharon!" He slapped me. As my hysteria subsided, he stroked my hair. "You'll have all the time in the world to fall apart and then tell me all about it later, but you must come with me now. Can you make it? Can you walk?"

"Wait, Dell," I panted breathlessly, "those keys won't get us out."

"God damn it, Sharon. What have they done to you? I got

in and came right up here without a hitch. There's nobody around. We can just walk out."

"The keys won't work, I tell you. Every exit is locked."

"We'll unlock them. Those keys unlocked the elevator. How do you think I ever got up here?"

"They won't unlock the elevator on this floor, or the doors. I tried. The locks up here have all been changed."

"We'll find another way." He looked at me as though he wasn't sure I hadn't lost my mind.

"Please, Dell." My voice was coming back. "Not yet."

"What is the matter with you, Sharon? Have they driven you completely off your rocker? We've got to get out of this place as fast as we can."

He shook me by my shoulders, his hands bruising, unaware of his own anger.

"I'm all right now, Dell, but it isn't that easy to get out. Please, please believe me. There's danger to both of us. They've kept me drugged for months. Even now I can't think straight. If you only knew. If I can only make you understand." I started sobbing again.

"How the hell did you know enough to signal with those lights then?"

"It was the only thing I could think of."

"Well, you thought damned clearly that time. So keep it up. Now come on, we can get out the way I got in."

"I'm trying to tell you—we can't! You must listen to me. Dell, I'm not under some spell. And I'm not drugged now. I know exactly what I'm saying. You've got to understand what we're up against before we start out. They're at one of their ritual feasts tonight. All of them. Nothing will drag them away for at least a couple of hours. We're safe here long enough for me to explain as much as I can, and then maybe you can figure a way out. I can't. Won't you please believe me?"

For a minute he looked at me, studying my face, trying to trust me.

"Please, Dell, you must understand. Every elevator and

stair up here is locked and that key you've got won't work. There's one other stairway I know of, but it leads to dead ends, and worse, to the place where they're all congregated now."

"You couldn't have tried everything. If I'm going to get you out of here, you're going to have to help me. I can guess what will happen to us if we don't make it. So, damn it, shut up and do what I say. First, tell me everything else you know about this building."

"There's only that one stairwell we can get into from this floor."

"Come on, then, we'll go that way. You said it leads to their banquet hall—but did you try every exit on it?"

"I . . . I don't remember. No! I didn't. I didn't have time. I was trying to get down—"

"You couldn't find a way out? Why—?"

I cut him off. "They caught me, brought me back." I was weeping, reliving my meeting on the stairs with Cheena. Cheena . . .

Dell realized I was dissolving again, so he decided to take matters in his own hands, counting on my reactions to warn him if he was choosing a disastrous direction.

"Think you can make it on your own? I could carry you, but it'll be much faster if you can walk." Dell's voice was softly modulated as if he were speaking to a backward child.

"I can make it. I'm only weak with relief. Seeing you, seeing you here."

He wouldn't let me thank him yet.

"You'll have to wear that robe. No time to change. Where are your shoes?"

He was right. I'd never make it barefoot. I scurried into the closet and slipped my feet into my sneakers, the first shoes I found. When I came back, Dell was obviously relieved to see that I was capable of following orders.

"Okay, Sharon, are you ready?" He squeezed my shoulder gently. "We'll have to walk all the way down."

"Listen to me! The stairwell only goes down as far as the kitchens and God knows who'll be in there now."

"What floor are the kitchens on?"

"The third, or fourth. I can't remember."

"Then we'll have to leave the stairwell before we get down to the kitchen level. We'll get out on one of those upper halls and use some other stairway or elevator from there. We'll just have to keep trying until we find a way out. Will we run into any of them on the upper floors?"

"Not tonight. Nothing is important enough to make them leave their feast. Not even if the building were burning down would they miss that."

He cut me off.

"Hey. You've given me an idea. We might need help. They took out your phone. Can we get to another one?"

"No. There isn't a public phone in the place. And we can't get into any of the other apartments."

"Then we're going to have to attract attention some other way, and baby, you've given me one hell of an idea. I may get twenty years for this, but come on. Bring all those sofa pillows out on the balcony. The chair cushion, too. Thank God it's blowing a gale out there. Have you got any cleaning fluid? Get it. Hurry up!"

I ran into the kitchen and under the sink found a can of cleaning fluid. Then I remembered I also had lighter fluid, two cans of it. I snatched them up.

In the meantime, Dell had dragged the mattress from the bed out on the balcony. Blankets, pillows, everything he could find. He even pulled out the overstuffed chair. I knew now what he had in mind. Running back and forth to the closet, Dell came out with all the clothes he could carry and dumped them in piles all over the balcony. We finally had it piled high with combustibles. Taking the large can of cleaning fluid, he doused everything within reach, but saved half the can's contents.

"Get back inside. Quick!" he yelled. "There's gonna be one hell of an inferno and plenty of smoke—I hope."

Dell touched his lighter to the pillows at the bottom of the stacks. Then to another, and another. He fanned the flame with his hands to get the fire started, but it only took seconds. Everything was dry and the wind was blasting about the balcony like smoke in a flue. The fire erupted and Dell ran back into the room. A trail of cleaning fluid spilled out behind him.

"We've got to get out of here fast. In a few minutes this whole damned place will be filled with smoke. I'm going to open the doors again so the fire will move into this room and then down the hall. We won't be able to retreat this way, but then, who the hell would want to?"

We both raced out the door and down the hall. I was in the lead, directing Dell toward the back stairwell. All along the hall he sloshed a trail of the cleaning fluid. He had the keys in his hands again and quickly opened the door, slamming it behind us just ahead of the fire that raced along our path.

Dell had been skeptical about the difficulty of escaping, but the moment he encountered the strangely antiseptic white walls, ceiling, and floor of the stairwell, I knew he was beginning to believe that nothing was impossible in this bizarre place.

I was already puffing from our frantic efforts to set the fire. Dell went ahead of me, moving slowly, but steadily descending the stairs.

As soon as we neared the first landing, he sprang ahead and tried the keys in the door. It wouldn't open.

We moved on to the next floor and the next. Each time Dell tried the keys, then became bolder and tried tugging at the doors. They wouldn't budge. He heaved and shook them. His face was red, running sweat.

At each failure I became increasingly discouraged. The old fear was creeping over me, wiping out the glorious relief I'd felt for such a short time. But Dell only became more furious and resolute. His hand gripped mine fiercely as he led me on down and down.

At last we reached the fourth-floor landing. The next floor

led right into the kitchens. If this door wouldn't open, there was nothing left but to face them directly. I didn't know if I had the courage. Then, we both saw two doors on the fourth-floor landing, one straight ahead and one on the left. On my last trip down these stairs I must have been too intent on getting down to the street floor to notice this other possible path to freedom.

"Which one?" he asked. I shrugged, then pointed to the door straight before us. Dell tried it with my keys and it unlocked easily, but he stopped me before I could barge through. "Let's try them both in case this way takes us right into your friends."

The second door opened smoothly as well. I was completely taken by surprise. "This has to lead to the banquet room!" I nearly shouted.

"Come on, then—let's go."

This hall was wide, unfamiliar. It had to be leading us to the reception room and the elevators where I'd arrived at that first dinner party. But when I'd left that first night, the corridor had been narrow. Could I be all turned around? We were running, my legs tangling in the baggy robe and loose flopping sneakers, but somehow I kept going.

The foyer came into view—the wide, golden room, with the golden drapes shrouding its silence. The regal assemblage had moved on into the rooms beyond but they'd left behind an aura of solemnity. There was no tinge of scent remaining in the air, no flowers, no misarrangement of any item in the whole empty room, yet we both sensed strongly that many people had recently sauntered through here. Now, thank God, it was empty.

Dell scouted ahead, running noiselessly across the heavy carpet, the keys still in his hand. He headed directly for the elevator, jammed the key into the keyhole. He rammed his finger on the pushbutton. We waited. Dell leaned his ear against the doors, looked back at me. I could read the answer in his eyes before he spoke.

"This God damned thing's another bust!" He cursed under his breath. Then he stopped, listened again. "Wait a minute."

He leaned down, replacing his ear to the elevator doors.

"I hear sirens. They're on their way."

"They'll never find us on this floor," I whined. I couldn't help myself. To be so near to escaping and yet to be thwarted again was more than I could bear.

"Stop it, Sharon." Tears were rolling down my face. "Stop that and listen."

The strength in his voice reached me. I was still crying, but I resolutely drew the robe tighter as I tried to pay attention.

"I'm going to set this room on fire. Just pray that if they can get into the building they'll see the fire through the elevator shaft. There are enough of these drapes to make the place go up like Hades. They'll smoke like hell too. We'll have to run fast to keep out of it." Then he stopped for a moment's thought. "But you can't run fast enough. First we'll go back and try that other door. You can just hide behind it. You'll be safe there. I'll come back here, set the fire, and then go back and wait with you. You understand? Sharon! Look at me! I said, do you understand?"

I could only nod. The very thought of Dell leaving me alone even for a few seconds—I couldn't face it. "No!" I shrieked. "No—I can't!"

"You've got to. Now come on, and be quiet, they'll hear you."

He pulled and dragged me back down the long hall. I fell and, as he yanked me to my feet, I choked back a scream. Deep in my abdomen I had felt the first stab of pain. Oh God, I thought. Oh no—not now. It was too soon. I didn't know how long I had to term, but I knew this was too soon.

Dell pulled me to my feet, clamped his hand over my mouth, and carried me to the door. Then, restraining me as if I had gone mad, he quickly unlocked the hall door, then the one beyond, inside the stairwell. It opened and he shoved me through. Once inside I became a bit calmer. The darkness afforded some protection and Dell was still with me. I clung to his arm, walking beside him into a narrow, dark passage. Then we noticed it was becoming more difficult to press on. The passage was sloping sharply upward. How far was he going to make me go, I wondered. There was a cloying odor and where my hand touched the wall I felt what seemed to be layers of grease. But my hand came away clean. The ceiling was hardly higher than Dell's head and he had to push me ahead of him as the walls narrowed so sharply we could no longer walk abreast.

"Must we go much farther?" I whispered.

"No, we'll stop here. I just want to leave you where they won't see you; where you'll be safe from the fire and smoke when it travels down that hall."

"What about you? You've got to get down there and back. Can you make it? Are you sure you can make it?"

His answer was lighthearted, but hardly convincing.

"I can if you're not with me. Now be a brave woman. You're almost out of this hell. You've kept your head all this time. You can do it for a few minutes more."

He leaned over and kissed me quickly, tenderly, on the lips, then slapped me playfully on the bottom. The kiss and the pat quietened me more than anything he could have said. In another second I could see the shadow of his figure disappearing the way we had come. I was alone.

I hadn't told Dell about the labor pains, but they were becoming more intense. I bit my tongue. Held my breath. Nothing helped. What if the baby wouldn't wait . . . right here in this dark, slimy tunnel . . . even before Dell came back? Before anybody came! The next minute I realized it couldn't happen so soon. The pains had begun to subside. If I could just hold on. I had to. Then the pains were gone. I was supposed to be timing them, but how could I? I was frantic, drenched with sweat. Then I saw it—a pinpoint of light far ahead. I remembered something. This tunnel had to lead to the balcony around the banquet hall, where the essences of food were wafted in. The tunnel had to give access to that balcony for some reason, maybe so they could clean the hundreds of vents that had to be around the balcony. It obviously was there for some unusual reason or it wouldn't be so slick, clean, and difficult to traverse. It certainly wasn't used often.

While I was concentrating, trying to fathom what lay ahead, I heard the click of the door behind me. My breath stopped while I turned around. It had to be Dell. It had seemed like an eternity, yet I was surprised that he was back so quickly.

He took me in his arms despite the cramped quarters; I clung to him.

"It's done. Thank God you had that lighter fluid. At first those damned drapes wouldn't catch, but thanks to the fluid they finally did, beautifully. I doused the whole room. Even the carpet is raging. I sprinkled the fluid all the way back down the hall. It's all a blazing inferno by now. You should have seen me fly out of there. Haven't run so fast since I earned my school letter. But I almost got caught. One of those bastards started out the door from the inside room. They must have this whole damned place wired for sound."

"Who was it?"

He almost laughed at the question.

"How the hell should I know? I wasn't about to wait for introductions. All I know is that it was a man. He saw me, but the heat drove him out fast. The only thing, though, is that now they can probably guess where we are. . . ."

Looking down at me, he saw the panic return to my eyes.

"Here, come on, baby. We're almost out of it now. Help is on its way. Those animals inside—it's their turn to be scared. They are all about to roast, one way or the other. I'll bet they're in there ripping each other apart to get out."

I didn't say anything, but I knew better. Those "animals" were too well-disciplined to fail in a crisis. Dell would never believe me. He could never be convinced of their superhuman organization. They could meet any situation.

"Suppose they come in here. What can we do?"

"Relax, Sharon. They can't get through that hall. I told you, it's blazing like hell broke loose."

"But—"

"I'll ask the questions. Does this passage go through to that room they're in? Could they get in here from where they are?"

"I can't remember. When I was there, all I noticed was a balcony high over the room. I think this passage leads to that balcony. But I don't remember any stairs leading up to it from the dining room."

"We're on the same floor they're on. There could be a door."

"No." I was more sure of myself now. "The banquet room is sunken at least to the floor below. We had to go downstairs when we got inside."

"This does seem to be a ramp of some sort. Think, think hard! Is the direction of this passage toward that dining room?"

"It must be." I nodded, unable to concentrate on what I'd seen so long ago. Had there been a doorway on that balcony or not?

While we were engrossed in deciding our next move, I felt the pains come again, more intense, longer. I stiffened to smother them, bit my lips to stifle my cries. I tasted blood in my mouth.

A smothering odor started filling my nostrils. They were going to force us out by sucking off the air, filling the passage with the stench of their feast. But instead of the usual exquisite scents, this time the air was pungently foul, laden with an odor I couldn't recognize.

Dell understood at the same time as I did.

"They're going to force us out. We can't go back. We'd smother before we reached the stairwell. Between the smoke and the tunnel, we have no choice. We'll have to go on, even if the tunnel takes us to that balcony. I'll have the advantage for a while; I can push them off if they try to climb it. Just pray for time."

Scrambling to our feet, half crouching, we scurried up the passage toward the light. Dell maneuvered me behind him as we neared the end of the protective darkness. We stepped out onto the narrow balcony rimming the room. Dell stopped dead in my path, transfixed. The shock of the panorama below hit him all at once. Before I could think, I started to step around him. He tried to push me back, but I couldn't stand it. I had to know.

We were at least fifteen feet above their heads, and they were all looking up as if they expected us. Drawn, bewitched, I let my gaze travel over the room.

The great hall was much more splendid than it had been the night I dined there. Everything was now draped in black; the tablecloth, carpeting, and drapes were all black satin and velvet. The thousands of tiny, flickering electric candles were reflected to infinity in hundreds of beveled mirrors. It was like looking off into endless space.

It was difficult to distinguish faces. They blurred before my eyes. The guests were all dressed in ornate evening costume, and each was seated on a throne representing his kingdom of the world. They all saw us gaping at them, but they remained placidly in their high-backed chairs. Waiting. Each of them was splendidly bejeweled, glistening, glittering like peacocks in their exotic robes, immaculately white ties, turbans, red ribbons slashing across white shirt fronts. Cheena hadn't exaggerated: Orientals, Aryans, blacks, Semitics—all were represented.

As my eyes gradually adjusted to the room, I sought out faces I would recognize. Across the room I found Sylvia Ahnesback, dressed in black, mounds of stiff satin folded about her neck. She was wearing a dazzling diamond tiara high over her twin spikes of hair. Somehow she had hung long, glistening diamond earrings where her ears would be. My eyes tore away from her and traveled quickly around the table. Others were easier to spot. Farther down I saw the rabbity head of Dr. Romano bobbing next to the brilliant red hair of his wife. Helga's was the next familiar face. Her charges didn't seem to be with her. Dressed in deep-red chiffon and heavy lace, she had succeeded in enhancing her prominent bosom with blood-red rubies dripping around her thick throat.

Dr. Schine! There he was, presiding at the center of the table. One couldn't mistake the black points of that devilish beard, that gargantuan frame, the shining, bald head rimmed with its crown of black hair. He was leaning back in his chair, absorbing, contemplating, devouring the festivity. He hadn't even bothered to look up.

Looking around the table, I thought I recognized others, but some had their backs turned and I couldn't be sure who they were in their fantastic array. Then I saw Cheena. She was seated almost directly below where we were standing. I knew it had to be she, even though I couldn't see her face. Her posture had always been impressive; tall and firm and sure. Tonight her black hair was dressed high and full, elaborately styled, not simple and chic as before. She was wearing a white gown, ruffled silk from her throat to her waist. She had never before worn frilly clothes. Fleetingly I remembered the day she'd treated me to a glimpse of her wardrobe. Every gown was designed to cling to her; nothing she wore had been allowed to compete with her figure. For an instant I caught a glimpse of her face as she looked up at the tall man seated beside her. It was ashen, the only spots of color the rouge on her cheeks and her shadowy black eyes. How she had managed to come to this dinner so soon after the operation I couldn't imagine. But the physical stamina of these people was amazing. Nothing but death could have kept her away from one of these dinner parties. She was one of them.

Desperately I looked for Philip, torn between the compulsion to see him and the pain the sight of him would bring. I found him, near the end of the circle, almost facing me. He was glowing. His white teeth flashed as he flirted with the woman at his side. I couldn't look at her, didn't want to know how beautiful she had to be. And how unpregnant. And she had to be one of them.

I looked to the center of the room. The dais had not risen yet; it was still just a large black circular depression in the floor, much too deep to see into, even from my vantage point.

A hush gradually came over the room. It was so still that I could hear Dell's quick, shallow breaths, and my own. Then the dais began to rise. The feast was about to begin. Essences began to waft into the room. I could detect the subtle fragrance of something familiar like curry. But it was combined with another aroma that my mind refused to define. As the scent wafted about the room, the tiny spotlight beamed down from the ceiling. It was directed into the deep hole in the center of the room, and the light grew brighter as the dais continued to rise. The altar of immolation was emerging.

The first ring rose slowly in silence. It was huge, draped in black velvet and set with hundreds of small bowls, steaming with a thick, reddish liquid that stood out against the black velvet. I looked around for the waiters, but this time there were none.

The second ring followed, bearing ornate covered silver platters. Dr. Schine rose and went to the dais. Slowly, enraptured, he lifted the covers and laid them aside.

On each platter, a different part of a human body gleamed in the light, glazed and steaming. My eyes bulged in stupefied horror. I could even distinguish the flesh, darkened, a glistening pinkish brown, decorated with sprigs of parsley and vegetables.

None of the participants stirred. It was like a heathen rite, a diabolic sacrilege. But none of the spectators were devils, or witches. They were human beings, just like Dell and me.

The center ring was about to rise. The hushed room was

charged with excitement. The dais rose slowly, tantalizingly, and Dell and I could both sense the sensuous gloating of the hosts. They were almost drooling. Suddenly it was all there before us. The beam of light sparkled down and illuminated the horror. On the dais, rotating slowly as the dais rose, was a spit. And on it was the body of a baby. Flames licked up from a cauldron, gently flicking at its tiny body. Its face crackled and popped blood.

I screamed. It made no difference to those below. They were all mesmerized by the sight before them. Bending double, I began to vomit. The bile flowed from my mouth and spilled over the balcony, spotting the black tablecloth and the dinner guests below. At my side Dell stood in stupefied disbelief, his hands white from clinging to the rail. Nothing happened down below. The ritual continued as if we weren't even there. All about us now wafted the putrid odor of burning flesh. But below they savored its pungency. They were ecstatic at the very aroma.

Dr. Schine began to chant softly. Chanting as he went, he stalked slowly around the room. Only as he turned our way did I notice that in his out-stretched arms he was carrying a black velvet pillow resting on a golden salver.

On the pillow was a head—the head of a beautiful woman.

Her hair was red, and her lustrous braids were bound into a high crown framing her face. The eyes were wide open. The lips were set in a sensuous grimace. Cosmetics had been artfully applied so as to give the head the illusion of life. Schine was gloating, lingering before each of the guests to allow them to share his pleasure in the jewel he was presenting. As each guest viewed the spectacle, he would acknowledge his pleasure by joining Schine's funereal incantation.

Dr. Schine proceeded in stately cadence around the room, the chant rising and swelling behind him. There was an unhurried, awesome solemnity to the occasion. Although someone had discovered Dell setting the fire in the hall they seemed to be taking no measures to protect the building or themselves. Our intrusion on the balcony seemed only to heighten their mad euphoria.

Schine finally returned to the dais. As he reached the outer rim, a grin spread over his face and he looked up at me for the first time, and I knew he was stimulated by my fear and horror. His spittle caught the light as it dribbled from his lips and down his immaculate beard. When he reached the dais he daintily deposited his gruesome treasure so that it faced his empty seat. Then he reached for the huge carving knife and fork that lay at hand. He started by carving from the big platters. The diners slowly and silently rose, one by one, and marched regally toward him. They chose for themselves slices of liver, heart, belly, breasts, and thighs. Dr. Ahnesback seemed hungry for the tongue.

The carver hadn't touched the baby at the top, but eventually he would. That I couldn't bear. . . . I clasped my hands over my belly. Spellbound, neither Dell nor I could move. The cannibals down below were so sure of themselves. The fire, the presence of two horrified spectators, were only minor diversions, further whetting their appetites.

Then I felt it again. The pain was sharper, like knives piercing my insides. They were coming again. Oh, my poor baby. I was about to have a miscarriage right here in view of the whole assemblage. Spasms tore through my body, searing like bullets. I screamed; I shrieked. Dell scowled, twisting sharply back toward me. All eyes below were finally looking up, but no one moved. They knew! They knew I was losing the baby—right here and now—and not one of them was making a move to help me.

Dell crouched down beside me. His voice was stern, which was what I needed.

"Hold on, Sharon. For Christ's sake, hold on. It will all be over in minutes. The firemen are coming. It can't be much longer. They probably had trouble getting through that front-door barricade, but nothing will stop them while that fire rages on the roof. And it's blazing like hell out there in the hall, too. Can't you smell that smoke? Those bastards down there know it too, but they're too turned on to care."

"They're not human, Dell. They can't be. They must have a contingency plan for anything, even this."

"Not this time, Sharon. Trust me."

Looking at Dell's face, I realized he still wasn't aware I was about to have a miscarriage. I wanted to tell him, but I could barely speak from the pain.

Then, as I felt I would faint from the agony, I saw someone moving a massive ladder into the room from below. Dell saw it, too. His eyes panicked, but the rest of him stayed calm, for my sake. He leaned over the rail. I pulled myself up behind him.

There they were—Philip and the General, carefully, quietly moving a ladder into place below us. There could be no mistake. They were coming to get us. We wouldn't be able to hold out. The ladder was the type that didn't need to rest on the rail. It stopped about a foot below the balcony, but anyone climbing it could reach us with ease. And Dell wouldn't be able to push it away.

The General held it steady and Philip began to climb.

The buffet line continued, slowly, toward the dais, each guest helping himself and returning to his seat to the rhythm of the chant. They were still ignoring everything else, sure that any problems would be remedied with the usual dispatch.

Philip's rise up the ladder was cool, dispassionate, as though he were merely replacing a festoon that had slipped. Staring down at him, almost hypnotized by him again, I suddenly caught the glint of metal. He was carrying an appalling knife! Philip and the doctors knew what my screams had meant. That knife was meant for me. Now I was dispensable. It was the living baby they wanted, and Philip was coming to get her.

The room began whirling around me. Everything was

turning black. As I began blanking out, I prayed I'd be unconscious and never know whatever was about to happen.
But even that blessing wasn't to be allowed me. The blackness dissolved just in time for me to see Dell throw his arms
out to grapple with Philip. Philip thrust out viciously, the
knife gleaming deadly above his head. Dell grabbed at Philip's wrist and hung on, with Philip now clinging to the top of
the ladder. They were only feet away from each other, claw-
ing with both arms, Dell kicking through the railing to topple
Philip or the ladder. It began to sway despite the General
holding on for dear life below. Philip was almost at the level
with Dell. They were in a stranglehold, Dell leaning down
over the rail, Philip reaching up to him. The knife waved
wildly over their heads as they fought for the advantage.
Then the impasse was broken. The ladder started to rock.
Philip lost his balance. Dell was still hanging onto the arm
with the knife. Philip's left hand lurched out and grabbed for
Dell's neck, and they both went over at once. About ten feet
of the railing tore away, hurtling down to the floor far below.
I could hear myself screaming, screaming over the insane
chanting that hadn't once faltered in its impassioned cadence. But nothing drowned out my piercing shrieks.

Everything went crashing down into a tangled heap, the
ladder, the railing, Philip, the General, and Dell. They all
toppled onto Cheena and several men and women below.
Not one of the others moved. Then Schine, Romano, Pavel,
and Warden Smith all broke into a run, heading for the spot
where the tangled heap of people still lay, kicking and
thrashing to separate themselves from each other and the
debris on top of them.

I had to look down. Blood was gushing over the floor, spat-
tering everyone. Oh, Jesus, Mother of God, I prayed.
They've killed Dell!

I forced myself to look closer. I crouched on the badly tilt-
ing, derailed balcony, clutching the broken cement which
had cracked away from the wall. Only the metal braces were

holding the balcony where I clung. If I leaned too far, it would all break away and fall, taking me with it. Cautiously I moved only my head. I was searching for Dell's jacket, which was lighter than the black suits of the others. Romano and Pavel were tugging at it, pulling him away from the pack. As they dropped him on his back, I could see that his jacket was covered with blood. He was a dead weight, his eyes closed, mouth hanging slack. They simply dragged him aside and left him lying there.

Neither Philip nor Cheena had moved from where they fell. I almost lost my hold on the precarious perch. My hands flew up to cover my eyes. The torrent of blood was pouring from Philip's throat. The knife, still in his hand, was imbedded deep in his neck. His throat was slit wide open; his vacant blue eyes stared straight up at me.

And Cheena, too, was lifeless, a broken doll lying on her back. The dress she wore, all those diaphanous ruffles, had been torn from her body and her whole chest lay exposed. It was covered by thick bandages, but through their virgin whiteness seeped quickly spreading stains of bright-red blood.

With rigid precision, Pavel, Romano, and the architect lifted the bodies from the floor. Then I realized that Dell was gone. As I'd stared, entranced, at Philip and Cheena, they somehow had taken Dell away. Only his blood remained.

Now the bodies had all been disposed of unobtrusively, and Dr. Schine was ready to proceed. Slowly he raised his hands above his head, disdainfully dismissing the disturbance. Wordlessly he shepherded the others back to their seats. There they sat, resuming their ritual as though nothing at all had happened to interrupt.

Then Schine gave another signal and they were all staring up at me, willing me down, willing me to obey, and I was succumbing. The room began spinning again, but this time I was rising to my feet. I was losing my grip on the crack in the wall. The chanting had never stopped, but now it was echoing mercilessly in my ears. The incantation grew, swelled, pulsated, faster and faster. I felt myself yielding to their power, as I had sworn I never would again. The searing pains saved me from knowing the end. This time I drowned out their chant with my shrieks. I couldn't stop. They all froze, rigid as statues, frozen in time. I covered my eyes and curled up in pain. Somewhere below me, around me, I heard the world exploding. From the center of the room, from beyond its doors, the whole world blew apart. And all went black, and red, and silent at last.

CHAPTER 38

"Mrs. Crane. Sharon Crane. Come now; open your eyes."

I heard the voice, but I didn't want to open my eyes. I couldn't bear to give up the bliss of unconsciousness. Even if I were back in the apartment, drugged and helpless, I wanted to stay that way. It was too late to care what was going to happen later. For now I couldn't take any more horror. A cry escaped my lips. I felt tears in my eyes. I was weak and defenseless, and I couldn't struggle anymore.

"Leave me alone," I wanted to cry out. "Go away! Please! Leave me alone!" But the words wouldn't come. A hand touched my arm. I pulled away. The hand withdrew.

"Mrs. Crane. Mrs. Crane. Come on now, honey, please. Open your eyes."

The woman's voice persisted. It was an unfamiliar, Southern voice, commanding but gentle.

"My dear, you're in a hospital. You are safe."

She was trying to trick me. I knew their tricks. I opened my eyes to mere slits. A greenish room swam into view. It didn't look like the apartment. They'd moved me to the other side! My eyes opened wider.

A round, black face blotted out the green. A broad, warm smile. White uniform. A nurse?

"Everything's all right now, Mrs. Crane. You're in the Washington Hospital Center. I'm Mrs. Dunn, your nurse. They tole me all about what happened to you. You been through just a terrible time."

"Are any of *them* here? Where's Dell? Oh, my God. Dell!" Everything closed in at once.

She spoke as though she knew all about me.

"Your young man? He's here too. He's fine. He'll be in as soon as the doctor sees you."

Christ, more doctors? What if he had hairy hands! Which of them was it?

I began to shake. "What doctor?"

"Doctor Parsons. You don't know him. He's been watchin' after you since they brought you in. You'll like him. Everybody likes Doctor Parsons. He's on the staff heah. We all love him. He wanted to check you soon as you come to. It's just routine. You're a mighty healthy young lady, and you're comin' along just fine considerin' what you been through."

She seemed to know a lot about me. Maybe she was one of them. Were they trying to trick me again? The nurse went on as I tried to assimilate what I was hearing.

"Soon as he sees how well you are, we can let your Mister Singleton come in. That man has been frettin' us crazy. He stayed here with you 'till they made him go back and get some rest. That man sure must love you, honey. So just calm down and let the doctor give his okay and you'll be able to see your man for yo'self."

Dell was all right? I had to keep asking. The nurse was patient with me.

"Yes indeedy, honey. He got hisself a bump on his head, slight concussion an' a broken arm. But all considerin' he's in real good shape. He could go home, but the doctor won't release him 'till his pressure goes down, and that isn't goin' to happen 'till they let him in here to be with you, when you're woke up. Now you just lay there and thank the good Lord, while I go and get Dr. Parsons. Sooner over with, sooner you can see your Mister."

Mrs. Dunn giggled as she started out the door.

She returned almost immediately, followed by a young man, wiry, homely, and cautious. He walked toward me, smiling. My thumping heart missed a beat as I saw how unfamiliar, how normal he looked. This was a real doctor, and his hands were smooth and strong. He had one of those eternally young faces. He must have been thirty-five.

"Hello, Mrs. Crane. I just want to check you, briefly. I don't like to admit it to a patient, but you certainly have been an interesting one. You've been thoroughly examined, though you didn't know it because you've been in shock for several days. We've been trying to bring you out of it—even with the help of Mr. Singleton. How are you feeling now?"

"All right, I guess. My mind—is it clear? Are you real? The pains are gone!"

Oh, God, my stomach was flat! And then he was answering, trying to keep up with the string of questions.

"Yes, young lady, I'm real, and I'm happy to find that your mind certainly appears to be clear." He took my hand. "But I'm afraid you have lost your baby. But you were lucky. They got you into the ambulance before you miscarried. I don't know what they'd have done if it had started before they got you off that balcony."

"What about the baby?"

"It was too premature to survive. It was a very strange fetus, unusually large. Mr. Singleton told us you were only about six months pregnant but the fetus was nearly eight pounds. That is completely impossible at six months. Are you certain of the time of conception? Mr. Singleton must have been wrong."

"No," I shook my head. "He was right. It had to be August, or even later." I answered mechanically, but in my heart I was weeping for my baby.

"Well, it was large but it wasn't even healthy. In fact, it was terribly deformed. It could never have lived. All of its inner organs were greatly underdeveloped. Its bones were soft and tiny. Its weight was due almost entirely to the flesh on its body. It would never have been normal. The researchers have examined it, but so far, whatever caused its deformity has completely eluded us. We've also been testing to find out what they were giving you. It is a complete enigma."

"Was it a girl?" I had to know.

"Yes. But hardly recognizable as a human."

"Thank God it's dead," I murmured, not caring what the solicitous doctor and sympathetic nurse thought of me.

They pretended to ignore the remark. Maybe they did understand. But they couldn't know how I'd feared that my child would inherit the madness of its father. Even if it had appeared to be physically normal, I'd have spent the rest of my life watching it, praying that it would lead a normal life, have a conscience, die a natural death. What if I had looked down at my child and seen Philip's blue, hypnotic eyes? The very thought set me trembling uncontrollably. The doctor must have seen it. He quickly changed the subject.

"Do you feel up to seeing Mr. Singleton now? We've had two patients on our hands so far, but I'm counting on his full recovery as soon as he talks to you himself."

Did I really have to say yes?

The doctor kept talking to me after the nurse left, trying to distract me until Dell could arrive. But I wasn't listening.

The door swung open. It was Dell! He was alive. It was true. Now I could really believe them. We *had* escaped. All my fears faded at the sight of him, his lopsided grin, his arm in a cast and sling. Slipping away from the nurse's helping arm, he ran to the bed and threw himself down beside me, kissing my face and grasping my hand with his good one.

Neither of us knew when the doctor and nurse left. Neither of us could speak; we only breathed each other's names. My tears were of joy, a joy only Dell could understand.

But my timing was as bad as usual. Here we were, both alive, and we were together. Now I knew that it was Dell I loved, and we would have all the happiness of a new beginning. But I said nothing of this to him. Instead, foolishly, anxiously, I asked: "How did you see and understand my signal that night? How are you alive? I was so frightened. If you hadn't come . . ."

He didn't mind.

"One thing at a time, Sharon. I'll tell you everything I can remember, but then let's never talk about it again. I know how you must feel. But thank God, it's all over. Let's let it go." I nodded my agreement, and he went on. "I had seen your lights go off and on once before, but only for a second. I thought it was an accident or something. I even tried to get into the building that time, just to be sure, but the doors were locked. There wasn't a doorbell, a knocker, or anything. I tried pounding on it, but nobody came.

"I even thought of calling the police, but what did I have to go on but my own wild theories? If it turned out to be nothing, I'd have looked like a damned fool—illegal entry just isn't based on the crazy notions I had. Particularly by lawyers. It could have proven damned embarrassing to me and to you, and your husband, if I had barged in and found nothing wrong."

"My husband?" I recalled having had one, long ago—James Crane.

"You *were* married to that guy, weren't you?"

"Philip? No! No! He never . . ."

"You weren't! I'll be damned. They certainly had every avenue covered. The last time I called, some weird lady told me you were getting married. After that I forced myself to stop looking over. I thought she was staying in your apartment and you'd moved in with your boyfriend."

"But what made you come running that last time? It was like a miracle. You were watching my windows that night."

"That wasn't any miracle. Just a few days before I received a strange letter from James Crane. He wrote that you hadn't cashed any of his checks for months. He thought you might have gotten married, and that I'd neglected to notify him. At first I didn't think too much about it, but it got to me. I knew

what that receptionist's job was paying. You would have
needed those checks for clothes, things for the apartment, all
the expenses of getting settled. And I knew you wouldn't
take money from a guy before you . . . It was that last call,
too. It didn't set right. That woman, the way she gushed, she
didn't sound like the type of friend you'd send all the way to
California for. Then I tried to call and the phone had been
disconnected. After that I stayed at the office watching your
windows every night. I even tried to get into the building
again. I thought about going to the police again, too, but I
still had nothing to go on. Nothing but your ex-husband's
question about the checks, my own feelings about that building, added up with the incongruity of that woman who answered your phone. The police would have sized me up as
your jealous ex-boyfriend. All I could do was stay in the
office until I saw your lights go out every night. Sometimes I
thought I was cracking. Once I was ready to chuck it and give
up. But I couldn't."

"How did we get out? I blacked out at the end, but before
that I was sure they'd already killed you. What happened to
them? Where are they now? I'm still afraid I'll blink my eyes
and find myself back there. Even here, they won't give up.
Cheena told me . . . They'll never . . . " I was almost hysterical.

"Sharon, Sharon, listen to me. They can't get to you now
or ever—you or anybody else."

"Then what happened? Where are they?" I clung to him
harder.

"Let me go and I'll tell you."

Dell laid me back on the pillows and smoothed my hair as
he spoke.

"I must have fallen on top of the others when the ladder
slipped. My wind was knocked out and I got this lump on my
head. I was out cold. There was blood all over me. In their
mad rush to get me out of the way, they must have just taken
it for granted I was dead. They only wanted me out of the

way fast so they could get on with their feast. They hauled
me off into some freezer, dumped me in with a bunch of carcasses and left. When I came to in that place I thought I was a
stiff, a very cold stiff. They must have thought I'd be safely
out of the way there, at least until they were ready for me. If
I'd been unconscious longer, I probably would have frozen
to death. As it was, I woke up in time and managed to stumble out. The kitchens were empty. I heard you screaming.
Then—I think it was about then—the freezer room blew up
right behind me. That would have finished me if the fall
hadn't. Anyway, there were explosions all over the building.
The whole damn place was disintegrating. But I didn't know
that then. I came running back into the dining room, just
about the same time the fire department came blasting
through the doors at the head of the stairs. Just then, that infernal thing in the middle of the room exploded like a bomb.
It looked like a volcano erupting."

"What happened to . . . to them?"

"Honey, that's the weirdest part of it all. They did have an
escape plan, but it didn't save them. I guess you could call
that part of it a miracle if you want. The police identified
their leader. His name was Schine. He was busy pushing a
whole bank of buttons beside his chair. He was the one who
started setting off the explosions. As soon as they started, the
wall right behind him lifted. He started for the opening. Behind the wall was a long staircase, winding down to the garage. The others calmly started lining up to follow him. God
damn, those people were cool. But that's where their genius
finally failed. Schine was halfway through the opening when
the whole wall fell—a foot thick—and squashed him to a
pulp. The others stood there frozen, then they all marched
back to their chairs and sat down. Not one of them moved.
When the firemen reached them, they were all dead. The police are still making tests, but they think the rings they all
wore held poison. A kind of last resort hari-kari. . . . If the
escape route had worked, they'd have all reached their cars

or the street and nobody could have identified them but you. And I'm sure they would have seen to it that you didn't live to do that.

"The interesting thing is, it was their own intelligence that brought them down. That back wall opened by some electrical device, and it closed by a spring so heavy nobody could have followed them once they'd gotten on its other side. As soon as they all got to the other side, another button out there would have released the spring. Bang, down would come the wall, cutting anybody off from following them. But the electrical device malfunctioned. Schine had rigged those explosions to destroy all the evidence. And the first thing he detonated was that abomination in the middle of the room. He disintegrated the evidence all right, but the explosion ignited flames all around it. By then the firemen were all over the place, chopping at everything around that hole. One of them must have chopped through the electric wires—the works for that door."

"Are you sure they got them all? Are you sure you saw them?"

"Did I see them? I'll never forget it. There they sat in those damned throne chairs just like statues with their eyes wide open, their black tongues hanging out. I saw a fireman touch one of them and it fell over onto the floor stiff as a board. Whatever they took was very fast-acting. The police looked into all that later. At that time nobody took time to check on the corpses. That whole room was erupting, so we got the hell out. Believe me, Sharon, they are all dead."

"But Dell," I whispered, "there are others who weren't there that night. And all those young ones up in Maine. They're preparing to take over."

"Don't worry about that, either. Nobody in that organization has a chance now."

"How can that be? Nobody realizes how much power they have. They're all rich. They'll start up somewhere else and no one will know till it's too late."

"Listen, Sharon, don't think I wasn't thinking the same

thing. But several detectives have been here to see me. The wires the firemen severed apparently prevented some of the bombs from going off. The dining hall, that freezer room, part of the basement are all gone. Some of the offices and labs, but Schine's office came out of it untouched. The firemen had to dismantle a bomb before they could get inside, but when they did they struck gold. Schine kept files on all the members, worldwide. Names, photographs, fingerprints, family backgrounds—everything. Of course the police haven't examined every document yet, but they're positive enough that it's complete. It names every one of the Maine gang, and anyone who had the least connection with them. Most of them were at the dinner that night—all except the prep-school bunch and two of the adults who had just had operations and couldn't travel. Dr. Parsons told me he could even account for every one of the bodies from that roster."

"You're saying that most of the members were at the dinner?" I still couldn't believe it.

"The police seem to be pretty sure they were. But they've got every national and international force searching down even the relatives of every person named in those files. I'm sure that cult, or whatever that was, will be wiped out for good."

We looked at each other for a moment, hardly daring to believe his words. Slowly I reached out to caress his wounded head.

"Does it hurt?" I asked.

"Honey child, nothing hurts now. But kiss me and make it better."

Our embrace was long and warm and impassioned. Dell pulled away first and kissed me on the ear.

"I'd better go and let you get some rest. By the way, the police and the FBI will want to ask you some questions when you feel up to it. Don't worry about it now; they won't bother you until you and the doctor say it's all right."

"I don't think I'll mind. It helps erase the horror, when I see normal people hearing me, believing me."

"Well, you can talk your head off now, whenever you want. The police will listen, I'll listen. Even Mrs. Dunn will listen. We all will, but it won't get publicity. Dr. Parsons and Mrs. Dunn had to be told some of the story so that they'd know how to handle your condition. Other than that there's been a publicity clamp-down, completely hush-hush. They want to move on the Maine compound before any of this gets out."

I leaned over and kissed him again in a way which told him better than words how relieved I was. He kissed me back, but when we drew apart, he looked worried, and I knew he was weighing whether or not to tell me something. He took a deep breath, then spoke low and quickly.

"There's one more thing I guess you should know. The other end of the building on your floor—well, it exploded along with everything else, and afterward they found six more bodies up there. They'd been torn to pieces by the blast, but it was clear that they were all women, and all pregnant."

I couldn't reply. Now I knew why they hadn't moved me to a stall when they were fully convinced I was ready. The poor thing who followed me must have succumbed instantly to the hypnosis and drugs. She hadn't even needed to be enticed into the apartment. And so all the stalls had been filled. What Dell didn't know was that it wasn't women who had died that night. With their minds taken from them, they'd only been shells by the time they died.

Dell watched me for a minute to see how I was taking this last shock. Reading my face, he could see that I had guessed about the other women many months ago. He seemed relieved, and resumed talking as though the subject hadn't even been mentioned.

"I'll bring you some clothes for when you're ready to leave the hospital, and whatever essentials you need to get started. You won't have to be carried out in a swaddling blanket, honey, I promise."

He saw the look of panic come back to my face as I realized I was once again going to have to start all over.

"It's only a loan," he said. "And you have those checks, re-member?"

"I'll have to find a job. . . ."

"You won't have any trouble. Don't forget, you're not alone anymore. But please, Sharon, don't talk to any new men. I'll pick out your next involvement myself: a conventional guy, but really nice, with a dog—a beagle, as a matter of fact; you like beagles?—a couple of cats, one four-year-old station wagon and a lot of friends who get together occasionally because they like each other."

"I'm not ready. . . ."

"I know. And until you are, I'll be no more than your friend."

"Mrs. Crane, Mr. Singleton. I do think you all had better rest yourselves for a while now."

The big nurse again filled the doorway. She was looking down at the floor, embarrassed. Surely she had heard our last few words, but neither of us cared. Dell rose from the bed, reluctantly letting go my hand.

I still didn't want him to go. Not yet. Not ever.

"Dell!" I called out. He stopped at the door.

"I think it will be very soon," I whispered.

He gave me one dazzling smile, then stepped jauntily through the door without even glancing back. Mrs. Dunn came and stood beside me wearing a broad smile. All three of us knew what I'd meant.

As I watched Dell's departing figure, I knew I had found myself at last. Never again would I be lured by a fantasy world. I had grown up. For the first time I knew that what I wanted, and always would, was the life and love that was within my grasp.

EPILOGUE

In the Maine compound, deep in the woods, Rudolph sat in Helga's enormous chair. His feet up on the desk, he gazed through the barred windows of the office, which gave him a view of all the approaches to the compound. Whenever the active members all congregated at one of their special events, he was left in charge by Helga. Usually it turned out to be a simple job of baby-sitting. But in the event of something serious befalling the active members, Rudolph was responsible for alerting all the inheritors and supervising their escape.

That, at least, would be exciting, Rudolph thought. But the members were always too well prepared. No one would ever take them by surprise, and he would never have to assume leadership of the inheritors. He stared out the windows, bored and sulky. Everyone knew he was being primed to assume Philip's role, but he had no intention of stopping there. Some day he would be a leader in the House of Games. Rudolph recalled the training films they had been shown—actual chapter meetings over which the present leader had presided. The leader's face had not been shown

282

on film, but his authoritative voice had cowed everyone he questioned. Rudolph also remembered the latest film, the Washington meeting where they had discussed the problem of Sharon Crane. Even Schine had groveled under the leader's interrogation. Rudolph knew he had those same qualities, and if the right time ever came, he would prove it.

For a moment the memory of that film reminded him of his own encounter with Sharon Crane, that moment on the boat when he had explored her body. He had always been able to sublimate his own reactions as he excited those beautiful women Philip brought to test him. But that Sharon had been different. He had reacted almost as quickly as he felt her wetness, and he'd almost made the inexcusable blunder of climaxing himself. He shook his head. That would have been a black mark against him. As Philip had taught him, he had to be above orgasm, except at his own choice.

He cursorily scanned the desk, and its elaborate mechanisms. Two of them—the red light and the telephone— would warn him of trouble in Washington. Even if he fell asleep in his chair, there was always Lester, curled up in a corner like a dog at his master's feet. The idiot's only purpose in the compound was to keep vigil with Rudolph, to alert his master if the telephone rang or the red bulb lit up while Rudolph slept or used the bathroom. His fingers played over the other lights, buttons and microphones. Each had its special purpose, but only he and Helga knew how to operate them. One combination of buttons controlled the vault a few feet behind his chair. Inside that vault were exactly fifty-one small pouches, each containing a packet of money, precious stones, the number of a Swiss bank account, and one or more priceless formulas which had never been released to the world.

Tomorrow Helga would phone to alert him to her return. He had her exact schedule, but the call was another procedural precaution. If the call did not come, Rudolph was to carry out the well-rehearsed evacuation plan. Every youngster would file through Helga's office, to be given a pouch and sent off in a different direction. As soon as it was safe, all would rendevous at the House of Games.

By Sunday morning Rudolph had not slept. He scratched at the stubble of his light beard. He was growing frustrated as the time for Helga's return approached. So far she hadn't called. She was nearly an hour past due. The very thought made his adrenalin pump faster. She had never been late in calling before. Rudolph thought nervously of the alarm button. But he didn't want to be hasty. If something had gone wrong, why hadn't Helga signalled him with the red light? Perhaps she was just testing his nerve, seeing how quickly ne'd panic. He decided to stay calm. His charges were already out playing and exercising all over the house and grounds. No need to alarm them yet.

Afternoon came and passed and still no word. No signal to disperse. But still Rudolph couldn't give the alarm. His superior position might be mortally damaged if he made one false move. On tenterhooks he waited. He was too excited to eat. The afternoon was an eon. The stupid Lester irritated him with his complacency. If only the alarm would go off. His dreams of power could be realized immediately, if he could just get the signal to go ahead. But the sun went down and twilight passed into darkness as he kept his vigil in Helga's chair.

Suddenly, with no warning, his domain was invaded. From the windows of Helga's office Rudolph saw cars converging on the compound from all directions. Headlight beams crisscrossed the open fields, split the darkness from between the trees. Dozens of men were running across the frozen ground toward the house from all directions except the cliffs beside the ocean. Rudolph could see them, hear their shouts. There hadn't been any warning! Even the electronic signal had failed! He didn't have time to wonder what could have happened. He could hear the screams, yells, coming from everywhere at once. He dared not use the microphone to summon the inheritors. It would betray his position and besides, they would have no chance of reaching the office. He couldn't save them. He had to think fast. He had to save himself. The men from the cars had crossed the fields and had reached the sprawling house. They were all over the place, the children and the men after them. He had to think and act fast— put into action one of those alternative plans he had dreamed about. He could save himself. He was more confident than ever.

Softly he spoke to Lester, who was running from window to window, intoxicated with the spectacle.

"Come here, Lester! Sit down in Helga's chair."

"Huh?" The excited boy barely heard him, but the voice of authority penetrated.

"Move, damn you!" Rudolph grabbed and shoved the boy down in the chair. "Open your God damned mouth!"

Terrified at Rudolph's anger, Lester slid down in the chair and dropped his jaw.

Rudolph smiled. Lester had no fillings; his teeth were as perfect as Rudolph's. The two boys, both eighteen years old, were also about the same size.

Rudolph stared into Lester's eyes hypnotically. "Now just you sit there, Lester. Don't you dare move until I come back. You hear me, Lester? Don't you move out of that chair or you know what will happen."

Lester nodded, sitting paralyzed on his spine.

Grabbing the duffel bag he kept in the office, Rudolph dumped its contents on the floor. He could hear them running up the stairs. They were coming closer. He ran to the hall door, slammed down the heavy iron bar to keep them out, then quickly ran to the desk and pushed the buttons to open the vault. Wildly he pulled out every pouch, pitched it into the duffel bag. In minutes it was done.

Throwing the bag over his shoulder, he pushed another combination of buttons. As he pushed the last one, a heavy metal door beside the vault swung open. He raced through it, hastily shoved it back into place, and drew down another thick bar to hold it closed. He jumped onto a long, steep slide, clutching the bag. As soon as he reached the bottom he ran through a long, deep cavern where fifty-one launches lay waiting in the darkness. At the end of the cave he stopped. There in the rock wall was another bank of pushbuttons. Carefully Rudolph chose two and pushed them hard. Then, quickly, he jumped into the nearest launch, started its motor, and sped far out into the open water. He knew that all the commotion above would drown out the little noise the boat was making.

Rudolph sped along until he reached a point where he knew he couldn't be seen from shore. Then he slowed the boat and peered behind him. The people looked like black ants, caught in the beams of headlights. Lights were on all over the building. He knew that his charges were being caught. He could picture the invaders trying to batter down the metal door to Helga's office, Lester still sitting there petrified with fear. They'd never break through in time.

Rudolph grinned. What could the authorities do to all those youngsters? They were all minors; they'd committed no crime. They were all too smart and well-trained to divulge anything about him or the organization. The worst sentence any of them might face would be a year or so of useless rehabilitation. Then they would be free, and they knew well how to lose themselves from further scrutiny. They'd head straight for him; even if they had to go halfway around the world, they'd come. And he'd be waiting.

All the elders, even the leader, had to be dead. The compound was their legacy. They would have tried to save it at all costs; if a single one of them had escaped, the warning would have been given. Death was the only explanation—none of them would have allowed himself to be taken alive.

Rudolph stared back at the house expectantly. He didn't have to wait long. With a tremendous boom, the sky lit up—first Helga's office, then the cave. The explosions were deafening. Eventually they'd find the body and assume it to be his own. No fingerprints, nothing but the charred remains were there for the enemy to find. He could see them commending themselves on rounding up every last person involved with the organization.

He started the little boat, going slowly at first. Holding on to the tiller, he sat back to ponder the distant flames and smoke. What could have gone wrong in Washington? Every senior member must have been there. Schine's chapter had always been so efficient—until that episode with Sharon Crane. Despite his triumph, hatred boiled through Rudolph's body.

Even the leader, his own father, was dead! How could their whole ultra-world have been overthrown by one insignificant, brainless slut? He should have warned Philip about her. He wondered for a moment if she, too, was dead. No! She must have escaped! How else would they have learned about the Maine compound? She had to be found and punished. She and whoever had helped her. He'd find them. It would be his first duty as leader to rectify that wrong in the eyes of his young followers. Since everyone would think him dead, he would have sufficient time to set his stage as well as establish himself in the House of Games. He would bring her there! But for now he could enjoy a leisurely trip in this little boat, riding the heavy waves through the night, savoring the pleasure of working out the just retribution for Sharon Crane.